# Grimes' Reckoning

## A Waking the Dead Novel

Written by

**H.A.L. Wagner**

Edited by

**Troy McElvoy**

©2020 Forker Media

Published by

Grimes' Reckoning A Waking the Dead Novel © 2020 H.A.L. WAGNER ISBN: 978-1-942657-15-6




For more information, please contact forkermedia@gmail.com
www.forkermedia.com

# The Grimes Collection:

Grimes' Punishment A Blood, Sex and Brawls Novel
Grimes' Retribution A Debt Paid in Full Novel
Grimes' Reckoning A Waking the Dead Novel
Grimes' Redux You Only Die Twice Novel

Other books by the author:
Blood Oranges A Chamberlain Cotton Novel
No Name Book – Collection of short crime stories
The Collectors-Co Author Jorge Sastre
Division 6 – Co Author Forrest Parham
....and many more in the works...

## The Grimes Collection:

**Grimes' Punishment A Blood, Sex and Brawls Novel**
**Grimes' Retribution A Debt Paid in Full Novel**
**Grimes' Reckoning A Waking the Dead Novel**
**Grimes' Redux You Only Die Twice Novel**


Thank you for buying this book.

I hope you enjoy this Grimes novel; I hope you enjoy all the Grimes novels.

    -H.W.

Instagram: @hal_writes

# Table of Contents:

# __Chapter 1__

The seagulls were squawking, calling to one another, making a hell of a racket this morning. There in the blackness of my closed eyes, I wondered if I had left the windows open again. Once my lids pealed back, I realized it wasn't the windows that were open, I was open. Nestled in a small dune, curled in the fetal position, my face was half buried in the sand. The waves lapped at the shore. A blazing orange sun bulged, pushing its way into the purple sky, burning off the morning haze. Maybe the haze in my head would burn off as well.

When my world stopped spinning, I managed to roll over by sheer will power, that heavy haze in my head made it difficult for my brain to communicate to the rest of my body except that I was cold. This was Florida and I was cold.

My watery eyes caught a blur of a gold shimmer to my left. Her hair was a heavy blonde that wisped freely in the gentle onshore breeze. *Alysa.* She found me, all the way out here, she found me. My gnarled hand with busted knuckles went out to brush the blonde from her face, a face I desperately needed to see. Something was wrong, I didn't know her name. Her lipstick was smudged and the deep purple bruise under her eye matched the bruising around her neck. The zipper on her black dress was down with the hem pulled up. I didn't have to touch her grey skin to know she was dead. I laid there as still as she and stared into a face I did not recognize. The black holes in my memory left me unsure of a lot, but I do know I was alone when I passed out in the dune.

On my feet I needed to decide; run or call in the cops. I reached in a soggy pocket and pulled my salty phone. I must have jumped in the water before passing out. The phone was toast. The girl who had no name rested peacefully in the sand while I began to pace back and forth. The set up was good, this body lying next to me was no accident. A creepy crawly feeling tingled up my spine, that sucker bullseye on my back spread out, but I had no idea who was taking aim. There were so many lately.

I stood at the top of the dune. White sand and a lapping ocean behind me, sea oats and scrub palms ahead of me. There had to be a road out there somewhere. Right?

# **<u>Chapter 2</u>**

I went down on all fours to climb out of the sandy bowl then stood over the sawgrass to figure out my location. We, the stiff and I, were on a deserted beach along the Canaveral coastline, at a spot where A1A runs into the marsh. Through the tall grass and sharp pointy scrub palmettos, I found the road I came in on. Something was missing that got my heart pounding. In its place, was one set of fresh tire tracks heading north. The dense pit in my stomach inched its way up into my throat. I knew the make and size of those treads, 33x12.50 all-terrain tires I mounted myself. I looked back over the dune to the grey corpse.

"Some stupid son of a bitch stole my Scout." I said to the girl that was no longer here.

I pinched my eyes shut and rubbed my temples. Flashes of memory lit up my mind taking me back over each step, starting with when I passed out in the sandy dune, still warm from the day's sun. The stars were out, and I gazed up wondering at their distance, my last thought until now. I had walked to the beach for some time last night, my Scout parked further up the dirt road where A1A ended. The top on my Scout was down when I drove along a dark A1A. It was late. Then I rewound more memories.

Images of the night were cut into blocks that I was trying to arrange. Drinks and random bars, pictures of faces came and went as I shifted the blocks around in my mind, visualizing my last memories first. I was at The Last Resort Bar with company that hated the world as much as I did. Before that, I cruised on in my Scout, south US-1 before I cut over to A1A south. Before that I saw her, Alysa.

Alysa was strong and too smart to hang around me. Her cold shoulder was more than I could bare, so I left Coopers, but why was I there. Rewind some more and I was at Coopers drinking heavier than I had in a while. She was on the opposite end of the bar. Sitting in a tight navy-blue dress with a copper zipper that ran up her back and disappeared into her blond hair. She turned to her glass of wine and that's when we saw each other. She pretended, poorly, not to notice me. I didn't blame her. Last time she got mixed up with me she went through hell. So had the blond I woke up next to as well.

Seeing Alysa, relaxed and smiling with friends, pushed a lump into my throat making it difficult to swallow the shot of Jack I held. I moved through the crowd, pushing past people having a better night than I. A smile to a friend showed a slight burgundy stain on her normally pure white teeth. I didn't care, her smile cured all that ailed me.

My presence faded her smile. She said hi and introduced me to her two friends. I paid no attention to them; my focus could not escape those green eyes I dreamt about so often. Alysa had been there with me in the beginning of all this. She was my bartender, the wise one, who could nurse me back to mental health. She was there serving me after I broke up the child sex ring and then got too close to my flame when I shut down a blackmailer. It burned her. We hadn't talked again until last night.

Alysa didn't have it in her to completely ignore me and asked how I was, then looked down at my hands. The red, swollen knuckles told her things in my life had not changed and those things she wanted no part of. She turned her back on me.

How did I get to Cooper's? The flashing images of my night before were smoothing into a hi-def film now. Cooper's was my usual stop after work was done, but I hadn't been in a while. I was hoping not to see anyone I knew. It was a busy night on Beach Street, and I had to park a couple of blocks away. I didn't mind, it was a cool night for the first time in eight months. A cold front had pushed the temperatures down into the sixties and my thin southern blood needed a long sleeve shirt. As I walked to Cooper's I saw a man ringing a bell in front of a red kettle. I shoved most of the cash I took from the meth heads into the kettle and kept going.

Tender, swollen knuckles reminded me of the latest assignment. A meth lab on the outskirts of town was quickly poisoning the beach community. The lawyer wanted them gone as part of our quest to rid the town of such venomous snakes. I went in on a white horse pretending to be St. Patrick to drive them out.

The job went quickly. The mobile home was still on wheels half sunk in a field of waist high green grass. Two pickups were parked outside. On a half-ass constructed porch, sat a fat toothless redneck resting his eyes. A shotgun stood between his legs. His plaid flannel was sleeveless, and he reeked of moonshine. I slapped him awake and then knocked him out cold.

Inside two pencil necks with twigs for arms wore white paper respirators. They stood perfectly still as I scanned the room and the meth cook-out they were preparing.

We exchanged a few words; I wanted them to know I was shutting them down because of the two deaths related to the shit they cooked. They threatened with the usual *you know whose meth this is* and puffed-up chests. It didn't impress me any more than the time before. Once enough of their brain cells collided, they realized I was not backing down. I went to work. The images of what I did to them shown in my mind like slides in a projector against a brick wall, jagged and smoky, but right now, I can't see their faces. I never see any of their faces anymore.

I do remember the pain, not mine but theirs. The brass knuckles dripped with their blood, reminding me to wear latex gloves next time. I wasn't worried about prints, this place would burn like all the others, disease worried me. These bugs carried diseases making this town sick, making me sick.

Before I torched the trailer, I tossed it. Going through the cupboards and closets. A plastic grocery bag sitting on the top shelf of the linen closet held some loose cash. Blood money, meth heads that would do anything for a high. This cash did not belong to them, to the cookers or the dopers. It belonged to the people they stole from physically and emotionally to get that cash and to get that high. I took it back.

I left there with the flames climbing, releasing a bright orange glow to the blackness of the wilderness night.

The case was handed down to me by Willis Sanford, the lawyer who employees me. Another one of our 'off the books' cases. Our partnership had started off rocky. He had visions of grandeur for him and me and the criminals we wreaked havoc on, but I wasn't ready and instead took my own path for a time. All I found was that I did in fact want to help people and so I embraced Sanford's creation of *the vigilante*. The city was sick, and the vigilante was the cure. Sanford had me on three cases in one month. I cracked a lot of skulls in that time.  I can still hear the bones break and feel the warmth of the blood sticking to my knuckles. We were doing good, that's what we celebrated anyway. Even the cops were recognizing our contributions to fighting crime, often leaving the scenes loosely investigated. If they looked hard enough my DNA would be there somewhere, but it never turned up.

As the jobs mounted, I became a nameless, faceless celebrity in town, with every photo of the vigilante nothing but a black silhouette. Newspapers shaped public opinion as write-ups in the local paper had started out unbiased and always finished with 'Detective Rhoshanda Camp not commenting either way'. The vigilante could not stay a neutral topic. Opinion pieces from editors were popping up villainizing my use of force without a court of law behind me. I didn't let it bother me and just avoided the news even more than I already had. I was killing bugs. Pimps, rapists, and thieves were all turning up beaten or dead. Feelings were put on hold with every assignment I completed.

# **Chapter 3**

The sun glistened off the dead black mirror in my hand. The phone was toast. I walked on along with my bare feet slipping in the white sand.

A yellow umbrella flapped in the cool breeze off the choppy surf. I found a couple of grey hairs sitting under it, wrapped in thick sweaters, hats pulled low.

"Sorry to bother you two,"

"Yes?" He asked, saluting me only to block the sun from his eyes.

"I need to call the cops. There's a dead girl back there."

After all the confusion and panic subsided, I got my sweaty palms on a phone and called Detective Camp. She was always by the book, which could land me in hot water, but she's the only cop I trusted.

# **Chapter 4**

On the seventh floor of the CBR Building, I sat in a chair with a rust-colored stain in the back corner of the cushion. A reminder of when I bled for the *cause*, Willis Sanford's white knight, taking back the streets of this fallen beach town and making them safe. I was the wrench he threw into the criminal machine. A tool to wield, his arm of justice firing a gun. The recoil of every fired round jolted my body hard. With each new assignment the recoil softened until I did not feel it, even when I expected it. The absence of caring began to concern me. I wanted to feel something for breaking their bones, for killing them, even if it was joy in their demise. But it was emptiness, a black abyss that could not be filled so I stopped trying. The machine broke down but was not dismantled. Criminals kept me employed.

"Uh-huh," Sanford pushed up on his brushed metal square frame glasses. A strained bloodshot look that stemmed from never sleeping peered a thousand yards past me. The white collar of a tailored dress shirt was undone, no tie, only a silver vest hung open. His long brown fingers rapped on the ebony desk.

My eyes went past his to the view of the city from the seventh floor. The corner office offered two views; one of a beach lined with tall colorful hotel pool decks lined with pasty bodies and parking garages lined with out of state plates. The other way view were homes pitched with swayback rooves missing shingles and cars parked on blocks. It was where Sanford grew up.

"And, and?" Sanford hated that I did not speak. He never stopped. We would sit in his office and have an entire conversation that only came from his mouth. He talked fast in short spurts like the burst from a Tommy gun, *RATTATTTTATATAT*.

I picked the loose sole of my Vans, fighting the urge to peel back the white rubber band holding the sole. Picking at it kept me from bighting my nails.

"Some detective named Waycross hauled me in. He tried to lay into me, get a quick confession then toss away the key. Camp came in and broke up the interrogation. She vouched for me. She has me on the books as a CI."

"That confidential informant bit is wearing thin. She's too close to you, Roger. You should have called me first." Sanford murmured a cuss word under his breath. He never swore aloud. Then he said, "What did you tell them?"

"Nothing."

"A lot like now."

"Yeah. What's to say? I know I drove down to the beach alone and woke up, hung over, beside a dead girl I couldn't identify. My truck was stolen. I tried explaining that to the cops. They asked a lot about my bruised knuckles because of the bruise on the dead girl's face. I told them to check with Saadon's Gym, that I teach MMA there sometimes and it's just part of the job. It was obvious, without a car, I didn't walk all the way out there with this girl. Then Camp retold my story, suddenly it all made sense to them. I guess they don't like PI's.

"Camp said to just stay in town and cooperate if I have nothing to hide, the usual cop crap." I paused picking at the white lip of my sole once more, "This isn't the kind of crime her new task force handles. Chasing the vigilante is top priority. She went on to ask about the meth lab."

Sanford grumbled something about not liking my relationship with Camp, then stood up. He swung around his desk with the gracefulness of the boxer he had been and made his way to the bar. His usual Remy and champagne went into a glass with ice. Three fingers of amber Kentucky bourbon went into another glass. He looked back me, at my darkened eyes and the way my sour stomach curled my lower lip. Next, he dropped in some ice and splashed a little ginger ale over the bourbon.

Holding the drinks, he said, "How'd that operation go?"

"Just as you laid it out. Found the lab, a trailer out in the woods. A couple of cookers, they didn't make it." I said then rubbed a sore left shoulder, another trophy for my efforts.

"Any cash?" Sanford asked handing me the bourbon.

I tossed it back in one gulp. Bubbles fizzled deep in the back of my throat, and I craved an antacid.

"I didn't count it."

"Did you deposit it?" Sanford resumed his seat across the desk from me.

"Yeah, dropped it at the Salvation Army. I kept a couple hundred for myself."

Sanford frowned then sipped his drink.

"I need new shoes." I said with a shrug. My tenure with Sanford was taking a toll physically. Mentally I had checked out, gone on permanent vacation a million miles from where my battered body lay. In order to destroy the machine, I must become one filled with gears and gadgets that spin to propel my fists and pull the trigger, when need be, and that need is all too often.

"That's why I pay you a salary. That target came from the list." Sanford said pointing to his safe then sipped his drink. He was growing tired of my general malaise over this whole relationship. The quality of my work was in decline and that would only lead to my arrest or worse. *The list* was something I stole from a drug dealer who decided trafficking kids in the sex trade was more his style. It didn't end well for him or his associates. Now, Sanford was spending his days deciphering the coded names and places of the criminal underworld around Daytona Beach. The state cops hadn't seemed too interested so Sanford turned to me to carry out justice.

As he went on about me putting him and Monique in jeopardy each time, something popped between my ears. I was certain Sanford heard it too, it was that real. The memory came back strong, shiny gold strands of her hair snaked against the soft white sand leaving the tiniest of curled tracks. Her left eye was half open, blue but maybe hazel. Single grains of orange and copper sand stuck to her pasty grey cheeks and tangled in the soft peach fuzz at the base of her jaw left her sparkling in the sun. Her lips slightly parted as if to ask a question she may not want to know the answer to. That's when I touched her, not to satisfy my curiosity, I knew she was dead, but to let her know her question would be answered.

My head hung now, cradled in veined and scarred hands, "I can't sustain this." The words dribbled out of my mouth past liquored lips. The acid splashed on the stones in my gut. Another drink was no use and more money never helped me sleep. Staring down at the waxy lifeless skin of a young woman who never set out to hurt anyone broke the light I clung to in the blackness of the abyss I had been falling into since I took on the role of an avenging vigilante.

"I didn't quit being a thief to become a killer. I want to walk down the street with my head up and not look over my shoulder. I want to go to bed at night without needing a sleeping pill except I'm too damn afraid of taking one because I'm convinced someone is going to kick my door in and put one between my eyes. I want to wake up after seven hours of sleep and have coffee without bourbon in it or need to take a Xanax before I leave my apartment." I couldn't hold it back anymore. Getting hauled down to the police station and interrogated was as close to going back to jail as I ever wanted to be. If it's not the cops, its criminals roaming the streets, all of them on alert now, knowing I'm out there. There is always an incessant splinter of thought in my mind, that at some point I won't have my guard up, and one of them will get lucky.

Sanford let air out in a whoosh, "I guess I have been pushing you, making you run on a level I can barely maintain myself. As a young man fresh out of law school, I made a commitment to do good in the end. Too obsessed, I began to believe the means were of no consequence, only the outcome."

He stood up and turned to face the window as he had done many times before. I've grown accustomed to that pose, the hands clasp behind his back, tipping up on the balls of his feet, gently rocking where he stood. His deepest thoughts were coming. He would watch out over the neighborhood he fought so hard to get out of and that is where he would find the direction he needed to get back on the rails. It was his grounding when he had been in his high-rise office too long.

"I searched a long time for you Grimes, for a man of your caliber. Yes, my *white knight*, you are a rarity." Sanford continued to look out over the city of his youth. Like a conjured spirit, I was somewhere in the reflection of the glass, just a shadow of the man he had found.

"I didn't know being so stupid was rare." I said as my finger picked at dry hanging skin in the corners of nailbeds. One nail pushed back the cuticle of another and scraped out dried rusty blood, blood that wasn't mine.

Sanford came back around to his plush chair, one he spent most of his waking hours in. Long brown fingers drummed against the desk.

"I want you to know I am proud of what we have done here, together, for this town. There are lives out there we have made better and the ones we have ruined needed it. You should sleep soundly at night knowing this. I know I sleep better knowing you are out there, Grimes.

"Let's take a break as crime fighters. If you have a hobby, go enjoy it for a few weeks. I'll do my best to keep the cops off your behind with this body dump business. So, rest up."

With a nod, I got to my feet and shuffled over the thick carpet to the heavy wooden door. I reached for the doorknob as Sanford asked what I would be doing with my time off.

"I'm going to find my Scout."

Outside it was night. The clouds were low casting the entire city in a silver dome. The air was dryer than it had been the day before leaving me with a static charge building on the short hairs at the base of my skull. A breezy cold front was bringing a rare winter to Florida. All my usual outdoor activities of surfing and fishing were now put-on hold. It didn't matter anyway, as finding my Scout was the priority.

My best friend Billy Horseblood was there waiting in the old white Ford F-150, looking at the end of his long braided black ponytail. The guilt and distrust of Willis Sanford kept him from going up to the office. It was Billy that got me involved with Sanford in what, by all accounts, was going behind my back. It was a turbulent time for all of us and I let any hard feelings go. We didn't know our place yet in this new business of vigilantism. Sanford wanted a guy that would brandish his sense of justice on the criminal community. Billy gave him me, not knowing Sanford's true intentions. The realization of what he had done crushed Billy more than anything I could do physically. He was not just my best friend he was also a mentor to me, sticking with me since I was fifteen, teaching me to steal cars and rob banks. We had been through so many stressful situations where trust was all we had. When it waivered, I looked back to the times it was strongest and I became stronger for it.

"I made some calls while you were with Willis." Billy said as he fired up the F-150. He pulled out onto US 1. "No one has seen a Scout in years, at least that's what they say over the phone. I'm thinking we need to go in person, see Jaffy, you remember Jaffy?"

I nodded. Jaffy was always willing to take a hot car off our hands.

"He should be our first stop." Billy went on about who else he talked with. I nodded again while staring out the window of the truck, watching the homeless meander among the massage parlors, strip clubs and bail bonds offices that lined Ridgewood Avenue.

"What's with you man? I thought you'd be all over this. Getting your Scout back is priority numero uno." Billy reached into the top pocket of his lined plaid flannel and pulled a pack of cigarettes. Then lit one. He cranked the window down and the smoke sucked out. I felt the cold air blow over my face, and I thought about Alysa.

"I saw her last night."

"Who, the dead girl?"

"No, Alysa."

"Aw, sheesh." Billy avoided swearing in hopes of avoiding drama. "Hey, she's not-"

"No, no. I really didn't know the dead girl or how she got there. The cops never told me her name. I saw Alysa at Cooper's last night. I said hi, she said hi and I moved on." I didn't want to tell him she blew me off. Billy knew what was coming, I had talked about Alysa for weeks after our only date and the ensuing kidnapping. That was not my fault and I got her out. My life was no movie, there was no passionate kiss after I freed her and killed the kidnappers. There were just two wide frightened green eyes taking in the ugly deaths I made them suffer. It was too much for her.

Billy didn't say anything. He nodded, smoked his cigarette, and waited the appropriate amount of time then changed the subject to finding my Scout.

# **Chapter 5**

Why does it take two hours every freaking time you go to get a new phone? I have never been able to get in and out of a place with a new phone in less time. The employees at the cellular store knew it too as they gave us that look of both frustration and dread as we entered. Their plan to get out right at closing time faded to disgust. I wasn't happy about it either, but I couldn't go the night without a phone.

Eventually we got out of there and I got a new shiny phone. Back in the truck, this time with the heater on, we rode along in silence. Tired and still hung-over, I struggled to form words that would have any meaning. Exhaustion left me hours ago. With a night of drinking and a day of police interrogation, I was running on pure fortitude. My attention needed to be on my Scout, it wasn't. The dead girl was there staring at me, asking me why she was there. She wanted answers and expected me to give them to her.

My head was held up by an arm resting on the door. "Why dump a body next to me and steal my truck but not my wallet? The killer didn't even take my keys."

Lost in his own thoughts, Billy took a few seconds to reply, "Maybe they thought you were dead?"

We hit some railroad tracks, rattling my head in my hand, and adding another crack to my splitting skull.

"Maybe," Billy hypothesized again, "it was just a coincidence, or they never saw you at all."

Billy had helped in nearly all my cases. Usually he does the phone work, like today, having called around asking sideways questions looking for any vintage four-wheel drives, maybe a Bronco or something like a Scout. There was no doubt he was good at finding things. The car shop he ran was mostly funded by his innate skills at tracking down rare car parts for collectors and other restoration experts. Not all the calluses on his fingers were from turning wrenches, some were from pounding keyboards and punching phones. Despite those strong attributes, I wasn't enthused about his current theory.

"No, it's almost as if she had something to do with me, like I should know her. They were sending a message. I don't know, just a gut feeling." In my gut or in my head, either way I needed to find the connection.

Billy let out a huff, flipped on the left blinker and cut the truck out of traffic. We were on a side street running along the rail line. He stopped hard at an empty four-way stop then gunned it on through.

"What?" I asked as I was jerked back in my seat.

"I guess we ain't going to Jaffy's tonight." he said with a snort.

We covered a couple more blocks before I was able to reply, "I'm so worn out right now I'll probably lose my temper and kill that fat redneck."

Billy smirked, imagining it. We had worked with Jaffy before and neither of us liked him. He nodded the alright and soon we were back at the shop.

Billy had moved shops recently. He found one with more square footage for less money than the previous one because it was tucked away on a side street that was more industrial than the commercial friendly US 1. He wanted to cut down on his customers and spend more time on custom builds. It was good timing for me as well. Just after Billy moved, I got an eviction notice for my office downtown. Landlord cited too many sleepovers and after the brake-in, other tenants complained they didn't feel safe. Billy moved me into the apartment above the shop office. Having an office for PI work wasn't necessary, being a detective was not my job anymore, my day started with an address and a list of wrong doings in an email. Mostly it was drugs or organized theft rings. I hated tracking down thieves through their fences. I just knew someone would recognize me from my thieving days. Luckily, I still had Smitty to call with back door channels so I could avoid the face to face. Sanford warned me to keep my distance from the old gangster, knowing one day I would be sent to end his crime syndicate.

We passed through the small office into darkness. With the lights flipped on I could see the fresh battleship grey paint on the cinderblock walls. The back seat of a minivan was against the wall, so I took a seat. Billy sat on a stool at one of the work benches. The shop was closed, Jose the master tech, had left for the day. Under the workbench was a small refrigerator. Billy pulled out two cans of beer. We sat with only the hum of a florescent light between us.

When my beer can was empty, I went upstairs to the room above the shop office. It was large for one person, fifteen by twenty feet. I had a queen bed, a couch I did most of my sleeping on, and a small kitchenette which was also my bathroom sink. The floor and ceiling were bare plywood, and the walls dull, grey drywall. Billy was not ready for me to move in when I asked.

The 1970's floral pattern on crushed velvet that covered the long square couch called to me and I answered by laying down. Overloaded and burned out, it was time to let my mind wander in the quiet stillness of an empty room. The multi-colored Mexican blanket covered me as I lay there. Though I had just left the company of a friend, I felt lonely, but not like I wanted to talk to someone, just have them there with me. The body of a woman was as foreign to me lately as eight hours of sleep. To maintain a relationship was more work than I was willing to put forth right now. What I needed was a dog, a mutt from the streets of Daytona. I was in no shape to care of a pup.

With nothing but the dead girl on my mind, I sent a text to Detective Camp for any news. With the phone on the floor, I stared up at the ceiling while looking into my mind. The images of the night flickered through. Alysa to April and back again. The trail carried on past, to Sanford, and on to the days of my life as a crook, a thug that if active now would catch a visit from the vigilante. Heat built in my chest and caught in my throat as I resisted a grunt. The fist into the pillow I couldn't hold back. The old couch took a few blows then I settled back down as a forced acceptance of the way things were gradually reminded me there was a killer out there to find.

A soft blue light broke the darkness and grabbed my attention. A text from Lieutenant Camp brought my phone to life.

*Sorry, not my case. Det Waycross is keeping a lid on it. Not even press* -Camp

*I'm staying clear of that guy* -Me

*If you've got nothing to hide, work with him* - Camp

*Sometimes I forget you're a cop* -Me
*Sometimes I think you should be* -Camp
I laughed at the idea and put the phone back
on the floor.

# **Chapter 6**

Chains clanked as the large metal bay door rolled up in the garage below. The morning sun was slipping through the cracks between the blinds. My left hand was still slumbering, pins and needles attacking it as I moved it from behind my head. I rolled on my side and my dead hand started the slow process of coming back to life.

The sound of boots scuffing up wooden steps filled the narrow hall outside my door. I lay still wondering what Billy would want with me this early.

The three short knocks were sharp and fast. They were cop knocks.

I rolled off the bed and stood up. As I grabbed the door knob another knock. I pulled the door open.

Standing before me was Detective Waycross wearing khaki pants, a polo and a gun. Behind him Billy stood jingling keys.

"Got a minute Grimes?" Waycross said with a smile. The only time he smiled during my interrogation was while telling me he knew guys in prison that liked fresh meat and he'd make sure they had some.

"No." I said.

"This will just take a minute." Waycross said then tried stepping into my apartment. I blocked his advance. Waycross smirked.

"You really want to play it this way," he said.

Detective Camp's words to *play along* sounded in my head. I stepped aside. He looked around, taking note of anything and everything.

"I'm having trouble lining up your where abouts the other night and –"

"He was with me." Billy said.

Waycross looked Billy over, "Ah right, Billy Horseblood. I'm sure that alibi will hold up, chief."

Billy stopped jingling the keys. His eyes narrowed and I knew that *chief* remark was about to get him in jail for assaulting a police officer.

"Talk to my lawyer." I said and nodded to Billy.

"Have a nice day." Billy said and held the door for Waycross. Waycross ignored the invitation to leave. He pulled a pen from his pocket and began circling the room. His eyes searching, the pen a pointer and tool to poke and prod.

"Oh, I will talk to Willis Sanford. I'm going to ask him all about each *and* every case you two have ever worked. Why you worked it, who paid for it, and them I'm going to go interview them." Waycross leaned in towards me, looking up with his brown eyes reading my face.

"Including April Ward." His breathe filled with old coffee.

So that was her name. I didn't know and didn't let the news reflect in my face.

"How'd you know her?" Waycross moved to the couch squealing the springs as he settled in. His hand slyly slipped between the cushions, running along the seams. I didn't think the police still used bloodhounds but here one sat on my couch.

"I told you already, I didn't know her, I've never heard of her." It was true. April Ward, a woman I met once in a sand dune, but she never met me.

Waycross bobbed his head after hearing me say it for the 100th time.

"What'd April do for a living?" I said, turning the questions back on Waycross.

He smirked, and said, "Reporter for the college paper and sometimes with the local press." He stood up and looked around at my small apartment. He shook his head and walked through the door. As he crossed the threshold he spun on his heels.

"She was a good writer. Liked to do write-ups on college events, politics and the vigilante." Waycross smiled then took the stairs down. Billy followed him out, shaking his head as he went.

As their steps on the stairs faded a weight pushed down on my chest keeping my lungs empty. Sliding prison bars locking shut filled my mind. I forced a breath. A young attractive reporter found dead next to the black silhouetted vigilante she was writing a story on. A couple of dead meth heads were my only alibi.

I sat on the bed as my hand dived into the side table drawer. My fingers sniffed for a pill bottle. It was on the other side of the room. I stood and took a couple deep breaths as I crossed the room and snatched the plastic bottle off the counter. Relief was only a pill away, but the cap stayed on. April's killer was out there and wanted the cops to pin it on me. The hell with those pills, I needed to be sharp, and I needed to feel sick about April's death. So sick that I would do anything for the cure. I would have to find out who killed her and make them eat the fear she felt the night she died.

Back on the couch, social media was my go-to, a free background check on anyone. Searches for

April Ward brought up a Facebook page that let me know everything. She studied journalism at the local state college. Her page was filled with "Thinking of you" and "Prayers" posts from people who may or may not have known her. Her last post was a week ago. A couple of nighttime pictures of her and a couple friends down at the same beach where her body was dumped. They were there to see a rocket launch. Maybe it wasn't the same dune we laid in together, but it was the same stretch of beach.

Scrolling down, I found only one post from a concerned friend asking to return a call about a class project. That was yesterday. To me, that puts her missing no more than two days ago.

She had several posts with a link to a local event scene paper, *Daily Daytona*. It was free, one you see in faded red plastic boxes outside convince stores. They run on advertising, the papers are filled with what bands are playing where, farmer's market news and a one or two stories that usually are more commentary than actual news.

I looked up the newspaper and searched her articles online. Many of them had political slants that were a week past the headlines and sounded unoriginal to the point of being plagiarized. Back-to-back pieces criticized the state for not doing enough or doing too much against the *current thing*. Then there was a piece on national protests and how to get involved. It was all about opposition without defining what they were opposing nor offered solutions. Click bait and sound bites from drive by reporting without investigation. Her latest piece caught my attention. Camp was right, she was not a fan of the vigilante.

Volusia County Sheriff's Department and surrounding city departments had kept a tight lid on what the vigilante had been doing, with the Sheriff never validating the rumors there even was a vigilante, making everything conjecture. April claimed in her article that the poor investigating was due to the police secretly admiring the violence I threw down on these *alleged* criminals. The piece started strongly but like the others, lacked depth. Citizens getting death sentences with no trial was her point. But two things she left out, a pair of burning red, water-soaked eyes of the real victims. From her ivory tower, still funded with her parents' money, she could easily look down at the filthy gutter I crawled through to give the victims the true justice they wanted.

Up until now, I had avoided any news on the justice I dealt ripping apart the criminal underbelly of this town. It was holding a mirror too close, seeing the blood and the tears caused by my hands then reading about it after the fact. Monique oversaw our social media campaigns, anonymously posting comments countering any negative press. She would also send in fake tips to the hotline to confuse law enforcement, keeping my actions clouded.

There were more posts and other social media to check, but my skin was scratchy with sea salt, granules of sand were settled in creases of my skin. The odor of not showering in three days hovered around me and I had to get out there and find more on April.

The shower warmed, before the steam covered the mirror, I stared at myself, at what I had become. The short bristly hairs around my temples were a shiny silver. The front tooth on my lower jaw was a bleak grey, damage from blunt force trauma. The tattoos on my shoulders, running down around my biceps, were now puckered with pink slugs from bullet wounds and knife cuts. The pink spider web of scar tissue on my side was blending in with the flesh around it, the first bullet wound I earned for profit in the war on crime.

Around my puffy eyes were brownish-blue rings, not healing bruises from fighting but from never sleeping. My nights prowling around, living as the criminals I hunted lived, were all taking a toll that I could no longer afford to pay.

April, a young reporter who was writing about the vigilante, had she seen these scars? Did she know I never slept?

No longer able to look at myself, my eyes fell to the counter, on the orange pill bottle. The label was off because I didn't get it from a pharmacy. Two rectangular white pills were left from a bottle I filled two weeks ago.

My hand snatched up the bottle and popped the cap. As the pills tumbled into my palm, I felt April's stare upon me. She was gazing deeper at the things buried beneath the scars and the yellow bruises. All the reasons for this life that were there before a landslide of pain covered over them. She needed to see the purpose in my change. The pills went into the toilet. As they slid down the white porcelain, I wondered what pieces of my soul could be saved and what was lost forever.

The hot shower brought some relief to my hungry brain. Winter weather was here for a week, mid-sixties and dry, so I dressed accordingly in a hoodie and shorts. In the office, a large coffee maker made of shiny metal and stick-on wood grain, dripped hot black sludge into an orange rimmed pot that was no longer translucent. Jose sipped from a metal mug; his eyes came over the top of the brushed metal to look at me. Billy was leaning back in his worn black chair, a pen twirled in his ever-busy fingers.

He reached into his desk drawer and came out with a small white bottle and tossed it at me. "You could use some."

Ibuprofen. I took two with my coffee.

Billy leaned back, squeaking in his desk chair, "Sorry about springing that cop on you so early. Maybe I should rig up some buzzer I can push at the desk and a red-light will flash upstairs."

I smiled, "Nah, don't worry about it."

Billy sat up in his desk chair, "I got *other* news for you."

Jose knew us well enough to avoid being within ear-shot of anything Billy and I discussed. It was a sure way to be labeled an accomplice.

Once Jose closed the door behind him, I said, "Yeah, me too."

"This is Scout info. I have a feeling yours is about the girl."

I nodded.

A frown deepened the creases already around his mouth from years of smoking. His head started to fan left and right slowly until his hand went up over tightly pulled hair on his scalp and down his black braid.

"Go ahead, I know you won't hear a word I say until you use me as a sound board about this girl." Billy went to the coffee maker to warm the quarter cup he still had.

I didn't say anything until I had some coffee in me. The black sludge dribbled into my mouth and down my throat. It didn't take long for my eyes to widen and my mind to come into focus. Caffeine.

"April Ward, seemed to have a thing for the vigilante."

"Shit. Did you know her?"

I shook my head, no.

"How bad is it?" Billy was doing his best to wait for me to get my thoughts out about April and how she wound up next to me on the beach. His focus was on the Scout. I appreciated that and up until recently I would have chosen my Scout over anything else in my life. For reasons I hadn't explored, I was thinking only about the forever stare of a lifeless April Ward.

Silence.

"Well, your Scout that we worked so long and hard on, has been spotted. Thought you might like to know."

I snapped out of my trance and felt my heart sink in my chest. Billy was right, I needed to move the Scout higher on the priority list. Right now, there was nothing I could do for April, learning more about her dislike for the vigilante was not going to fix things in my head or anywhere else and looking into her death would just put me in the way of the police investigation, which is the one thing I don't want to be in the way of. After I started working with Sanford again the money started rolling in, I was able to get started on the Scout restoration. Every bolt was removed, cleaned, and put back. Billy was there beside me, giving up his nights and weekends to get it done. My C10 had been shot to pieces and the last time I borrowed a car from him it was nearly destroyed, so his motivations to get me my own ride were not all altruistic.

"Good ole' Jaffy says he has us a lead." Billy was smiling.

My head was clearing, and I wanted back in the game. Finding my Scout could lead us to who took it and that was likely April's killer.

"You're right. Let's go find it." I shot out of the chair. Billy bounced up ready to be on the hunt.

He stopped at the door to the shop and shouted to Jose then we went out to the parking lot.

Jaffy's shop was back off Segrave Avenue, not far from the tower Willis Sanford had his law office. As we drove by, I looked up at the windows wrapped in grey clouds and felt Sanford's deep brown eyes penetrate the mist and zero in on me.

The chop shop was single story concrete block painted and repainted several times. Today it was mostly red with the old colors bleeding through the single coat. The driveway was gated and there were no windows facing the street, just a single, dented, black metal door. Leading to the metal door was soft powdered dirt that plumed with each step. I stomped my shoes on the concrete to shake any fine powder off before knocking.

Sounds of metal on metal screeched out from the open bay doors just on the other side of the tall chain-link and razor wire fence. It took some more pounding before the door opened. A young black-haired kid with olive skin popped his head out. He wore protective eye wear and gloves.

"Yeah," He said.

"Jaffy's waiting on us." Billy said with a shout.

He jerked back on the door, getting it fully open and we went in. Distinct smells of grease gave way to transmission fluid as we weaved through cars and shop tools. A haze filled the air, as welds arched and grinders threw sparks, as burnt offerings to the metal gods. Air compressors drowned out any verbal communication, so we relied on the guy's open palm directions. The bare cement floor was stained, gouged, and cracked from years of cars coming apart and going together. Two other mechanics worked, one appeared young like the guy leading us, and the other, who was around when Henry Ford started him on the first assembly line. They glanced over at us but were more focused on the hot torch they were using on the door frame of a late model Tahoe.

Ahead of us was an office door covered in stickers from companies like Holley, Edelbrock and Hooker Headers. There were a few more, the kind you get free in the box of new parts. The adult prize in a cereal box. Slapping that Crane Cams sticker in the lower right corner of your back windshield was always the finishing hallmark on any build.

On the other side of the stickered door sat Jaffy. Yellow foam sprang from the cracks in the black faux leather desk chair. The wheels squeaked under the sheer weight of the bald man. Wispy blond hair circled his crown leaving a leathery tanned scalp full of dark brown sunspots. His face's complexion was no better than his scalp. Years under the Florida sun will do that. Jaffy's whiskered jowls pushed out at the sides, hiding his chin as he looked up at us over his reading glasses. A dark blue work shirt with even darker grease stains needed buttoning to cover his sparse chest hair. He had on blue shorts and black work boots with white tube socks that hung around the tops of the boots.

When the door shut the decibels from all the grinding and cutting diminished. We could all speak without shouting.

With blackened fingertips, he removed the glasses and stuck the end in his mouth and chewed.

"Whatcha all want?" Jaffy said with a twang that won't leave your ears for days. The arm of the glasses popped out of his puckered lips with the suction of a grape lollipop.

"I called you about the Scout." Billy said friendly but to the point. Billy went further back with this car thief and was the one who dealt with him when we had a car to sell.

Jaffy nodded knowingly. Having information, we did not, gave Jaffy special tingly feelings throughout his wide body. Slobbering over the kernel of knowledge like a warm apple pie. Fat fingers intertwined like snakes in a den, twisting as he savored the tiny morsel of knowledge out of our reach.

"Yeah, and I told you it weren't here." Jaffy swiveled in his chair.

Billy took a seat on a stool to ease the tensions. I was not about to move, this fat man acted like he knew something and if he were holding out on me, I would tear him apart. He didn't know that and worse, he danced around the Scout like he didn't think I would.

"Jaffy, we ain't just searching for a client, this here Scout is personal." Billy reached over his shoulder and straightened his braid. Turning, he looked at me then back to Jaffy.

"Billy, you know the way it is around here, there's a code. I can't just start blabbing who might have what. Maybe you just been outta the game too long."

Billy looked back into my eyes. I hadn't spoken yet, not because I knew my place or because there was nothing to say. My silence checked my rage, I had to remain still.

"Jaffy, it would mean a lot to us," Billy was cut short.

"Nah listen here," Jaffy snorted, "maybe back in the day you bring a hot car around and tell me what to do with it. Well, things have changed. I moved up, I got serious partners, and I don't take shit from no washed-up Red-man and his boy Robin here." Jaffee jutted a grease-stained finger at me.

Time was wasting with every second another bolt was removed, or another buyer lined up for my Scout. As the seconds ticked, a forklift carried my truck closer to the crusher or a boat to go overseas. I had grown accustomed to beating people to get what I wanted. Just because Sanford put me on vacation didn't mean I wouldn't beat this man to death.

I groaned and taking the hint, he started talking again.

"Well, I still don't know. Red Scout, huh? Red? I don't see no red 'til I see some green." Jaffy smudged a bulbous finger and thumb together. Yellow teeth peeked out at me from his parted lips that pulled back into a sneer.

My hands were around the collar of his open shirt faster than Billy could get from the stool. I synched them tightly together choking the fat man. Gurgles bubbled from a slack jaw as a loose tongue dangled between his lips. His eyes bulged. A high-pitched whine leaked from his closing throat.

"I don't care who I have to go through to get my Scout back." I said with a look in my eyes that let him know he was close to death.

Jaffy's bulging eyes fluttered, he was about to go under. I eased up and let the oxygen in. Billy had a hand on my shoulder now, no pressure, just to keep me from the edge before I lost myself. My friend's hand almost worked, I almost let the fat man up until I saw his black boot stretching out to press a red button at the lower end of the desk.

With a jerk, his large blubbery mass fell to the floor. Wheezing, he remained on all fours.

"Who has it?" I growled.

"Jaffy, c'mon man, we just want the Scout back." Billy reasoned.

The metal office door opened, and the olive-skinned kid came in holding a long extension to a one-inch drive socket wrench. His eyes went large and before he could reel back the bar, I tossed him into the desk. He hit sideways and rolled off. I snatched him again and tossed him into the old warn leather sofa. Questions came from his mouth along with spit and heavy breathing.

With a sharp finger I pointed, "Shut up. This doesn't concern you."

He was a loyal employee, but this was as far as he would go for his boss. There was no fight there.

Billy was close in to Jaffy now, "This could end badly for you. My friend here has put everything into that truck. He wants it back and so do I."

Jaffy flopped to his wide ass. He sat like a toddler who fell after learning to walk.

"I ain't no rat." The fat man spit.

The back of Billy's right hand caught Jaffy in his fleshy red lips. Jaffy tasted the blood then spit it out.

"Ain't gonna be enough." He grinned with blood at the corner of his mouth.

I stepped up and reached in my back pocket. Jaffy flinched when he saw the dull finish on my brass knuckles. Used over and over again left them tarnished with others blood and scratches from broken teeth.

"You tell me when it starts to hurt." I said and grabbed him by the unlaced boot.

"Alright, damn it, alright. I ain't know no for sure but," Jaffy reached out for the toppled over desk chair. He righted the chair. With heaving breaths, he sat looking at both of us.

"Since you two been outta the game, been some new players take your places. They got connections, the kind you can't get around." Jaffy's face was covered in moisture, even around his eyes. He smudged the sweat bubbles with his wide grease-stained palm and looked at it before wiping it on his thigh.

"I haven't done any business with them. I swear." Jaffy put his hand up, palm out like he was swearing an oath. "I think they part of a new MC, that's probably who you want."

Satisfied by what the fat man said, I made my way for the door. Before I opened it, he said one last thing, "You watch yo selfs." Jaffy grabbed a red shop rag and blotted his still bleeding lip.

Billy drove us back to his new shop.

The beer helped lift the fog of the hangover and I started to feel like myself again.

"Did you notice any motorcycle tracks where your Scout was parked?"

I shook my head no, "MC's." I said sorrowfully. "Jaffy's not too far off than. I'll start asking around."

Billy scoffed, "No you ain't. Leave the clubs to me." Motorcycle clubs in Daytona Beach were an institution. You hear of blocks in towns cops won't go, there are clubhouses in this town the cops won't go unless in large numbers. They would never admit to being afraid, the cops here like to shoot first and blame you later. At least you know where you stand with them. Something about this beach town collected a lot of trash, cheap hoods looking for big scores. I can't really blame the local PD, they do the best with a town full of transients, policing is difficult. That's why I did what I did in the middle of the night, the things the cops can't do.

Being a new club, whoever their connections were had to be big. Like any other gang in any other city, turf is important. A club can't just show up in their cuts and start rumbling around on hogs and think nothing will happen. There must be something or someone backing them.

Leads dissipated as my mind wasn't all together yet. The cool breeze off the ocean held me there in the dune with the dead reporter. Her gaze, eyes held open, held me there. I stood up, knowing going out there alone was dumb but my mind needed my body moving or else I'd be stuck thinking of April Ward all day. Having Billy at my side was a smart move. He had a way about him, his broad smile was soothing and inviting, and he knew everyone in town. The custom car and bike culture in Daytona was a tight community. New club or not, there was a chance Billy knew someone there.

"You're right," I said and started pacing.

"No resistance?" Billy chuckled and sipped some more beer.

"My mind's still spinning." With each sip of golden ale, I tried to clear the static, and go back to that dune, the sand, the moon, her face.

"The girl, huh? No recollection of who she is?"

"Nope," My head tilted back, and I closed my eyes to see things as I saw them before. "Young, about twenty with dyed blond hair and a small black dress." I opened my eyes.

"Sounds like you should have got to know her." Billy smiled with lifted eyes in amusement at his crude joke.

I didn't acknowledge him or the joke, "I'm sure I never saw her before."

"Could she be somebody Sanford sent you after? Maybe she has ties to a club."

Billy had a good point. Like the Daytona cops, I had avoided the bikers in town. Sanford didn't seem concerned with them and their activities. It could be the demographic or geographic reasons that lead him to choose where and when to strike against the criminals of this beachy town. We never discussed where he got his information. I was given a name or address and a list of crimes against the city. Then I went to work. A one-man cleaning crew, enforcer to some and death dealer to others. I had not killed them all, most just needed corrective behavior and others could just be run off. Somewhere among the beaten and the dead was this girl, beaten and dead herself. Was I to blame?

"No, we've avoided direct contact with any clubs. Besides, any of the real mean criminals I put down are dead." I have a recurring dream; I'm knee deep in a shallow grave holding a man by his t-shirt. His face is smudged with black damp earth, the kind of nutrient rich soil you get in a can of worms. My hand smears the earth away but more springs from his flesh like sweat from pours. My feet begin to sink, and I can either go down with the corpse or let go and escape. I clear the dirt one last time to see the man I'm holding is me. I wake up before I make my decision.

"No coincidence here brother, whoever dumped the girl knew you were there. I'm sure Camp will get back to you with more details." Billy said.

"That's what I'm afraid of, I need to know how I'm connected to this girl before the police come with more questions. One slip-up, one inconsistency in my story and you know they'll lock me up for good this time." I emptied the beer into my mouth. Billy chugged his beer and was up to get two more. I declined the second round. I needed sleep, not alcohol, but sleep would never come, it never does anymore.

Billy was disappointed when I told him I'd see him and made my way to the stairs that lead up to

my single room apartment above the office of the
auto shop.

# <u>Chapter 7</u>

The next morning, I slid out of bed. Just having slept the night in bed was an accomplishment leaving me hopeful the rest of the day would produce more.

In the shop office Billy sat at his desk punching on his grease-stained keyboard. Out in the shop I could hear an air ratchet zip off and on.

Billy waited until I was seated in one of the customer chairs before he looked at me. "Talked to Jaffy last night.", he said.

"Good."

"Maybe. It's stuck in a field south of here."

"Fitting, it was built by a tractor company." I smiled, knowing the truck was nearly home. I sipped some more coffee, "What do you mean maybe?"

Billy sat up, "The field is out off Tomoka Farms Road. Near some new clubhouse for the Dead Ends. I never heard of them. I made some calls. It's some kinda new club for, ah, *millenniums*." Billy's voice went up an octave nearing dog whistle levels. He reached out at a scrap of paper next to the phone, held it close to his nose then all the way at arm's length.

He nodded, "Millenniums." His eyes rolled off the note covered in his chicken scratch to meet mine.

"Millennials?" I asked.

"Could be what he said. What the hell is a millennial?"

I could feel my brows push together as my mind raced to catch up with the news he found out and make it make sense.

"Me, I guess. People under thirty-five or so."

Billy smooshed his lips in an effort to think. Then he said, "So, what am I?"

"Ah, you're a Gen-X'er." I studied the lines around his eyes and mouth trying to remember the last birthday he had. We had been friends for half my life, and I remember my milestone birthdays he celebrated with me. My eighteenth celebrated at the dog track where I got to know the infamous Smitty for the first time and had beer in public. Twenty-one was celebrated with a trip to Las Vegas where we hung around casinos trying to talk ourselves up to robbing one. It was a lot of talk and daydreaming, no one ever robs a casino and lives, for long. After that there was maybe a birthday or two spent together but never really celebrated. He showed up at the county prison to visit me on my birthday, never actually acknowledging it was my birthday, but I knew he knew. And in all those birthdays of mine, I can't remember one of his.

"Yeah, I guess I'm getting old." The wrinkles around his mouth smoothed as he relaxed his face. "Any way, these young punks seem to think they can come to Daytona and start an MC and just start stealing shit. Sorry mother fuckers, gonna learn though."

I nodded. If they had stolen my Scout, they would learn you don't mess with classic cars in a car town.

"Seems kinda easy for them. It's like Jaffy said, they've got to have some kind of protection." I pondered how a group could start up with full colors riding around on display and not get torn apart by the Outlaws or the Pagans. Clarity of thought came with an empty coffee cup. I needed another then we would have a plan to get my Scout back.

"Well?" Billy stood up. "Sitting around ain't gonna answer nothing. Let's go get your ride back." Billy's smile showed a missing tooth on the top right side of his mouth.

We went to the war chest and gathered all the tools we would need to pull the Scout out in case it was stuck. Billy didn't have a wrecker for the shop, so the F150 would have to do. Billy's eyes glanced at the pistol in my waist. It was always on me now. Bringing my set of knuckles crossed my mind. That would mean work, and this was about my Scout. I wanted to know more about this new *biker gang* before kicking in doors and shooting the idiots that stole my Scout. I must admit the irony in being so upset over a stolen car. How many times Billy and I had taken away someone else's pride and identity with the pop of a lock or turn of a broken ignition. Times like these, it's hard to say I do not believe in Karma especially when it kicks me in the teeth.

We hit the trail to take back what was mine. I had my best friend/mentor by my side. He had his red skin in the game as much as my white ass. That Scout meant a lot to me, car guys get it, others not so much. Memories and meanings were wrapped up in the broken bolts and busted knuckles we had bringing the rusty hulk back from the brink of the bone yard. To Billy, that Scout was me, with every turn of the wrench he fixed my ride but also fixed me. I was lifted out of the darkness with every new part bolted in place. I may not have reached the light yet as the numbness of purgatory continues to keep me wandering, but nothing gets me closer than firing up that 345 ci Binder motor. There in the fog of exhaust and warmth of the V8, I am restored.

It was time to get her back.

For the most part there wasn't much on Tomoka Farms Road once we got south of the city. We passed a gas station and next to it was a blacked out single-story block building with a tall chain-link fence running out from both sides. Each stretch of chain-link had dark green fabric pinned to it. On the metal door was a yellow Dead End street sign and under it hand painted was M/C making it unmistakable.

Billy swung the F150 into the gas station, putting us a hundred yards from the front door of the Dead Ends' club house.

"We might as well have a look." He said and plucked a cigarette from the pack.

I had binoculars looking down the road to the clubhouse, trying to catch a glimpse of something in one of the blacked-out windows. It was a waste of time; they did not want to be seen. There was nothing to do but wait.

Fortunately for us, the cold front was still dipping into the most southern state. The greenhouse effect in the cab kept us warm and we even had the windows down about half-way. We waited and watched. Drank a couple Red Bulls and waited and watched some more. The clubhouse did not stir.

After discussing it, we decided it was safe to get a little closer. I got out and walked while Billy pulled the truck closer to the clubhouse. Just short of being across the street, he flipped on the flashers and popped the hood. I walked by a few minutes later and casually strolled over the crunching gravel to the fence. I got a look past the green fabric into the yard. On the other side was more grey gravel and an open barn with four stalls on a concrete slab. The stalls were empty. Standing in the shadow of stall one, were two men in black leather vests. One had a grey skull cap and the other a mesh snapback hat with the bill curled up at the front. Neither one of them were dirty. They looked well-groomed down to the shape in their straight beards. The ink on the guy in the ball cap looked fresh and bright. The other had no visible tattoos. Their faces were both round and pinked by the cool air.

The ball cap pointed at sides of the stalls and walked around them like he was laying out a plan to build or add on. The skullcap nodded and agreed to everything.

Ball cap was looking at his phone now. He sent a text and they both turned towards me, I had to remain still. Movement would give me away. Their gaze was nothing more than their paranoia scanning the yard. I took a slow and soft step back, losing sight of them behind the green fabric. As gravel crunched under their feet, I kept on a slow retreat to the road, keeping my eye on the gate but my body pointed away from it.

Not wanting to chance them seeing my face, I sped things up as I neared the road. Without looking back, I did not know if they ever emerged from the gate or went into the clubhouse from a back door.

Back at the truck, Billy was wiping his hands with a blue shop rag then shut the hood. We both got in the cab, and he pulled out into the street and headed north.

"That didn't take long." Billy lit a cigarette and cranked down the window.

"There were two in the yard. If it is a car theft ring, they have a lot of work to do. There are just stables out there leaving the cars exposed." I shrugged. We still didn't know for sure it was them that stole my truck.

Billy nodded in silent contemplation. His eyes flickered and asked, "So what's a millennial biker look like?"

"Like a couple of snowflakes in leather cuts. I'm not sure how they've survived this long without some other clubs ripping them apart. Maybe those two I saw don't represent the whole organization." I shrugged. "If they are stealing cars, they must dump them fast."

"Like in a field." Billy pointed with his burning cigarette.

The blue and red lights flashing in a field led us straight to my Scout. Problem was the cops had beat us to it. Billy waited in the truck as I made my way out there. The officer in charge would not let me in it and said Detective Waycross was on his way with the crime scene unit, the same detective who hauled me in and tried to get a confession until Camp shut him down. He didn't like that, so I thought it was best to split.

Billy had the F150 already moving before I climbed in. He was about to pull out but hit the brakes. We watched a parade of Outlaws rolling like thunder as they each took a turn at us in the field. For the rest of the ride back, every wide-open throttle on a Harley got my head to turn despite knowing Billy would have spotted a tail better. I could not let it rest. Any of it. There was no way to tell if this young biker gang playing dress-up had dropped the dead girl in my lap and took my Scout or if they simply saw an opportunity while I was passed out drunk. Then they leave the truck in a field less than a mile from their clubhouse. Nothing was making sense and that was making me nervous.

Back in the shop I peeled off my jacket and grabbed a water from the fridge. Jose had a fresh pot of coffee going when we got in and Billy poured a cup. I sat holding the water with one hand and flipping through my phone with the other. Then I would switch to warm the other hand. My finger scrolled through Facebook looking for April Ward's page. Routine took me first to Alysa's page. She updated her profile photo since I last cyber stalked her. It was far from real stalking, I checked in from time to time. Her page was locked but I could still see activity and that new profile pic. It was from the other night at Cooper's. She was in the blue dress with her two friends. I zoomed in to see those green eyes, but my fingers missed, and I enlarged the side of the picture. I spotted a familiar shirt and tattooed arm coming out of it. It was mine; I was partially in the photo. Past me, further down the bar, I caught sight of another familiar blond. April Ward was sitting at the bar looking my way. My back to her, I saw her, but I hadn't been looking for her either.

It was impossible to be certain she was there for me but considering we wound up together on a beach, it was not a stretch. I immediately found April's page.

The news was out, and people continued to post their condolences. I switched over to the local paper and looked for the story. It was brief as the cops were not releasing any information, just that she died. Then there was the line about leads and suspects. I took that one personal. The rumblings of the vigilante were sounding. It would not be long now before someone tried to connect dots that were not there.

Billy was on his phone as well. His focus was still on the Scout. Now we knew the cops had it, Billy wanted to know how it got in the field. Was it a joy ride or the deal fell through, so they ditched it? If the Dead Ends had an empty stable, then they had buyers. In our day, we would have moved a truck like that out of state or even out of the country. Usually classic 4x4's fetch good money in places like Europe or China. So, it came down to either the Dead Ends were hired locally to steal this specific truck, or they really were as dumb as they looked. As a part time gambler, myself, I'm betting both.

Calls went out on Billy's end asking around this time not looking for a chop-shop but looking to buy a Scout. My attention was on my coffee and my phone. As each of his calls ended, I looked up, he would shake his head no, and I would go back to Facebook.

Candice Burke had posted another message to April. Again, it was about their journalism class. She posted the name of the class, 'all of us in JL3404 miss you'. I cross-referenced the course number in the college catalogue and found out it is a current class. JL3404 wouldn't be in session until tomorrow at 9am. Going back into Facebook, I screen shot a picture of Candice from her page. She didn't list a job or any other current classes.

Billy was still on the phone, so I had no clue if he was on to a buyer or not. A text from Sanford came through.

*I have a job for you. Need it done today.*

So much for my winter break.

# **Chapter 8**

The sun was out but the air was cool and dry. Billy grumbled when I took the F150, so I'd need to find wheels of my own soon. I left the truck parked in a spot on the street and walked up to the CBR building. Inside the curly haired security guard smiled and waved as I passed her station to the elevator.

On the seventh floor I entered Sanford's office.

Monique was sitting at her usual post and dressed down like she came in on her day off as a favor to work. Even on dress-down day she was well put together. Her aroma, a floral scent, light and airy with just a hint of spice that let you know there was more to just stopping and smelling the roses. Her kinky black hair was pulled back tight and flat with not a single strand free. A white V-neck t-shirt with the gold letters of some designer covered her midsection but left open her soft round cleavage. Her left leg was tucked under her right thigh and covered in expensive denim. I could not see her shoes but figured they were expensive as well.

Monique's hand went up, "He's on a call." She pulled the hand down and went right back to typing.

"Okay." I said and continued for the door.

"Not this time Grimes. I need you to take a seat."

I stood for a moment, then chose a seat among the row of chrome chairs under the African motif of crossed spears flanked by twin zebra hides on the wall. My eyes fixed on the only noise in the room. Her posture was true, and her fingers were quick as long nails picked at keys, entering data, and completing files. My brow pushed together as questions log jammed at the front of my head. Was my name in those files? What was she logging?

Sanford was smart, he would keep me out of most things. There were a few above-board jobs we took, where I caught the cheating wife or found the missing designer dog. Those were the jobs I thought I would be doing day in and day out when I first got my private investigator license. It doesn't happen often enough. Soon, those will be the only jobs I take. What could Sanford possibly be talking about that I couldn't hear? I was the guy that trudged through the gutters of this town to tear apart any of the dirt he saw unfit. It made no sense.

My palms grew damp, and my knee wouldn't stop bouncing as I waited for the buzzer and the sound of Monique's voice letting me through.

We never talked much, her and me. In a year's time we had maybe five whole sentences pass between us. Her focus was on the computer screen, the fury of typing, this time I knew she wasn't online shopping. I remained silent, thinking about April at Coopers then later dead next to me. Just as I began to repackage all the paranoia, I had unpacked in the silent waiting room, Monique told me to go in.

The gold carpet in his office was plusher than the course Berber carpet in the waiting room. My Vans left honeycomb tracks as I took my seat.

Willis Sanford stood behind his large mahogany desk looking sharp in a baby blue button up and black vest. The top button was undone and there was no tie. This was a dress down day for him as well. I never dressed up, so every day was dress down.

Sanford gripped the back of his tall burgundy leather chair. His nostrils flared as I took a deep breath and let it out with similar force.

"You want a drink?" Sanford nodded to the wet bar tucked in the wall between wood paneling.

"I'm good." I said eyeballing his tall glass of pink grapefruit juice.

"Yeah, I'm trying to lay off the sauce. Cut back at least. Monique's been keeping an eye on the liquor bill; she says it's too high."

The way Monique had a handle on a boss like Willis Sanford confounded me. She stood up to the lanky former boxer in ways I did not. Feminine charm goes a long way and so did her legs. Still, she stayed employed. I had always liked her for more than her looks even if she usually was all ice. It made the times she was nice that much warmer.

"No, don't say anything," Sanford said waving his hand. He looked at me from the corner of his eye with a half grin. "You weren't going to. I know because you never talk."

Sanford enjoyed jawing and he did so across the office, floating like a butterfly, pver the Daytona skyline, his feet never crossing.

"Detective Waycross has been calling. He wants to talk to you some more. They have found your truck in a field off Tomoka Farms." He clasped long fingers together and pressed two to his lips.

"I know. I got there a little late." I rubbed my temples trying to sooth the ache that was building. Catching breaks wasn't in my fortune.

Sanford dropped his hands flat on the desk. "Okay, anything you want to tell me?"

I shook my head without saying a thing.

"Probably best you don't." Sanford pushed back from his desk but remained seated. "This job is coming at a bad time. We'll get to that in a minute. I know you were supposed to be on vacation, I'm sorry. Don't worry, these cops have nothing so the guy with the criminal past is suspect number one, that's all. And there's this." Sanford clicked on his computer and then turned it around.

I looked at a screen loaded with the local newspaper website. He clicked the play button, and a small video box showed a man in a mask beating a man in a wheelchair.

"You know Shoeless Sam?" Sanford closed out the website.

"Yeah, the double amputee panhandler. Usually off Mason Avenue."

"Well, this video is supposed to show the Vigilante beating him."

I ran my hand over my bristly scalp. "His crime?"

"Panhandling, I guess. Obviously, a copy-cat or something. The media seems to be driving this as much as the cops. What's worse is somehow my name has surfaced. I've been getting calls from news outlets, people pretending to *be* news outlets even fake police. It all just feels like..." Sanford licked his lips. He wanted his Remy.

"Like it's about to fall in on itself." I said sitting still in my seat. I used to be a thief. There were jobs that imploded just like this was imploding. When you run an operation long enough, at some point shit goes wrong. So far, I had been careful. The people I ran out of town were gone and the ones that stayed alive never saw my face. The rest were dead. As a thief I never got caught, as a vigilante I will not now.

"We're still ahead of this thing. Don't worry." Sanford said getting on track and walking back his moment of hysteria.

"So why send me on a job now?"

Sanford could no longer hold out; his eyes were fixated on the wet bar. His feet no longer fluttered, now heavy and flatfooted, made the arduous trek to the liquor. The marble countertop did not receive the thick glass well. The Remy went into the glass, but it didn't last long. He doubled the next one.

"A call came in from a woman I haven't spoken to in years, I haven't seen in decades even. Her name is Sheela Richards. We go way back." Sanford pointed towards the west facing window. He held the glass near his lips but did not drink, his eyes cast off in a stare that went for ever. Then he nodded, drank, and said, "Her grandson was busted stealing cars. She called me for help. I helped her grandson, Terrence, legally. He quit stealing and was signed up for college classes again."

Sanford didn't speak as he walked back to his desk chair and sat in it.

"This *gang* or what have you is now threatening him. They beat him up pretty bad a few nights ago. He locked himself in his room for two days before Sheela found out. Now they're making threats." His hand was open and flat on the table. Slowly he curled his long fingers into a tight fist.

I don't like threats. I never have.

"Is the gang afraid he will rat?"

"I suppose. Terrance won't open up about it. I would love to cut you loose to go do what you do best, but the timing of it all." Sanford's chin went down as he shook his head, "Really, I just want you to investigate this, find who is responsible and kick it over to the cops." Sanford pushed up off his desk to his feet.

I stood up as well.

Sanford said, "Go do some real investigating for once." He smiled and I let myself out.

In the lobby I smiled to Monique who actually smiled back.

"I've emailed you the file on Terrence."

"Thanks," I paused with no words to follow.

"Go get 'em Grimes." Her smile was full of energy.

I nodded and walked out.

# **Chapter 9**

All the information on Terrence was in the file on my phone. This was a personal case for Sanford so I should have just driven straight there. Instead, I found a stool and a cold drink at Cooper's.

It was just after eleven and the old wooden doors with faded brass hardware had just been unlocked. The downtown business lunch crowd had not been released from their cubicle corrals yet, so I had the place to myself.

The TV's were on but the sound off. A news broadcast showed a familiar street in Daytona. Yellow police tape flapped in the wind. I didn't need the volume on to know what the reported was saying. Noise came from the kitchen, drawing my attention. Clanking of pots and other processes cooks went through to get their day started. I sat patiently with my phone out. Instead of looking into Terrance, I had April's photo up. Then I heard a familiar voice.

"Grimes."

I turned in the direction of the voice and my heart lept off the high board and splashed deep into my chest.

"Hi," was all I got out from the goofy smile on my face. I was caught off guard. The last time I saw her she was shutting the door in my face and locking it behind her. It was the end to a horrific thirty-six hours. Getting close to me nearly cost her, her life and mine in trying to get her back. Her kidnapping went unreported, and I was thankful for that, but it cost me ever getting closer to her.

"I didn't know you were back working here." I said turning in my seat as she passed by to take her place behind the bar.

"Wayne needed me. He called and offered me the moon to come back." Her face was tight with her lips barely moving as she spoke. Seeing me wrapped her up in that trauma. She broke loose of it with a slight smile and then moved some glasses around. Alysa wore a Kelly-green polo with Cooper's yellow logo embroidered on it.

She began to remove all the little white paper cones that covered each open bottle of liquor lining the glass shelves. It was nice to watch her stretch up on tiptoes to clear that top shelf. As I watched her calves bulge and butt tighten, I suddenly became aware of how thick I had become around the middle and looked down at arms now less defined as they used to be. The man in the mirror across the bar was far from what he had been when I first came into Coopers last year.

Back then, my office had been down the street but, Cooper's was the place I did a lot of business from. A place to meet with clients and friends. Alysa was the bar tender and we hit it off, but only ever had one date. Regrets, I had a few.

Another Cooper's employee came out from the back. He was just south of 5'10" and had a small pot belly. The lines around his tanned face and streaks of grey put him at about 45 years of age. I knew him, his name was Wayne Ayers, the owner of Cooper's.

He said something to Alysa about meeting a liquor rep, then turned. "Hey there Roger." His arm stretched across the bar. We shook. His hands were large for his frame with an incredible grip strength from lifting kegs and twisting off beer caps.

"You still catching cheating spouses?" Wayne's smile was genuine.

"Yeah, Grimes, keep any insurance companies from paying injured clients?" Alysa's smile was crooked and faded quickly. Ouch, I felt that cut through my chest. I smiled through the pain. What else could I say? Alysa sounded bitter and I didn't blame her.

The silence was broken by a guy in a blue polo dragging a rolling case with booze in it. He smiled to Wayne who stood up straight with a smile and walked off to escort the liquor rep to his office where they could do shots of the latest liquors.

"So, you still drink that oatmeal stout, or you want to go straight to the bourbon?" Alysa gave me a smile that felt rehearsed.

"Actually, I'll take a water."

She let a frown slip through then brushed it off and brought me an ice water. She put it down with a coaster and said, "Everything okay?"

"Yeah, what do you mean?"

"Health wise."

"Oh, other than a little out of shape I'm fine." I said then arched my back in a stretch that crackled and popped in different areas. My shoulder ached once more, and I rubbed it. She searched my eyes for a hidden truth. It was on my face and in my posture. My eyes were different now, changed by what they had seen in the dark. Her own eyes, the fancy green gems, had undergone a similar transformation. They had seen things, things that separated us but also joined us forever by events we would not talk about.

She watched me sip the water. Her hand went out but laid flat against the resin-soaked bar. I put the water down. My hand responded but stopped short of hers. She withdrew and wiped her hand in the white bar towel then turned back to setting up the bar for the day.

"So, if you aren't drinking, what brings you in?"

As much as I wanted to flirt and tell her she was the reason, I was here to find out about April. It didn't matter who my bartender was, I had questions to ask.

"You ever see this girl in here?" I passed my phone across the bar.

A crease imprinted between eyebrows as she studied the expanded image. I hoped she wouldn't zoom out of the picture to see it was her Facebook post we were looking at. She didn't and put the phone back on the bar.

"Seems familiar. Was this recent?"

"From the other night."

"Missed connection?"

"Work."

"Oh," Alysa said leaving the words on the bar as she walked down to the large double door cooler to inventory the bottle beers. From behind the glass, Alysa began to disappear, fade out as it fogged with condensation. I sat and wondered about her, what she had been up to and if there was anything still left between us. We had always had a bond, a sense that we should know each other more than we did. Simple life situations kept us apart until she was kidnapped, then she made the decision to stay away.

A smart, sexy, wonderful woman was the price I paid to be a shadowed vigilante. Someone no one could actually thank when the man who raped them was begging for his life through busted out teeth. No cards in the mail or message posts on social media giving praise when the pedophile was punished. I was nameless, a blacked-out silhouette on the evening news.

Alysa closed the cooler doors and put a single shot glass down on the bar. Next, she filled it with Don Julio. No salt, no lime, she held the glass close to her mouth, pinched her eyes shut and sucked it back. Her head shook as she tried to eradicate the taste in her mouth.

"I needed that." Alysa said with her tongue hanging out. "Okay, so, the other night when we saw each other here, I noticed that girl watching you." A sheepish grin smeared across her face, "I saw you before you saw me. That's when I caught her watching you and when she looked at me, she looked away, but it was quick like she knew she was busted."

I sat back and crossed my arms. A smile crept in at the corners of my mouth. So, Alysa had seen me first and on top of that she was scoping out the bar to see if I was with anyone, like a twenty-year-old blond named April.

"You've got a good eye, Alysa. Maybe you should quit this job and come work with me as a PI."

"I'm not ready for that kinda action." Her smile rounded at the corners. She walked off down the bar, I watched her go in those tight khaki shorts reminded me she was a CrossFit trainer on her days off. I missed this view, sitting at the bar watching Alysa bounce around from one end to the other. Looking from her legs to her smile and then back down again felt like home.

"If I did see her the other night, I didn't know her. Not yet anyway."

"Well, who is she?" Knowingly or not, Alysa poured another shot. She held the shot glass out and I nodded that I would take one as well. She poured the second shot and handed it over. We both took the shot.

When the burn subsided, I said, "April Ward, twenty-year-old college reporter."

"Why are you looking for her?"

"You haven't seen the news?"

She shrugged, "I worked, yesterday, both jobs."

"I found her, dead, lying next to me on the beach."

Alysa frowned. I wasn't sure if it was because of a dead girl or that I was laying on a beach with a girl or the memory of the dead men around my feet the last time we saw each other.

"So, you did know her? I'm confused."

"No, after I left here, I had some more drinks and passed out in a dune down in New Smyrna. I woke up and she was there beside me, dead. Choked to death, but also beaten."

"Oh shit, Grimes. That's awful."

She didn't ask. I was reaffirmed she didn't think I was a complete psychopath.

"My truck had been stolen, too. The cops are keeping me on the suspect list because they need someone to point a finger at, but they have nothing."

"So, you need to prove your innocence." Alysa washed out the shot glasses.

"The evidence will do that. I just want to catch the sons of bitches that did it."

"You said *sons,* like you think it was more than one person."

Damn she was quick.

"The only clue came from some motorcycle tracks. I don't know for sure it was them or not." I finished the rest of my water.

Alysa grabbed the glass and started to refill it, but I waved it off. There was still Terrence and his troubles to deal with. More Alysa and more liquor would have to wait.

"Hey Grimes, snapshot me that picture and I'll show it around today. Maybe one of the other staff knows her." She smiled with genuine enthusiasm and melted a little ice around my heart.

"Thanks, be careful. I wouldn't--"

"Don't worry about me. I want to help you find out who did this to such a sweet looking girl."

"Text me if you find out anything." I said and put a twenty on the bar. She tried to slide it back, but I turned and headed out the door.

A text came in from Sanford letting me know Terrance was home. His auntie Sheela was home as well. She knew I was coming and would let me in.

The house sat in a neighborhood I frequented in the cover of night wearing a mask and a hand ringed with brass. The recent negative press on the vigilante sent a static charge in the air that had people around here on high alert. Neighbors were casting glares at neighbors, taking in every nuance, wondering if they had been out the night before. Outsiders like me went directly under the microscope. Criminal or not these people were being fed a lie like the story of a panhandler beaten that made the vigilante out for anyone's hide. All my actions at night meant more police presence and with that more citizen interaction with police. The people in the neighborhood were beginning to feel targeted, singled out. Tensions were building, snowballing into an avalanche.

I pulled up past some kids in the street with x-ray vision, eyeing people that didn't belong, especially a white guy like me in their neighborhood.

I found the house soon enough. It was red brick with a white tile roof that had more roof sealer on it than tiles. I walked over a dead yard and broken concrete bird feeder. Flaking white paint covered a rusty iron screen door. I rang the bell but did not hear it on the inside, so I knocked. The iron screen rattled. The kids in the street froze their play to watch me once more. I smiled and nodded. They did not.

The door opened. Sheela stood tall and straight at five foot nine and slender with wisps of pure white through dark stormy gray hair that was neatly curled. She wore a baby blue zip-up fleece and a pair of white slacks. The fair wrinkles around her mouth and eyes told me she was a few years older than Sanford.

"Yes?" Sheela asked.

I expected her to know who I was. The noise from a TV gameshow broadcasted from inside along with the thud of a soft bass of rap music deeper in the house.

"I'm Roger Grimes." I said with a nod.

"Oh," Sheela hesitated, running amber crystal eyes over my white skin, then opened the screen door. "Willie, he didn't say, well I just wasn't expecting, anyway, thanks for coming so soon, Mr. Grimes."

"Sure." I smiled out of awkwardness.

Inside the carpet was an egg white and free from stains. The couch was floral, mostly a seafoam green color. The accenting furniture, end tables and coffee table were a whitewashed salmon color with gold trim. The whole living room set looked like an ad from the 1990's.

She stood staring at me; much the way Sanford does when he expects me to say something. The humidity under my hoodie increased. I felt like I was in a line up at the police station. Her eyes pinched as her study of my face continued.

At once, her face smoothed out, "I apologize, Mr. Grimes. Willie didn't say much about you." She led the way into the living room. She held out a long arm and I took a seat on the couch.

"Something to drink?"

I shook my head no.

Sheela moved to a lime-colored recliner and sat on the edge. Her posture was straight as she folded her hands in her lap. I was leaning forward as well, afraid to touch anything in this time capsule of a living room.

Drops of sweat rolled down my back as we stared in silence for a moment then I said, "Terrance has been having some trouble."

"Um, yes." She pulled her hands apart then folded them back together. "He got in with the wrong crowd as teenage boys do. But he learned from his mistakes and got outta that gang. Now they have been harassing him."

"Auntie!" Terrance was standing in the hall. He stood about six feet and weighed in around 225 pounds, but not much was muscle. He wore red basketball shorts, white socks, and a grey sweatshirt.

Terrance headed for the door, but Sheela was quick to cut him off. Her hand went out in front of him, and he changed course. His head down as he stomped back down the hall.

"This man here is gonna help you, Terry." She called after him.

I stood, "I'll talk to him." And moved down the hall.

After I knocked, he said yeah, and I went in. His room had dark blue walls. A couple of posters of rappers with gold chains, cash in hand and blowing smoke were tacked up. Terrance was laying on a single bed he was too large for. A television displayed a paused video game. A backpack lay on the floor.

"Are you from her church?" Terrance said without looking at me.

"No."

"Okay, so what are you a cop?" Terrance started playing his video game.

"No."

Terrance looked up at me with one eye pinched nearly shut. He shrugged and waited for me to explain the who, and the what. I honestly wasn't sure how to do that.

"Willis Sanford sent me to talk to you. He's a—"

"Yeah, I know who he is. I don't need no lawyer." Terrance went back to his game now that he had me all figured out.

I moved between him and the game. He waved his arm as he began to protest. I snatched his wrist and bent it back. He moved forward and I swung his arm around his neck and applied pressure, choking him with his own arm.

"Man, what the hell?" he squeaked out.

I let up. He rubbed at his wrist.

"Dude, what the hell?"

"Sorry, just getting your attention. I'm not so good with words but now you get what I do for Sanford, right."

"Kinda, yeah." Terrance wore a sour face.

"Tell me about this gang giving you trouble."

He shook his head like he was not going to talk then he saw me looking at his sore wrist.

"They ain't nothing."

"Look, I won't let any of this come back on you."

Terrance eased up, "They don't scare me none."

I looked around his room at nothing in particular. Then I moved past him and flipped his pillows off his bed. He tried to stop me from lifting the mattress, but I shoved him away. A Smith & Wesson Bodyguard .380 lay between the box and the mattress. I pinched it around the trigger guard and held it up like it was a dead mouse I had by the tail.

"Is this why you aren't scared of them?"

"Man, gimme that." He demanded but made no move to take it from me.

"I get it. This makes you tough. It's a nice pocket gun, something for emergencies right up close. But it won't stop a home invasion. You think you can keep your Auntie safe with that?"

Terry remained silent. Gunshots cracked from the videogame. His character died.

I lifted my shirt so he could get a look at the double stack hog leg of my Glock 30. "That will stop someone. The only thing that beats a large caliber is knowing where to put to the rounds. Have you ever shot this?"

He shook his head no.

"Do you know how to use it?" I released the magazine and pulled back the slide. He didn't have one in the chamber.

"It was loaded but not ready to fire. Even if you had got to the gun before me, you couldn't have shot it without loading a round by pulling back the slide."

Terry was standing, watching everything my hands were doing with the small .380.

"How old are you?"

"Twenty."

"So, you're not even old enough to have this. It's probably stolen, which doesn't help if you get caught with it."

I put it in my pocket.

"Man, don't! I need that." He reached for my pocket but stopped short of coming within arm's length of me.

I nodded in agreement with myself, "I get it. Auntie Sheela. That's why you quit school and won't leave the house."

"They threatened to mess her up and shit, if I ratted."

I loved bullies, I loved to beat the hell out of them.

"Where do they stay?"

"Around man."

"Okay, is there a place they all hang out?"

He nodded, "They usually hang out around the basketball courts off Derbyshire."

"That's not far." I stood and pulled a business card with my cell on it. Terrance looked it over and laid it on the bed.

"C'mon, get dressed. I want to take you somewhere."

"But what if they show while I'm gone?"

"I just proved you won't make much of a difference being here. I'm going to take you somewhere that will make sure if they do show, you will have a chance."

"What about the gun?"

I pulled it back from my pocket. I picked up the magazine and slid it in grip then chambered a round. The Smith had an external safety that I switched on. I repeated the safety action a couple times so Terry's large brown eyes could soak it in.

"Now, switch it off and you're ready to fire. Keep the safety on always unless you see the trouble coming your way. Now," I started to hand it over to him then reeled it back, "this is about trust and responsibility. Don't play tough, be tough. Use this as a last resort." I stuck the pistol back under the mattress.

"What's the first resort?"

"They'll teach you where we're going."

We waved goodbye to Sheela and drove across town to Ben Saadon's Gym. It was set back in a strip mall wedged between a vape shop and a tax specialist. The windows were tinted and there was no sign on the door. Terry stopped as I reached for the handle.

"You sure about this?" He said looking down at the ground.

I opened the door and let the smell of stale sweat and disinfectant wash over me. An instant adrenaline rush filled my veins as the grunts followed slaps on the mats. Heavy metal played in the back corner where the boxing ring was set up. Large blue mats two inches thick joined to make larger squares over the floor with three-foot pathways between them. Along the right wall was a small variety of weights and on the left were the different bags and dummies for striking.

Ben was quick to come from the back office. His time as a Moosad agent taught him not only enough about fighting to open this place but surveillance skills as well. I bought all my spy tech off him. He stood about 5'10", roughly fifty years of age and had mostly silver hair he wore in a classic man's style, tapered from the neck and around the ears up to about two inches of hair on top. He had thick forearms covered in black coarse hair and was rounded all over. He wore a black t-shirt and black shorts.

"Roger, how are you?" His Israeli accent was nearly gone.

"Doing well Ben. I'd like you to meet Terry." I stepped aside and let Terry shake hands with Ben.

Ben let go of Terry's hand and said, "Again."

Terry looked at me and shrugged so he stuck out his hand. Ben squeezed, not to crush, but to make sure Terry could not let go. "Stronger, huh?"

Terry squeezed back and Ben nodded his approval.

"I'd like Terry to get some training."

"Sure," Ben turned to Terry, "What would you like to learn?"

Terry shrugged, "MMA stuff." He started to sway side to side. He was feeling it, the rush of the fight coming. He had it in him, the decision to fight not flee.

"How about I teach you to put a man on the ground, maybe he wakes up, maybe he doesn't."

I peeled off a couple hundreds. Ben waved it off. I said, "For your fighter Pete to go pro." Ben tucked them in his pocket. He put his arm around Terry and started walking him back. Terry looked back and smiled.

"I'll be back in a couple hours." I said.

"Couple hours?" asked Ben, "I will drive him home when he is done."

Terry was in for a long day. I waved and headed out.

There were calls to make and intelligence to gather on the Dead Ends. They were new to town and so far, managed to escape being squashed by the other MC's. Was it inevitable or were powerful forces propping them up? Sanford and I never went after any of the MC's in town. These clubs were nationwide, stomp one out and three more show up in town to take over and expand. Taking out drug dealers and sex traffickers was not without risks. Being killed was obvious but also being caught by police. I hoped in some way my deeds were having a positive effect by freeing up the cops to focus on bigger fish, like established MC's.

A text from a young skinny part-time drug dealer named James came in. He's smart and I've been encouraging him to stop dealing. Our first conversation was with my fists but now it's just big brother advice. He coughs up the word on the street and I don't go after his supplier, if he stays in college.

The text said one of the Dead Ends buys pills from him. A mixed-race kid, white and black, about 20 years old, goes by the name Hitch. He said to check out the Carnival Bar. I thanked him and told him to stop selling his mother's prescriptions.

I drove around waiting on the night to come. The streets around The Carnival Bar were mostly residential. The bar rested in a part of town you do not want to run out of gas in. It's known as the highlands because of the large ancient dunes making it the highest point in town. The bar sat in the middle between a fish fry joint and an independent dollar store. The neighborhood once housed doctors, engineers, and professors. Long ago they fled and slowly it was filled in with the less desirable people in town. The big four-bedroom houses were now broken into duplexes. The cars in the driveways were still Cadillacs but now they were up on blocks. The Carnival Bar remained, becoming an institution of sorts.

The white flight out of the highlands did not affect The Carnival, it still had a mostly white customer base. Though not as wealthy as it had been in the past, the bar now catered to mostly bikers and NASCAR fans. Loud Harleys and Rebel flags seemed out of place now in the highlands, but somehow this bar has remained and even grown into neutral territory with no colors, patches, or racial divides. That's the strange thing about money. The super-rich only see green and so do the very poor. It's all the people in the middle that get caught up in skin colors and pedigrees.

I sat at the far end of a bar topped in fresh plywood still salted in sawdust. Apparently, sections of the bar were under construction and rather than close to finish it, the owner just worked around the patrons. My seat was cracked green vinyl and was not ideal as my back was still exposed to the hall that went to the pisser, but I had to pick a spot to be seen without giving up too much security.

The fat guy behind the bar had curly brown hair springing out across the middle of his head. His hands looked like they were covered in thumbs as he wiped out a glass with a rag, I would not wipe my ass with. He flipped the toothpick from the right to the left of his mouth then asked what I was having.

"Miller Lite." I said and unfolded a twenty.

Jackson's face disappeared under the barkeep's meaty hand. When the sausage fingers came back it dropped a beer and my change. He said nothing as he walked off to the other end of the bar and stood to light a cigarette. He exhaled, letting the smoke rise through the green and red neon beer signs humming in the purple tinted window. He leaned in towards a skinny guy sitting across from him. The bar tender mumbled something and wiggled his brow and shook his head. The skinny guy nodded but said nothing.

It took three Millers before meat hands said anything to me.

"What'ch you got going on today?"

"Just looking for work." I said as I dropped another Jackson on the bar.

The bar tender eyed it then rolled his eyes to the stack of Jacksons it came from.

"Seems you're doing alright."

"This," I said putting away the wad, "It's all I got until I can find work."

"What is it you do?" The bar tender said making his way to the other end for another cigarette.

"Lost and found."

"Huh," He said and looked up at the old box TV showing an action movie, lots of shooting and explosions.

I sat sipping my beer waiting for something to happen. Thoughts floated through a fog in my brain, only to be interrupted by sudden electrical storms. Focusing on specific thoughts put them at a distance, just out of reach of a clear idea. The Xanax at the bottom of the toilet came back to me. Right now, my brain needed me to dive in after it to lift this fog. Cold turkey was coming home to roost.

The beers were making me sleepy. It could be the wrong night or just be the wrong bar tender. Maybe another guy would have caught on quicker than meat hands here. The Carnival was slow tonight and it didn't make much sense to keep on the bar stool sipping beer hoping the gang would show. But that is just what happened. I heard the roar of straight pipes on a late model Evo bolted to a Harley-Davidson Sportster. Sounds of other modified exhausts accompanied it, but the Evo was the loudest. Finally, some action was about to come through the door at the Carnival Bar.

The first guy through was in a new dark blue denim jacket with shiny copper buttons. He had a bandana over his thick black hair and his skin was a soft yellow brown. Behind him were two more guys. One was a tall lanky young light-skinned black guy with a high block of kinky black hair on his head. He had on a denim vest over a leather jacket. The vest had patches on it, but they were the generic ones you buy at shops on Main Street. The other guy was a white kid, shorter than the first two, a clean shaved face and wavy yellow hair. He was well groomed, clean black leather jacket and thin zip-up hoodie underneath. His hands were clean but tatted up.

The white guy blew into his hands to warm them as he looked around at who might be looking at him and then sat down. His companions joined him, giving the place a once over like they were old time cowboys off a great train robbery. They were all Ike Clanton, there were no Earp's here.

The fat fingered bartender put down three cans of PBR and then cracked each one open.

"Cold day to ride." The bartender said.

The three nodded and sipped their beers. They talked amongst each other for a little while. The bar tender had forgotten about me down on this end and kept his attention to the three newcomers. I studied their faces, young, early twenties, soft but with ever cautious eyes, looking for anyone that would look back at them. So, I did.

The little guy glanced at me a few times then said to the bartender, "What's new Sal?"

Sal shook his head.

"That so?" The little guy slowly turned his head towards me.

"He looks new Addison." Said the first guy through the door. I noticed his denim jacket had a name tag sewn on it, *Hitch*. James's tip was right.

"What's up man?" Addison called to me from the front end of the bar.

I frowned and shook my head, silently explaining nothing was up.

"Get him another beer Sal, maybe then something will be up." Addison turned back to his pals.

Sal poured more foam than beer in a pint. "He says he's looking for work." Sal said trying to gain approval of these young punks. What went wrong in his life that at about fifty, a guy who was strong once, now plays nice with shiny copper buttoned punks.

"What is it you do man?" called out the lanky guy.

"Not much if he lives in this neighborhood." Cackled Hitch.

Sal put my beer down. I nodded and sipped the foam.

"Well, whatever he does, he does it well." Said Sal.

They all moved as one collective down the row of stools towards me. Hitch sat while Addison and the other one stood.

"So, what is it you looking to do?" Addison said leaning back, his short frame catching the bar high in his back. He interlocked his fingers and grinned.

Four beers in and my smile was lazy. "A little of this and that. Depends on where the money is."

They all laughed with too much enthusiasm to let me know they were on to my way of thinking. Introductions went around. I gave my name as George, a go to for me. The lanky guy was Jackson and the other two I already had figured out.

"I know you from some place?" Hitch said as his smile faded, and his eyes raked over me.

I shook my head no.

"You ever been in county?"

"Not around here." A lie, I spent nine months in county lock-up on a trumped-up charge.

They all nodded and looked at one another attempting to communicate telepathically.

Addison stood up and turned to Sal, "Let's get a round of shots!" that's when I saw the patch on his back, Dead Ends. He slapped the bar with loud open palm and turned back with a smile. I lifted my pint and nodded.

The shots were poured, first in the glasses, then down our throats. Slowly we all started opening up. Telling stories and laughing more sincerely. The booze helped to lubricate the conversation. It was tricky dumping each shot I was handed; I couldn't get them all. The liquor eased the social tensions as we all got to know each other. It wasn't long before the invite went out.

"You ride?" asked Jackson.

"I can, I don't have a bike right now." I said.

"Well, we can take care of that if you're willing to put in some *work*." Addison said slapping me on the back. Earlier I would have slapped his round face, but I was feeling relaxed.

"I can wrench." I said. The three self-proclaimed bikers laughed.

"Not what we mean Georgie." Hitch grinned with a knowing behind his eyes.

My eyebrow went up, "Oh yeah. I can *work*." I said and we all let the booze push out laughter.

With bellies full of liquor and blood that was thinning fast, we spilled out of The Carnival Bar and stood around the small parking lot out front. I got a look at their rides. Addison rode a newer Harley Sportster with after-market bars stretched wide and trimmed fenders with a dirt tire in the rear to complete the dirt tracker style. The other two bikes were Japanese from the late 70's or early 80's. Each one with low, short swept back handlebars, flat seats, and no fenders for classic café style rides. Not your typical biker gang rides.

Addison straddled his Harley. He reached in his pocket and pulled out his phone. In it he looked at a list, but I could not make out what it was.

"We have to help a friend of ours find his car."

"Thing is though, he lost his keys." Jackson chimed on with a grin.

"Yeah, so you think you could help with that?"

I nodded that I could.

"Let's ride!" Addison shouted and they climbed on their bikes and fired them up. "You ride bitch for now until we find what we're looking for."

I tensed wanting to clobber this guy's head, crack his skull and let his brains seep out, but then he laughed. It was the kind of laughter that was at me but also with me. "C'mon, they have to double up too." His smile started to fade then I laughed, and he laughed again. These were the guys I was looking for. In order to get enough on them to take to the cops, I'd have to play nice and ride bitch just this once.

My chin cleared the top of Addison's blond mop. With a twist of his neck, he flipped his hair out of his eyes and let out the clutch. Hitch climbed on the back of Jackson's bike and away we went.

The cool air felt much colder at forty-five miles per hour. We cruised up Mason Ave then took a right along Clyde Morris Boulevard. The street ended with a much higher end neighborhood then the one we left. The residential street started to wind and as it did the houses grew larger, going from one story to two story. The garages got larger too. We passed a two-story brown brick house with moss covered wood shingles. The yard was well manicured. An island in the middle with accent lighting showed off two curving palm trees.

We stopped one hundred yards away and everyone killed their motors. I hoped off and stood in the cold with my hood up and blowing in my hands to bring back circulation.

"This is the security code." Addison showed me his phone. I put it to memory. Then he got off his bike and pulled what looked like a blood pressure taker. The black bulb pumped up a small air bag at the end of the black rubber hose.

"You ever use one of these?"

I took the air pump, knowing what to do. The thin bag slipped between the door and jam pumped until it separates enough to slip in a rod and hit the unlock button. But on a new car, especially a luxury car like Mercedes, there would need to be a way around the alarm. This isn't some old time smash the column and twist some wires. They would need more than an airbag.

Back in his saddle bag again, Addison pulled a small laptop with a plug hanging down. I knew what it was, the male end to an OBD computer scanner. With that plugged in under the passenger dash, I would use the software on the computer to reconfigure the keyless ignition, tricking the computer into thinking the key was detected. I had done it a few times, but with the ever-changing technology I wasn't sure my skills would be enough.

Hitch took the laptop saying, "We're going together, in case you fuck up."

"With a set up like this, I'm not worried."

The alcohol we ingested was in full swing making straight lines an impossible task. We made it to the house. Hitch pulled his bandana from the top of his head and tied it around his face then ran up the driveway and punched the code. The door rolled up. We were in.

The Mercedes-Benz was tall and boxy. The iconic design of a G Wagon. My heart fluttered. It had been some time since I boosted a G-Wagon. Billy and I had lifted one in Atlanta just for fun and decided to ride north through the Appalachians, along the Blue Ridge Parkway and see what kind of off the beaten path trails we could find. Any uneven unpaved road sufficed. It was dirty and it was slow going but it was also one of the best trips of my life. Now in front of me was another G Wagon waiting to be tested.

The pump worked and the door popped open. The smell of the new Mercedes slipped through my senses and filled my lungs, the leather and suede seats, and carbon fiber panel accents, everything soft, new, and clean.  It was German engineering at its finest. Hitch rushed in, plugging the computer in. The alarm blurted out then stopped. Rust broke from my nerves as I fought my knee from bouncing me all over the garage. I quickly got them under control and my hands stopped sweating. I was back in it, the life I left a few years ago was here, a return to familiarity brought new confidence.

Hitch punched the start button and the 400-horsepower turbo motor fired. He climbed into the driver's seat. I rode shotgun. We coasted down the drive then he hit it and the motor wound up pinning us in the seats as we rocketed down the quiet residential street.

In the side mirror, two head lights as close together as the front of a single car hit my eyes. Addison and Jackson rode side by side behind us. Then Addison shot out, whipping around us and I watched his taillight fade into the blackness.

"He's taking point. If there is trouble ahead, he'll let us know." Hitch said without looking at me. His eyes darted and I sensed his fear. The adrenaline was pumping a little lighter now starting to make us both twitchy.

We back tracked past Mason Avenue and I said nothing. Hitch was in control and these three had a plan before they met me tonight. There was no point in interfering. I had to start a plan of my own now that I found the gang. Maybe it was the booze or that smell of adrenaline-fueled danger that kept me from seeing these guys as the ones who stole my Scout. I had not asked enough questions at the bar. Now Hitch was in control, he was behind the wheel if the cops come after us. He was maybe twenty-five and I didn't know how many cars he had ever stolen. I had been lazy, now I might have to pay for it.

"You have a plan for this rig, right? This isn't just a joy ride?" My voice felt tight in my throat. Sweaty palms raked over my blue jeans as sobriety cleared my thoughts.

"Relax man." Hitch checked his mirrors several times, enough to make me wonder if he was even watching the road ahead of him. "We've done this before."

His confident words would do nothing for my rapid heartbeat. Stealing cars was nothing new, I had done too many times to count. As we headed west then south, I watched Jackson on his motorcycle behind us, I found myself wiping sweat off my palms more and more despite the air-conditioned seats. The road was familiar. I was headed into the den, the clubhouse of The Dead Ends.

Questions swirled only adding sweat to every pour in my body. I needed more air. The window went down, and the cold winter night brought relief to my body but not my mind. Had this been a set up?

Did they find me when the whole time I thought I found them? *Think damn it, remember that night in the dune!* Nothingness and then a headache and the damn seagulls screaming at each other.

The long dark road led to the clubhouse Billy and I had sat out in front of just yesterday. This time it was dark. The windows were blacked out in the front but from the road I could see glowing from the back of the building. I was one man against an entire gang now, but I knew if these were the guys that killed April and stole my Scout, I had to ensure I would be leaving there with blood on my hands either on my own or in a body bag.

Addison was out front at the gate when we arrived. He quickly closed the gate behind us as Hitch steered the G Wagon into a stall.

I jumped out and moved away from the stall. Anticipating a fight, I did not want to be trapped in there.

Hitch was out on his side and tossing moving blankets over the G Wagon. Addison hustled across the gravel yard to meet us.

"Clear sailing all the way. I jumped on the police scanner when I got here and not a word, hasn't even been reported stolen yet." Addison's round cherub face red from the ride was filled with a smile.

Now inside the gates, I could see the yard much better. The two flood lights lit up the corners of beams on the barn and sloping roof but left sharp black contrasting shadows to the depths of the stalls. The ground was nearly all gravel with sparse clumps of grass. A couple stalls were filled with motorcycles and parts to motorcycles, the G Wagon took another. Two were empty. At the back of the clubhouse was a door. Two picnic tables were out, and a metal barrel was burning pieces of broken pallets in it.

The door opened and two top heavy guys with beards stepped out, each holding four tall cans of PBR. They were dressed in flannels with black leather vests over it. One guy had a ball cap on with the bill curled up and the other was in a skull cap. I recognized them both from the day before.

"Good work guys." The taller of the two guys said and pulled a beer from the plastic ring and handed it to Addison then handed one to Hitch.

The new arrivals looked me over.

"This is George," Addison said making the introduction. Then added, "This is Leonard and that's Dennison."

"Lenny and Denny." Hitch chuckled.

Lenny was the taller one, "Shut the fuck up Hitch. You can call me Wino." His voice was deep and crunched like the gravel beneath our feet.

"And you can call me Denny." Denny said with a half-smile and stuck out a hand with a beer attached.

As I reached for the beer, Denny said, "Hey, do I know you?"

I took the beer and cracked it open, "Nope." I said and drank it down. I wanted to say yes and smash his face in, then before he passed out or died, show him a picture of April, and ask him why. Instead I followed the group over to the tables and trashcan fire.

"So, when's the buyer coming?" Addison asked.

"Later." Wino said as he and Denny silently made up their mind about me. Addison must have filled them in on how we all met because they weren't asking any questions.

Hitch recounted how we stole the Mercedes making it clear I had done this before.

"So, you do this for kicks or you in the life?" Wino asked finishing his beer and starting in on another.

"I'm reformed. These guys caught me at a moment of weakness."

"All that whiskey helped." Addison laughed, his face glowing in the red firelight. Everyone's breath came out in crystal vapors as we stood around shivering, sipping on cold beer.

"Let's go inside and thaw out." Denny said and turned for the door not waiting for any signs of agreement. I took my cue from the others that followed, and we all began to move our frozen limbs and crunch the gravel under our feet heading for the door. That tingle in my gut reminded me this could be a trap and going inside would make it a lot harder to get out.

As I reached the two wooden steps up to the clubhouse, I saw Wino grab Addison by the collar, snatching the little man back and then using both hands to hold him up.

I moved slower buying time to catch words or phrases. I caught neither, just grumbles about me being involved.

Inside, the clubhouse had the esthetics of a high-end coffee shop you find in trendy Miami neighborhood like Wynwood. A small bar was constructed out of pallet wood with an old door for a bar top. The floors were made from pine that had been milled one hundred years ago from two-hundred-year-old trees. The dim wire bulbs were screwed to tin shades with mason jars over the bulbs and suspended from the ceiling by galvanized pipe. An old juke box in the corner was lit yellow and green and played real vinyl. There were a couple of couches, one long and rectangular, and the other comfortably worn leather. A coffee table held motorcycle magazines and a copy of Psychology Today. The music was some bluegrass rockabilly fusion. Along with the classic Steve McQueen poster and other random antiques, the place looked like someone designed what they thought a biker clubhouse would look like but had never been in one. Overall, it was warm and inviting, the kind of place you take a first date, miles from the rough oily smelling biker club I expected.

At the bar was a jet-black haired beauty covered in ink. Long and lean, she stretched over the top of the bar and came back with a bottle of Jim Beam. The bourbon went into a pitcher of iced tea.

"Kentucky sweet tea anyone?" she said with a bit of twang buried in her breath. She wore a sleeveless denim jacket buttoned just low enough to see a red and white poke-a-dot bra and below her waist were jeans ripped out at the knees.

Denny went over and took a glass. He said, "Thanks Carry." with a hand on her ass, marking what was his.

From a hallway came another girl. Her hair was natural brown. She had on a backwards trucker cap and a black and white striped long sleeve shirt. The angles of her face were thin and long, and she liked bright red lipstick and heavy eyeliner.

"Hey Lexi," Addison said raising his beer can to her. She nodded to him, made time to look me over, and then turned for the jukebox. Addison's face transformed from a cherub to gargoyle. I was an invader now, new genes in a pool that had belonged to him.

The twangy vocals of Hank Williams softly pinged from the corner.

I slid a battered metal chair out from a chrome wrapped mid-century dinette table. Hitch and Wino sat with me. Addison sat on a high back stool near the bar and Denny along with the girl mixing drinks sat on a couch. Jackson poured himself some tea and took the other couch.

Now that everyone was comfortable Wino started his interrogation.

"Where you from George?" Wino said slurping his beer to completion.

I said New Jersey. Someone asked what part and I detailed a town on the shore. In reality, I had been there with Smitty and Billy. We were there to steal art from an aging rockstar's home. I fed them details they all processed, passing little glances between each member, searching for a face that had been to New Jersey. When they failed to debunk my story, Hitch bragged about my skill working the door to the Benz, that loosened everyone up. They liked that and wanted stories. I gave a couple, mixing them up along with imagined details to throw anyone off who might have been in the business when I was. Smiles followed knee slaps as I described jamming a screwdriver in a steering column of a '69 Chevelle. Each cheer of my stories proved them all novices at the car theft game.

My brain told me I had the wrong group for the killing, but my gut twitched with nervous anticipation to keep me searching for clues. I still thought they stole my Scout, but I was having trouble picturing them killing April. Addison always had one eye pinched a little more than the other that gave a shifty appearance at all times. But the baby face didn't back that up. Denny was low to the ground and broad. Along with Wino, I knew they could fight. They both looked like prior servicemen. I didn't pay much attention to Jackson or Hitch other than skinny, young, and always on their phones. Someone wanted me framed, they knew April and knew I would be suspect number one. Whoever that person was, they were pulling these puppets' strings.

"You guys ever steal anything classic, American steel?" I said throwing a question back their way.

Laughter faded as the music took over. No one said a word. I sat back in my chair. The record played on then Addison said, "Dead Ends.", and pointed to his denim vest with a giant patch of a Skull and two crossing lightning bolts behind it. Just like the rest of the clubhouse this too, looked fabricated out of someone's head who had never seen a real cut of a biker gang. This is Daytona Beach, birthplace of speed, with chapters of Outlaws, Warlocks and Pagans. Biker gangs are serious business in this town, it's not some TV show here.

"Nice." I said faking agreement to Addison's prideful smile. "Where you guys based?"

No one said anything. I had exceeded my limit on questions. I looked at each of them for an answer. When I got to Denny the bruising on his knuckles stood out this time, something I missed in the shadows of the burning trash can. They were fresh, the kind you get from beating someone.

"We don't discuss club business with outsiders." Wino grumbled. He spread his ringed fingers out from a tattooed hand and stroked his brown wiry beard. The chrome metallic skulls and wolf head rings looked sharp and pointed. Ready to rip the flesh from cheek bones.

"Sure," I said coolly. I finished my beer. After making eye contact with Denny's chic, I got up and poured some Kentucky Sweet Tea. At the bar I turned to the group, "So, can I ask what we do now?"

"Spoke runs the show 'round here. So, we chill until he shows." Denny said getting to his feet. He made his way to the bar where I stood. He poured a glass of tea for himself then went back to the couch and his old lady.

Wino let out a burp and said, "Spoke ain't coming tonight. He's busy."

"Okay. So, what's up with the Benz?" I said leaning my back against the pallet wood bar.

"It sits until Spoke says move it."

"Yeah, so you guys will find me when it's time to get paid or what?"

No one said a word. Jackson and Hitch both looked up from their cellphones. The tension in the air burned off the cool vibe the décor had set. Lexi looked over and smiled with a slight giggle, a giggle that only twisted Addison's face more. These amateurs really had no idea what they were doing.

"Tonight, was for kicks, just a try out." Addison said, then killed the rest of his tea.

"I'm not some rookie and I don't work for free." I put the glass down and moved to the end of the small bar so nothing or no one was behind me. "That's a two-hundred-thousand-dollar car out there and I want my cut."

I was pushing these wanna-be criminals. Finding out what they were made of was a necessity to tearing them apart.

"Who tha' fuck do you think you are?" Denny said rising from the couch and bowing his shoulders. He was the basher, the fighter in the group, no doubt. The blood flowing through his muscles, making them larger, that was creating a fire in my gut. I suppressed a growl as it clawed at my throat.

Addison was on his feet now and that made Wino stand. Jackson and Hitch were watching but not doing anything.

We all faced off. Denny and Wino had folding knives on them as did Addison. I had my gun in my waist band but shooting them all was a bad idea. I didn't like it. If they came at me in a rush, I could lose my gun.

"Guys don't." The Carry said in a whiney voice.

"Shut up Carry." Denny said without looking at her.

"C'mon, remember after Eric, we gotta cool it with the violence." Lexi said from the back.

Denny looked over at Lexi, "This don't concern you."

"*You* concern me, Denny." Carry sat up from the couch. "It was a shit storm after you got tough with him."

I looked to Carry. She had a worry in her eye, not from me but from Denny. The kind a girl gets when her man has a berserker side to him. The kind of rage that gets the cops called and assault charges filed. That's the kind of fight I was looking for. I like a guy that likes to throw hands and bust people up. I liked him so much that I want to tie him in a knot in front of his tough friends and with his old lady watching would be icing on the cake.

Coolness on my part would have to prevail. If these were the guys that killed April then I would have to get evidence, do this by the book to get out from under the frame for good. No killing and no burning the clubhouse down.

I put my hands up, palms out, "It's cool. We can work something out later. Doesn't have to be tonight."

Tensions simmered. Denny had to back down his rage, something he wasn't used to or didn't like doing. I didn't either. I preferred we let our fists work it out.

Once Wino sat down the other two followed. I was still standing. The juke box stopped, the silence heightened my sight, as I waited for someone to move.

Denny pulled back his shoulders as his lips curled into an 'O'. Then he let out a wild-man howl. He let out another prehistoric shout and said, "C'mon, let's have some fun."

Lexi got on her phone started playing music from a Bluetooth speaker somewhere in the clubhouse. Then she met Carry in the middle of the room, and they started dancing, silly at first, just getting loose. Wino waved me over and I took a seat. Addison joined us. We started talking about cars and bikes and the mods we've done or want to do if we had the money. And the conversations carried on through the night.

# **Chapter 10**

The pneumatic gun zipped off lug nuts below my bed as Jose started his day waking me to drool on my pillow. I wrapped the pillow around my head, but it was no use. It hurt to think but spinning in my head were tasks and ideas that needed worked out. It had been early morning before I got home. I had left the clubhouse with an invite to return. Last night didn't feel like work, it felt like relaxation. Going in I had a lot of anger balled up inside me evoking images of dismembering the gang fluttered past my mind's eye. Looking at it from the inside, it all had changed, those guys weren't the menacing violent types they wanted to portray. Amateurs, all of them. It was like looking tough was more important than being tough for them, and by the end I could let my guard down.

I sent a text to Sanford asking if he wanted updates. He said no. I put the phone down on my bed and stared up at the plywood ceiling. *ZZZZEEEZZZ,* *ZZZZEEEZZZ* the pneumatic gun went off. After several more of those my concentration was shot. I sat up and grabbed my laptop off the nightstand and went downstairs to the shop office for some black sludge Jose makes every morning.

I sat in the shop's office while Billy and Jose came and went, getting coffee, exchanging keys to cars, and growing greasier each time. After a third cup of joe my knee started bouncing independently, I knew it was time to start investigating.

Searching the internet, I came up with Hitch's real name, Daniel Ramirez. It wasn't hard, he had every aspect of his life on social media. The others, Lexi, Carry and Jackson all had their accounts locked. Denny and Wino were nowhere to be found. Without knowing their last names, I came up with nothing.

I ran Daniel's name through arrest records in the state. One arrest for shoplifting but the charges were dropped. As far as I could tell he was the only one with any real 'record'.

A review of my notes on April got me back to checking the local college. I needed to head up there and ask around about April and come up with some leads to talk to.

*ZZZEEZZZ!* It was time to head out on the street.

The college took up a couple blocks of International Speedway Boulevard, not far from the NASCAR track. A large parking lot sat in the front and then the main administration buildings. The buildings beyond were of different sizes and shapes reflecting the decade they were designed. The smaller plaster white buildings were original from the 1960's, then the tan brick from the 1970's, the square 1980's architecture and finally the 2000's with lots of mirrored glass and stainless steel.

I took a few law enforcements courses here, enough to get me ready to take the state test for my private investigator license, so I knew my way around. If there was a shot at finding the girl posting on April's page, she would be among the journalism classes.

Across a courtyard, tables were out for student organizations trying to recruit new members. Multitudes of young eighteen to twenty-year-old co-eds meandered about, moving across the square on their way to or from class. Many were gathered around the club tables, reading pamphlets, and talking to club presidents. I looked at the screenshot of Candice with her big kinky black hair and light brown skin color. She had a smooth rounded face with large inviting eyes. The rest of her was large and rounded yet proportional as well. I scanned the crowd for a match and found none.

I made my way up a chatter filled stairwell. Students with books skimmed past or shuffled ahead. It was tough getting the timing right on the steps as students followed no protocol on who was going up and who was going down. On the fourth floor I found room 4120. Looking through the skinny rectangular window, I saw it was a small class. I hoped for a large auditorium class that I might sneak in and sit in the back. No way could I do that here. So, I wandered the hall.

I didn't have to wait long. Candice came out of the stairwell talking to another student. They both held textbooks and carried large satchel bags over a shoulder. They talked with smiles as they entered the classroom.

An hour and half went by then the silent hall erupted in clatter as students began pouring out of classrooms. The professor was shouting something they needed to remember as they left. Candice stood at his desk and talked with the man. He was long and lean relaxed in his desk chair. His hair was curly brown but without the body and hung like a mop. His skin was pasty white and thick glasses bulged his eyes. He wore an old ash grey sweatshirt with purple lettering for North Western on it. So, he likes people to know he's smart.

Our eyes locked by steel cables as the door closed. The connection held through the tiny rectangle in the door as it closed. When he looked to Candice, I stepped aside, breaking the connection.

The busy hallway packed with individually wrapped college coeds slowly disseminated and soon I was alone. My phone was opened to Facebook.

April Ward, twenty-year-old journalism major nearing graduation. She was alive in her photos. Dirty blond hair pulled back in a bun with a pencil as she played Lois Lane. Pointy glasses could not contain her big eyes, the kind that take everything in deep and store it for winter to feed off later. A green long-sleeved shirt hung on her like a flag without wind but was worn for comfort not beauty. That is how she lived. I met her when she was dead. She dyed her hair yellow blond and painted her nails. A little black dress wrapped around slender curves that provided free drinks. She wore heels that night to accentuate her calves and grow beyond the five-six frame God gave her. Earrings, but no necklace, it wasn't that fancy of a bar. An earthy sent of spice and burnt Cherrywood mingled in the rejuvenating fruity shampoo used in her hair.

April's killer was still out there, with a face as shrouded as their motive. The police were shaping a narrative that had to do with her reporting, her vocal dislike of the vigilante. The city's best detective was not on the case. Detective Camp was sent out after a ghost, a vigilante that was righting wrongs all across this filthy windblown beach town. She had all the information, evidence, and witnesses, but she had not made an arrest. The vigilante carried out the justice she was not allowed to deliver, and she liked that. Pressure was mounting now as innocent bystanders fell victim. Our crime fighting honeymoon could only last so long. Then she would have to come for me too.

Candice walked out of the class and looked at me standing by the water fountain. Her eyes narrowed and her mouth opened a bit to suck in a breath. I didn't like it. She turned and headed for the stairwell. I let her go.

Inside the classroom the professor was hunched over his desk with one hand in his curly hair and the other fidgeting with a pen, clicking it and twirling it then clicking it. He had a nice cadence going until the door shut behind me.

He looked up, "Yes?"

I covered the room to his desk. I reached in my back pocket and pulled out a black business card with just my phone number and email.

"I'm a private investigator looking in on the April Ward case."

He took my card, scanned it then flipped it and flipped it back. He placed it on his desk keeping an index finger on it like a paperweight.

"Are you going to tell me your name? Your card here is lacking in the information department." His thin lips parted, and he wanted to smile but stopped when he saw I was not.

"Roger Grimes."

He used his expensive education to study the lines in my face and examine my scarred hands before telling me his name, "Doctor Blaine Igo," without getting up, he extended a baggy sleeve of the sweatshirt that ended in a slender hand.

Igo took my hand in both of his and rotated them. He held it for a while. I took my hand back wiping my palm on my jeans. I already didn't like this guy and him holding my hand for that long just made it worse. He smelled like a tie-dye of earth flavors, but it wasn't from gardening, that would be too natural. His odors were too concise, more on the artificial side. Like he hung out in head shops just to absorb the odors.

"Tell me Blaine," I started but paused as Igo fluttered his long fingers in a dismissive manner, for my lack of formality with his title. "How well did you know April Ward?"

"What makes you think I knew her at all?"

"A P.I.'s hunch."

"A professional." Igo sat up from a slackened position in the chair. "Yes, ah…" He let that thinker's pause drag on, the one where you wait on every breath that what he will say will be so mind blowing that you need a mop to soak up what's left of your brain. When in fact he said little.

"She was in three of my classes."

My silence forced an elaboration.

"Intro to News and News writing, Deadline Writing and let me think, Professional ethics." Igo put a right index finger to his mouth and tapped his lips lightly.

"She was also on the paper, correct?"

He nodded she was.

"And you edit the paper?"

Igo stood and started putting books and notebooks into a satchel bag. "Yes, now a question for you. Who hired you?"

I shook my head, "No one."

With his eyes focused on stuffing his bag he said, "I supposed you wouldn't tell me." Then he stopped and looked up at me, "Yes, Roger, yes. I bet you want all the juicy details. How we worked together on the school newspaper. Late nights and rushed deadlines, things like that." He kept his head pointed down to the desk but lifted his eyes to meet mine. "We worked very closely."

He swung his lanky frame around the desk, threw the satchel bag around his neck and stood close enough to me to make sure I knew he was taller.

"I already told the *actual* detectives everything I know about April. It was a tragedy of senseless violence and I'm deeply saddened. Now please, stop trying to sensationalize this tragedy. Let me remember the good."

"I'm just trying to find out who killed her." I said.

"The police didn't come out and say it, but I suspect she was not alone on the beach." Igo sauntered his long gate to the door. Holding the doorknob, he paused, "There's a reward out now for this vigilante and I hope it works."

I stood there processing what he just said. My thoughts were so scattered even breathing seemed difficult. A reward for the vigilante?

Igo cleared his throat, snapping me out of my internal panic. "That is whom we all assume killed her. She was his greatest adversary. And I plan to expose him." He waved his hand motioning me out. We walked out into the hall together then chose different directions.

As I made my way down the stairs, I couldn't help but focus on every set of eyes that was looking at me. Anyone of these students could recognize me, call out, report a tip, get me arrested. At the bottom of the stairs, I was breathing rapidly and leaned against the cool painted cinderblock wall. I had been on autopilot going after criminals. Sanford was worried and now for good reason.

Outside I caught a lucky break and spotted Candice in the courtyard standing around the club tables. She had a digital recorder held closely to a fellow student who was holding a pamphlet. Beside the two, a chubby guy with bad acne, wearing a tight green t-shirt was taking photos.

I meandered in the background while Candice conducted her interviews. She moved from table to table, asked questions, recorded answers, and posed for pictures. When she wrapped up, her and her camera man stood off to the side talking, then parted ways.

I moved in.

"Candice."

"Hi," She smiled like she thought she knew me. As she studied my face her smile faded.

"I saw you interviewing fellow students over there for the paper. You mind if I ask you a few questions?"

"I can't right now, I, um, I have to go to the writing lab and write this up for tomorrow's edition." She turned and started walking with precision, like there were suddenly landmines hidden in the sidewalk.

"Please," I called to her, but she increased her speed. "For April."

Candice stopped. She turned halfway and looked back at me. The overhead sun pinched her eyes as she gripped the recorder in one hand and held the strap to her backpack with the other.

I trotted over and pulled a business card.

She looked at it but didn't take it.

"When you're ready to talk about what April was in to." I said.

Candice turned and walked off.

# **Chapter 11**

There were two texts from Billy. The first one was about the Scout, wanting to know if I'd talked to the cops. The second one was about a customer call I took last week and forgot to tell him about. That was a long text explaining how the lady was mad and he didn't really care if she came back or not. I wanted to tell him that attitude is why he doesn't make any money at the shop but then I would be forced to take customer service seriously as well and I just didn't want to do that.

I pulled up to the shop. Jose was under a 2008 Mustang GT as I made my way to the office. I said nothing, leaving him to work.

Inside a window with bars on the outside was open giving the air a freshness it hasn't had in a long time. Billy was at his desk punching on a keyboard. In my usual chair was a customer. He had a pointed nose and an extra chin. Dressed in a shirt and tie, he kept an eye on his watch hoping to make it back to the office within his lunch hour. Billy's typing was that slow.

I leaned on the counter, between the customer and Billy.

"Seems to me an auto tech should have more dexterity in his fingers." I smiled at the guy.

He half grinned, unsure of who I was to make such a joke.

Billy looked up only to shake his head at me then went back to punching out a receipt so this guy could leave. After it printed and the yellow copy was stapled to the credit card receipt, the customer finally left.

I sat in the already warm chair. My legs went out and feet went up on the small table that was covered in old muscle car magazines. I glanced up to the small television in the corner played local news with the sound off.  Images of a street corner surrounded by police and yellow tape filled the screen then the reported stepped in front and started talking. Another criminal, another victim.

I pulled my phone from my jeans and saw a message from a number I didn't recognize.

*Monique had a tail coming back from the courthouse today.*

A chill waggled my spine and I sat up in the uncomfortable chair. Monique did not scare easy, and I believed she had a level head. Lazy or overconfident, coming back from the college, I hadn't paid much attention if I had my own tail. I wasn't sure. This wasn't the work of the Dead Ends, they were amateurs but whoever was backing them sure wasn't.

I didn't like *them* going after Monique. It came across as desperate and desperate people are unpredictable.

"What's the word on the Scout?" Billy asked still working at the computer.

"Nothing yet." I shook my head, "It's just getting deeper. I don't like it."

Billy stood up and refreshed his coffee. He leaned his thin frame against the counter.

"That worry in your voice?"

"If it isn't, it should be. Monique was tailed today. I don't think dumping April next to me was a mistake by her killer."

Billy fiddled with his long-braided ponytail. "And the Scout?"

"Last night I met up with the boys who might have taken her."

"And you killed them?" Billy smiled; he wasn't serious.

"The Dead Ends are alive and well, I helped them steal a G Wagon."

"What the hell for?" Now Billy was the one sounding worried.

"I wanted to get to know them, see what they are about. This new biker gang is running around town wearing their own cut like it means something. They're not criminals. None of them have a record."

"You didn't for a long time."

"That's because I had a good teacher." I smiled and Billy took the compliment well. He plucked me before I was out of high school. We had a long run stealing cars together until things progressed into bank robberies and eventually higher end burglary. I was never smug or boasted about being a thief. Inside I resented it, always looking over my shoulder, never getting close to anyone except Billy and our fence and financier, Smitty.

"How do you figure the dead girl's involved?"

"You know," I scratched at the whiskers on my jaw, "I've been trying to connect those two dots."

"The timing is there, if they're the ones that stole the Scout."

"If you'd met these clowns, I think you'd see they don't have it in them to kill a girl. All I know is I was alone when I passed out."

"She was a reporter, right? Maybe she was onto something."

"She had a thing for the vigilante. Maybe what she was on to was me."

"I hope not." Billy said.

I opened my texts. Sanford was waiting on a reply. I let him know I was okay and let him know I thought Terrance was a good kid. Then I shot a text to Detective Camp, asking for any new info in April.

"I put the feelers out. Let's see what comes back."

"And the Scout?"

"Yeah," I said leaving it hanging. I had become more concerned about catching April's killer than exacting revenge for stealing my Scout. Had I matured? I still had a deep love for that hunk of steel. "There's a good chance I'll be killing two birds with one set of brass knuckles."

I left without telling Billy where I was going. He knew it was back to the clubhouse, but he didn't know why. He figured the gang for the killing of April, but he wasn't there, he hadn't spent time with Hitch and Wino or Lexi. Sure, stealing cars for kicks was still a crime but they were just thrill seekers. Exploits to post on social media, building an online world with no consequences, personas that only existed there and couldn't be touched in the real world.

There was a tingling in my gut as I drove back to the clubhouse. Not for wanting to burn it down but to join it. To sit on a leather couch and drink beer with my feet up on a coffee table made from used pallets. There, I could spend my time talking about music instead of criminals, and action in movies instead of the violent ones from memory.

# **Chapter 12**

I drove straight over to the Dead End clubhouse. The F-150 bounced over the wavy asphalt as I slowed to make the turn onto the gravel parking lot. I hit the brakes hard, kicking up white dust, and stopped just short of the closed gate.

I went up wooden steps to the tan steel door and knocked. Then I waited.

From inside I heard a few bolts throw back and Lexi swung the door open. She looked up at me and smiled wide. "Oh, hey, George." She said leaning on the open door, letting it swing side to side as if caught in a breeze. She wore a Guns and Roses t-shirt with the neck and sleeves cut off exposing the edges of a black bra underneath. The blue jeans had tears in the knees and blacked out Chucks covered her feet.

"Anybody home?"

She pinched her eyes as the smile drifted letting me know she thought she was enough for my visit. "Nah, everyone is home sleeping it off."

"Big party last night?"

"No, pulled an all-nighter and finished a job last night." She said as if I should have known.

"Gotcha. I see the Benz is gone."

She nodded, "Yeah but it was a different kind of job." Her hand covered a yawn, she turned her slender body, leaving the door open, then said over her shoulder, "You want a beer or something?"

I watched her swing tiny hips that could barely hold her size 2 jeans up. The pallet wood bar was her first stop. Out of the fridge she pulled a 16-ounce PBR and cracked it open. She left it on the bar and made her way to the couch where she sat with her skinny legs tucked under her. Reaching to the side of the couch she picked up a steaming mug and blew gently then sipped. Her eyes came up to mine patiently waiting for me to say something.

Instead of talking, I looked around the club house. Being now sober, it looked a little different than the other night after we stole the Mercedes. The trendy décor was still there, but I noticed a hallway that went somewhere.

"So?" Lexi finally queried after our silence.

"You think I'll finally get paid?"

"Man, you don't beat around the bush."

I shook my head no and sipped the beer. It was cold and went down smooth.

"I really didn't expect you back. I don't think anyone does." She sipped the hot tea.

"Like I said before, I don't work for free." I moved to the couch and sat close to the arm leaving my back half exposed. This way I could grab the grip of the Glock tucked in my waist.

"I was drunk the other night and maybe came across a little loud. I'm sober now and just want what's mine. So, what do you think, will I get paid?"

Lexi giggled. I was unsure what to make of her. She rolled creamy brown eyes over at me. When she giggled again, I figured out why. It was a look I got before from girls; one I should pick up on faster but never do.

"Maybe," She shrugged, "Maybe not. Depends what Wino says."

"What about Spoke? I thought he called all the shots."

"Sure, him too. It's his call but he don't come around much." She looked around at the clubhouse as if he were hiding and she expected to find him. I got the idea that whoever Spoke was, he had the power that kept the other biker gangs away, like a true Viking in stature with a blonde braid and forged helmet carrying a battle axe. Or all tatted up and quick on the draw, killing without care one way or the other, just because he could. He would have to be something of the two, someone that might be able to beat me.

A whirl kicked up in my gut and spread through my body. I liked it, a man big enough in size or reputation to keep the Dead Ends from being ripped apart by the Outlaws or Pagans. And now sitting here waiting for him, in his arena, to do battle while Lexi watched, was starting to push the worry and contemplation of my predicament out and fill it with pure animal instincts that had been so dormant I might as well have been dead.

That old hibernating caveman was waking up and suddenly I noticed how red Lexi's lips were and the divots of her collar bone where her neck ended and all the small freckles dipping into her low-cut shirt. Too much time had passed since I last bothered to be alone with a woman. My track record was not the best and things usually turned south quick with this new private investigating business I was doing. It seemed like every nice girl I met turned out to be nicer with a gun. This little tart across from me was no exception. The distinct shape of a folding knife pressed against the pocket of her tight jeans. This cat had long claws.

"I can't wait to meet him." I grinned that communicated something right back.

"He's nothing special." She frowned for the first time since I was here. "Everyone listens to him because they have to or some shit. I don't really, though."

The whirl slowed. Maybe he wasn't so tough. All these bikers know is strength. If Spoke isn't the Viking in stature, then, it is the size of his bank account. Being rich and boosting cars doesn't add up either.

I stood up and ignored Lexi's eyes on me as I walked for the hallway.

"Hey, where you going?" she called over her tea cup.

"I gotta take a piss." I said over my shoulder. I could hear the leather sofa creak as she sat up.

"Wrong way." She said as my hand grabbed the brass knob of a door. I twisted; it was locked.

I turned around and she was pointing at a door next to the jukebox.

"My mistake."

I made good on my promise to use the bathroom and came back to the couch. Lexi was still balled in the corner. When I sat down, she unfolded her legs, then scooted along the couch until we touched. The air in the clubhouse became thicker as my breath shortened. That look was back in her eyes, communicating without speaking, I knew what she wanted. Something primal filled my nose as the little waif was replaced by the cave girl.

She slid down into the couch, extending her legs out. Her neck was bent forward at 90 degrees against the back cushion pushing her brown hair out, giving her a wild look.

"We're a pretty tough group you know."

I raised an eyebrow in doubt and nodded with sarcasm.

"Oh, we are. Some of those beatings that they blamed on the vigilante, we did it. What a rush!" Her brown eyes rolled up to the ceiling then back to me. "I know why the vigilante does it, for the high." That giggle returned, this time deeper, more of a groan. "You think you might want to join our merry group, George?"

"You guys ever take it too far beating these assholes up?"

"What's too far?" Her voice was soft and still as she talked about beating people who were already victims of circumstance, or bad luck. It did not make sense.

"Someone died, it's in the news," I said.

Lexi shrugged. "That wasn't us, but we're making a change out there too."

The green recycle bin was full of beer cans, above it was a corkboard covered in small Polaroid pictures. The light was on the Keurig and next to it a K-cup tree that spins so you can decide which fancy imported coffee strikes your palette.

"I don't get how a bunch of socially conscience bikers go out and beat-up *undesirables*." My gut wrenched and I wanted to think she was disturbed, that these twenty-somethings were messed up from too much YouTube or something. The truth was, they were bored. They wanted another high that recreational pot and regular beer drinking didn't provide. They had no purpose outside of posting their meaningless lives on social media for others who were even more meaningless could like, share, and comment. And I had been seduced by them and their social media lifestyle.

Lexi's eyes glazed over like I was a teacher giving a lecture or an angry parent when she broke curfew.

"It's for the greater good dude. Also, we get paid. Spoke gives us a cut of what we take off 'em. Besides, it's how we really get our kicks. So how does Georgie get his kicks?"

I wanted to demonstrate on her how I got my kicks alright. I've kicked in plenty of heads, busting up criminals in their own homes. There were no high, only deeper lows that follow. And it was never about money. Every dollar I took went to charity. Sanford made sure of that. The fog of companionship lifted, I was not one of the *gang* and never would be.

"Look dude, there's a guy out there killing drug dealers and pimps. So, what if we take on some ourselves?" The slack from Lexi's body was gone as she sat up on the edge of the couch.

"The guys the vigilante goes after are hard targets, the worst kind of criminals."

"We just took out some undesirables. A druggie and homeless dude. The kind nobody misses." Her eyes looked away, when they came back, the red had faded to the milky brown once more, "We're helping same as that masked clown."

"The beating the other night of the drug dealer wasn't the vigilante. There were two of them. He works alone."

She cocked her head to side and tightened her lips, then said, "How do you know so much?"

I sat back in the couch and shook my head. Was I the cause of this? Did I, in fact, kill April because doing the dirty work at night was who I had become? This gang of wanna be criminals was moving on from people's property to people's lives. Igo's news articles were right, the city didn't need a vigilante justice warrior, it needed someone to stand up for the beaten and the poor. The beast that fed on the criminals had become too fat. The Dead Ends were filling in the cracks the vigilante made. They wanted justice too, but it was their own version of a fairness that didn't exist in nature. Fairness through a warped perspective isn't fair to anyone. They were on the brink, and someone could tip them in either direction. Two paths lay ahead, criminals or rescuers.

Lexi kicked off her shoes and put a small bare foot up on my knee. Her toenails were painted black, and she had a tattoo on her ankle of a black and white panda bear face.

"You may not get paid right away, but I bet you could join the MC, you know, pledge and stuff."

"Think Denny and Wino would approve me for the club?" I smiled and touched the cold beer can to her foot. She giggled and retracted her foot then rubbed the wet condensation off on my thigh. The afternoon beer and relaxed feel of the clubhouse brought me past the wickedness she claimed the club displayed. We had all done bad things, I wanted to move on beyond the violence. Maybe she could too.

"I'll vouch for you, but you don't need me. The way you stole that Benz, you must be awfully good with your hands." Lexi began to knock her knees together softly at first then fanned her legs like she was trying to fly away. This time, I scooted closer.

"Thanks. I'm not sure this is the kind of club I would join."

Her smile faded and there would be no giggle. My stupid mouth just blew it. Lexi straightened up.

"Too much of a loner, tough guy, George?" She asked running small fingers through her brown hair.

"Something like that." I said turning away, looking at the trinkets decorating the clubhouse, antique motorcycle parts hung on the wall and a brightly colored Mexican woven blanket was perfectly draped over the back of a worn leather chair. It looked like a Cracker Barrel for bikers. The mood was spoiled. I wasn't sure what I was expecting to happen but either way it seemed it needed to.

"This is a family here, family that I choose, not the other way around." Lexi stood up then stomped off for the bar. She turned and leaned against it. The cell phone came out of her back pocket, and she was swiping through social media.

"I'm sorry. I don't have a family so it's just not something I'm looking for." I moved to be with her at the bar. This was going sideways. I wasn't done with Lexi or this club yet.

She didn't look up from the phone. I cupped her slender shoulder in my hand and give it a soft squeeze. This time she looked up to meet my eyes.

"Probably better to not have a family then have the one I had." She wiped at the corner of each eye then assured me with a smile the sad talk was over. I tugged on her finger, and we went back to the couch.

"Hey, I didn't mean anything by it. Tell me more about the club?"

The phone went back in her pocket.

"I knew Jackson and Hitch in high school. Back then I rode a 250 Ninja. They knew I was into bikes and when they joined up, they offered me a spot. Like I said, we're family. Everybody came from some place different. I grew up here, but Denny and Carry are from South Carolina and Wino is from all over." Lexi picked at her fingernails as she spoke, not interested in what she was telling me. Talking was not why she invited me in.

"What about Addison?" I asked, noticing she left him out of the origin story.

"Founding member. His dad and my dad worked together so I kinda grew up with him. He thinks he's my big brother or something."

That look he gave me the other night was not the kind you get from an overprotective brother.

"Founding member and he gets talked to like that by Wino?" I didn't mean to say that out loud and so fast.

"He listens to Wino because he is the only one of us with any crimes on his resume, you know. And Denny was in the Army. Jackson and Hitch are just useless." She smiled there at the end.

"What about Spoke? Did he just throw this together one day?" I struggled to hold back the dam, as questions I needed answered swelled.

Lexi shrugged, "I was last in. Not really sure how it all got started."

Useless. I felt my shoulders drop as the wind blew out of full lungs.

"You ever have someone leave the club?" I asked regaining some excitement.

Lexi wiggled around on the couch like she just couldn't get comfortable, but it wasn't the couch that cramped her muscles. Her one leg went up and crossed over my lap, settling her down, "Yeah, just last week. He rode an older CB 750. Nice bike. I remember when we did the seat and handlebars."

"What happened to him?"

Lexi shrugged, "Spoke don't make it easy to leave. This is family and Eric decided to abandon us. You don't just leave your family. He got what was coming." She took a deep breath then let out the fury of someone leaving the family. Fire burned the softness from Lexi's brown eyes as her lids closed into slits and her brow crinkled together. She was raging. The gull, the audacity to leave the family after they were so tight, just boiled her insides.

The club may be new, but the physiological tactics used to keep people loyal was not. Same old brainwashing, isolate the member, beat them down and then build them up in the club's image. They were no different than the Hell's Angels or Outlaws, just their dress and the motorcycles they rode. Like I have said before, I do not join clubs.

"Sounds rough," I said and finished my beer. When I came up for air, we both stared at one another through a few moments of silence. She ran two thumbs inside the waist of her jeans, across white fuzz on her flat stomach, pulling them away just enough to catch a flash of skin below. The earlier anger was over with and her focus was getting that itch scratched so she could relax.

"It got rough for E, but we had to cut him loose." She leaned a little closer, "Somehow I don't think you'd ever let someone rough you up."

I turned towards her, so we were face to face. "I don't know, that Wino looks like a tough character."

"He is, but he's also smart. Denny does all the punching around here." She reached her hand out from her waist and laid it on mine, "So how are we gonna kill time before they all get back?"

I spread my fingers, interlocking them with hers. I drew her in, and our mouths locked. Our size difference was tangible as my long arms wrapped around her waist. This was about to happen. To hell with the chaos around me, here with Lexi, things seemed to fade away and my focus was on feeling good inside filling the void the pill habit left.

My hands ran up her sides and over the lace of her bra. She leaned back and lifted off the t-shirt.

She held my head as we kissed, sloppy at first, searching, until we found the rhythm of back and forth. Her sharp tipped fingers clawed my side as she lifted off my shirt. Her eyes grew large as her fingers traced over the body art of my tattooed shoulders. Then one finger found the lumpy tissue of a scar, a knife wound I got last year. As if metal detecting she paused and went back over it. She leaned back and looked at all my scars and yellowed bruises. A toothy grin was pushed apart by a red tongue. She licked the scar on my shoulder then went up my neck and nibbled at my earlobe. Her nails dug into my skin.

I pulled her in and popped the clip on her bra. My hands came around to cup her two white puffs tipped in pink. I needed to see the rest of her.

She went for my belt then the button on my jeans, but it was not to be, the sound of straight pipes filled my ears as tires crunched gravel out in the yard. The gang was back. They would be coming through that door any second and being in Lexi's arms was a bad idea.

I let go, she hesitated, holding me there. Then suddenly her arms went limp. She rolled off my lap. We slipped on our shirts. She stuffed her bra in the couch cushion and put distance between us just as the steel door flew open.

Addison's rosy cherub face was all smiles, "Lexi," the smile faded as he gleaned me over. "Hey," he said nodding his head at me.

The rest of the gang; Hitch, Jackson, Wino and finally Denny and Carry came in one after the other, all wearing their club vests. My being there did not deter any of their smiles like it had Addison.

Wino went behind the bar and started pulling out bottles and beer cans. He mixed himself a bourbon and coke then opened a cold beer. Denny stepped up, took the beer, and gave me the once over before drinking from the can.

Denny wiped the suds from the whiskers around his mouth and said, "And the cat came back."

The others filled the space between us, pouring and taking drinks. Carry popped in a K-cup and the room filled with the smell of chi tea. Wino had both hands on the bar looking at us, the referee before the fight. I would let Denny's hubris mouth dig his own grave.

"George, you came back! I hope we can score some more hot cars like that Benz." Hitch said taking his beer. He fist-bumped my hand and made his way to the couch.

"So, what's new George?" Wino said getting to the point of my return.

I shrugged, "Just seeing what's going on. I see the Benz is gone."

Smiles faded from the room. Wino frowned as he and Denny shared a brain. They never planned to pay me. I hadn't been welcomed back like I thought I would when I left the other night. I was an outsider who demanded too much. Their size checked and their power shelved as I entered the scene out of nowhere and heisted a nice payday. The jovial banter the time before had to be reined in. Even if they did want me to pledge, it would have to come at my humiliation and not getting paid was their new plan.

"Well, Spoke took care of that." Wino said.

Lexi went to the counter and refilled her coffee. She took a seat on the other couch, her feet once again folder under her. Her eyes held silent conversations as she looked at each of us. Our exchange had put thoughts in her mind, things that had not been there before I showed up. The bonds that tied her to this group were beginning to fray even if she hadn't realized it.

The group was chatting as beers went into hands. I did not join in any particular conversation, just waited patiently for my chance to say something. Wino came over, his boots clopping on the rough pine floor.

He leaned into me and said in a soft deep tone, "Lemme talk at you a minute." Then his boots clopped to the door.

I followed, feeling eyes on me with every step as we made our way out.

We stepped out getting hit with a breeze that watered my eyes. The sun began its ritual dip into the west as the winter days grew shorter. Long black shadows spread out over the grey gravel in the lot. The stalls were empty of any stolen cars.

Wino sat on top of a wooden picnic table; his boots went up on the bench. He rested flannel covered elbows on his denim knees.

"I talked to Spoke about you today. I told him you helped with the Benz."

I nodded.

He went on, "Addison and the others jumped the gun bringing you along. Not sure what you got them hyped on in the bar that night, but they didn't want the fun to end. You weren't supposed to be on that job. Spoke don't think you ought' a get paid."

"Okay." I said and waited for him to tell me something more.

He didn't.

Now I know why my friends get frustrated with me. So, I had to ask, "Now what?"

Wino scratched at his beard. "Stick around, hang out, be of some more value and then we can see about getting you a patch."

"Sounds good." My hand went out and we slapped hands. "I thought there would be more of an initiation."

Wino got off the table. We stood eye to eye, "Oh there is, trust me brother." His ring covered hand slapped like iron on my shoulder, and we made our way inside. I felt like puking up all the horseshit I just swallowed to keep a straight face. Lying was what I did as a thief, dressing like a repair man and telling a security guard you were called in to check the wires is not the same as staring a man in the face who is willing to take you into his confidence. This wasn't lying it was more like acting. I had to get into their heads, their mind set and try to think like them.

Tough guy routine worked on the last guy that left and probably other people they bullied as well. Their problem was they never met a guy like me. Bully buster. I can punish someone for bullying a guy or for dealing drugs or whatever the crime. But not splitting the cut when it's time to pay up?  It cut me to the core, an old rotten core I thought I had moved past. A special kind of beating was reserved for this group.

Back inside everyone was on their phones. Jackson looked up from his phone, "Hey guys, we made the tracker!" His glee echoed through the mellow setting of the club house.

He jumped up moving to the bar. I watched everyone gathered around him but kept my distance. Lexi moved over near me with Addison again shooting me the stink eye, an eye I planned to pluck.

Jackson held his phone showing a website. The map of greater Daytona Beach had red dots and red lines linking the dots. He clicked on one of the dots. "See, the druggie we beat up the other night."

I stepped towards Jackson and felt Denny's shoulder lean in as hand went up and took the phone.

"Says here, the mayor just announced they have upped the reward for the vigilante," Denny looked back down to the phone for details, "$25,000.00 leading to his arrest. There's a protest planned against the cops for not doing anything about the vigilante. We all need to be there."

I felt the air escaping my lungs at a rapid pace and refilling it took longer than I had liked.

"We can make signs." The gang all smiled at each other, and Addison looked for someone to high-five, but they were all focused on Jackson as he read the news statement.

"The cops are finally going to do something about this asshole." Jackson said.

"Not too soon, I hope, so we can have a crack at him." Wino said. This time Addison found a hand to high-five.

Denny puffed up, "I can't wait."

"We don't even know what he looks like." Carry pipped up, giving Denny that look of concern.

"We're going to find out." Wino said. "Spoke called a meeting again tonight. He says he has the dope on this shit bag that's been terrorizing the hood."

"If Spoke knows who the guy is why doesn't he turn him in?" Jackson said putting his phone away for the first time since entering the clubhouse.

"Not my plan, it's his." Wino cracked another beer.

"You in George?" Jackson asked.

I had been quiet, observing the gang in its natural state, trying to figure their angle. Nothing about their existence seemed to make sense. They were not scary or tough. They stole a few cars and beat up a deserter and a homeless man. So far, I was not impressed.

"Why waste your time going after a killer like the vigilante for peanuts when that Benz must have brought five times as much?" I asked to a blank faced audience. There was no electricity to the light switch in their brains. It was basic math and the safer route.

"Chicken shit." Denny said, then puffed up awaiting my response. I ignored him which hurt his ego more than my fist would.

"I get what you're saying," Wino said. In another life I thought he and I might be friends. "But this guy needs to go. He's bad news."

"Isn't it kinda hypocritical? You're an MC that steals cars and probably other crimes the way you all talk. This guy goes and busts up criminal organizations." I could feel my heart rate increase. This thing was about to go down right then, if they really wanted the vigilante, here he was in the flesh.

"Where'd you say you were from, New Jersey? Maybe they don't take the trash out up there like we do here. Down here we kick it to the curb." Addison said.

"And curb stomp it!" Denny shouted, driving a boot into the floor with a thud.

I looked around at the group. They wanted blood of the vigilante and I could not reason why.

Then Wino finally laid it out for me, "Look George, we bust this racist douche and the Dead Ends become major players in town. We would be free to really branch out."

I did not respond. These were fools and fools cannot be reasoned with. I was convinced they were all living in a TV show or in a fantasy land. Their dress, way they talked, all of it felt so scripted. I have lived the last fifteen years of my life around real criminals, Billy, Smitty and all the others we worked with to steal and burgle. These puppets were just having their strings pulled. The bond they had was tight, something I had been lacking in my life. This wasn't the way I wanted to get it.

"So, are you in?" Addison asked.

I looked each one in the face, "There's not enough money in it." I made my way to the door. A couple of them let the air out with a hiss and Denny reminded everyone I was a chicken shit. It would be comical if I were not coming back to burn the clubhouse down.

# Chapter 13

Billy and I had just got back to the shop from having a much-needed home cooked meal at his sister's house. She was his half-sister and nearly 20 years apart but the only family he had in Daytona. His mother moved back to the reservation in South Carolina years ago. Billy had some internet searching for old car parts to do and I just wanted to crash on my couch upstairs. Alysa called just as I was flopping down on my old couch. It felt good to see her name pop up on my caller ID. She had news on April Ward. Another server at Cooper's knew April from high school and though they hadn't talked in years, knew her friend Candice as well. Candice, as it turned out was at the bar now.

Billy said nothing as I bustled down the stairs and shouted to him, I was taking the shop truck.

I pushed the limits on the old inline six to get me downtown to Cooper's before Candice left. She knew more than anyone where April was getting her information on the vigilante. Main Street was blocked off due to the anti-vigilante march that had grown to incorporate a police brutality march. I had to cut downside streets and not run over any of the marchers.

The bar was sparsely populated with the after-work crowd bellied up and talking shop in loosened neck ties and kicked off heels. Age wise the bag was mixed well from mid-twenties to mid-sixties. There were lots of over exaggerated laughter and arguing over who will get the tab. I didn't fit in with my dark blue mechanic cut jacket over a flannel and blue jeans, staples in every blue-collar wardrobe.

Alysa was seated at the end of the bar near the dart boards. Her golden hair was down with a curl to it. She had on a touch of makeup, accentuating her already beautiful face. With the one month of cold weather in Florida, she wore blue jeans with brown riding boots, a cream-colored sweater and grey scarf tied loosely around her neck. She was talking to Chastity, a curvy bar tender.

"Hey, off the clock?" I said.

"Hi, yeah I can't get away from this place." Alysa said then scooted over one stool, to the empty one next to the server station. The seat was always empty due to the server traffic fetching drinks for customers at tables.

I sat down, smiled at Chastity. With her raspy tone, she asked if I was in last night. I said no and ordered the oatmeal stout. She jiggled her way down to the tap.

While Chastity was off pouring my pint, Alysa and I sat nervously grinning at one another.

"What are you drinking?" I asked, pointing at her half empty pint glass.

"Jai Alia. A not so hoppy IPA made over in Tampa. Wanna try?"

I nodded and she handed over the pint. I liked that she drank beer, real beer, not light and not seltzer. Being a bartender, she was always trying new beers. I liked the IPA but was content to stick to my stout.

"So, *she* here tonight?" I said then sipped my beer. It was a local craft brew with a soft coffee flavor.

Alysa smiled and bobbed her head agreeing. She pointed to the left, over to a table. I turned slowly and scratched at the back of my neck making sure to cover most of my face as my eyes scanned the room. There at a table of three twenty-somethings was Candice.

"I thought a seasoned PI like yourself would have spotted her."

"You're pretty good."

"I get better." Alysa grinned once more and sipped my beer. "That's good. I'll take one of those."

"My PI skills also tell my you're a little buzzed."

She nodded again. "I've been here a while." She leaned on the bar and called out to Chastity, "Two shots." Alysa looked to me and asked what I wanted. I shrugged and she called out for two baby Guinness shots, coffee liquor topped with Irish cream.

We took the shots and then I wanted to get back to business.

"Can your co-worker that knows her get me over there?"

"Don't worry about it. I already interviewed her."

"Maybe I should hire you on."

"Yeah, then we could sit at the bar and get day drunk together all the time."

"Is that all you think I do?"

"Isn't it perks of the job?" She laughed and leaned forward. Her hand brushed along my thigh. "Anyway, she writes for the college paper and has done some work for the city paper. She knew April was writing stories on the vigilante. Candice believes April knew who he was and planned to expose him and that's why she was murdered."

I straightened my posture and said, "You think the vigilante killed April?"

"Well, yeah. I mean the guy has done some good, but you can't defend his serial killer tendencies. Who put him in charge of the court system?" She said with a smile expecting me to agree. The noise of the bar faded away as I stared into her eyes, round and green, unblinking. She had no idea. I never said it bluntly to her before, but I always assumed someone as smart as her with someone as drunk as I had been, could put it together. The bruises on my body coinciding with the violence on the street was too much of a coincidence to overlook. My chest began to burn with guilt. Alysa had been placed on a pedestal long ago and from there she looked down at me. If she knew the truth, I would never see her again. There was still time to turn this around.

"I don't think the vigilante killed her." I said.

Alysa looked past me, further down the bar to Chastity. She pointed to my pint and held up two fingers, Chastity nodded and went about getting another round. I turned my attention to Candice and wondered how I was going to get over to the table. Alysa had found out some good stuff, but there were pieces I already put together. I needed to know who was feeding April her info, who was her informant and just what they had on me.

"Yeah, that would be too easy." Alysa said looking down at the soggy cardboard coaster in front of her.

"Hey," I said, and she lifted her chin. "I'm blown away you're even taking part in this investigation."

That got her to smile.

"Really. I appreciate all the foot work." I said as Chastity delivered our next round. "Whatever happens," I said to Chastity, "Don't let her pay for a thing tonight. It's on me."

Chastity laughed and said something about it being an expensive night.

"I'm going over to her table." I said and started to get up. I felt Alysa's hand on my shoulder. I paused and that is when I saw the long lean curly topped professor make his way to Candice's table. Tucked under a tweed arm of this sport coat, was an anti-vigilante protest sign. Around his neck a scarf and the familiar satchel slung over his shoulder.

Dr. Igo stood among the young women seated at the table showing off his sign which read *Justice for All*. Not overly clever for a news writer. He stooped and said something which then prompted him to lean back and thrust his hips forward in back breaking laughter. Vomit rose in my throat. The PhD gave me the creepy crawlies up my spine and turned my stomach at the thought of touching him, even if it were to break his neck.

"Creep," Alysa mumbled under her breath, not totally aware she said it out loud.

I looked back at her and nodded. She touched her lips realizing I heard it.

"I met the guy, don't like him." I said. "He was April's professor and mentor."

We watched in silence as Igo took a seat and mingled with the women half his age. He touched Candice on the back and pointed at the bar. Then he made his way over.

There was space on the other side of the guy next to me. Igo slipped in there and waited, with his back to me, for Chastity to take his order, a dry martini with three olives and a lemon twist. Now I really hated him.

The guy between us, slipped a five spot under his empty beer bottle and slid off his stool.

"Take a seat." I said to Igo's back.

Dr. Igo turned, looked at me then to the empty high back stool.

"Ah, no thank you. I've got a table." He looked to Alysa then back to Chastity who had the shaker in her hand reminding us how jelly her body was.

"I wasn't asking Dr. Igo." I said. I felt Alysa pull away slowly from my right side.

Igo stooped to rest his elbows on the bar and without looking at me said, "Private Investigator Roger Grimes. Is that your professional title, Private Investigator?"

"If it makes you feel good to say, I don't care much what you call me."

"I just want to get it right, you know," He turned slowly, his long curly locks dangled over his round eyeglasses. "For the article I am writing."

"And what article is that?"

"Well, you see, I'm picking up where April left off. Carrying her torch, as it were. She knew who the vigilante was and that is why she was killed." Igo twisted his neck a few degrees left and smiled at Alysa. "The police may not be on his tail, but it won't be long before I unmask him."

Chastity dropped off the doctor's martini. He left a twenty and a wink. She took the money asking if he wanted change to which he replied no but he would be back for another round. Then he nodded his head in a slight bow and turned to head back to his table.

I reached out, touching his arm. His reflexes were faster than I anticipated as he rolled my grasp. He brought up his hand brushing off where mine had laid.

His face turned towards me with a slight grin.

"I must legally warn you Mr. Grimes, I am a level five in combative Thai Chi. You can expect me to use deadly force if threatened."

I withdrew my hand, trying not to laugh. He was serious which made it all the funnier.

"Thanks for the warning. I just wanted to let you know I'm working on the April Ward case and not chasing some phantom avenger. Remember not all villains wear masks."

"Avengers, villains, oh my. Mr. Grimes, still reading comic books?" He shook his head disapprovingly. "This psychopath avenges nothing. He is merely a racist, socio-economic bigot, who refuses to evolve past his fraternity boy world views, assuming he even went to college. There is no room for a creature such as this in our society." Shiny teeth covered his face as his lips curled back in a smile. He walked off. My blood began to boil forcing sweat to collect along my hairline. Of all the faces I smashed, it was his I wanted to the most. That sly grin and the way his curls fell in his face made a perfect target for my fist. I had to let him go, it was not the right time to press him hard. He was investigating something the same as I was. His newspaper had made it clear the vigilante had to be stopped, he was a killer, but Igo didn't know the vigilante hadn't killed his star pupil. I respected his need for revenge, but the fact was he didn't have all the clues and what he thought he knew was wrong. All of his *wrong* was going to press, I couldn't take that chance.

"Slimy." Alysa said with a shudder.

I nodded.

Igo could feel my eyes on him as he sat in full animation with the young women. Candice looked over at me and I didn't bother looking away. I wanted her to know something was not right with her professor. Whoever April and Igo got information from was dangerous. She could be next.

"We've got to warn Candice."

"About her professor?" Alysa asked.

"Not just that dirt bag, but whoever killed April won't hesitate to kill her."

"When she goes for the bathroom, I'll make a move."

I looked back at Alysa with a raised eyebrow. I said nothing, agreeing to her plan. She had a better chance of convincing Candice, especially if Candice suspected I was dangerous.

We had to sit and wait.

We sipped our beers slowly. Alysa grew bored with me dodging all her personal questions. Her intentions were pure, and she knew me long enough that I should feel secure opening up, but there were too many skeletons screaming in my closet. She filled the silence with stories of her own. One ear listened but I had to keep attention to the table across the room. Our first date had not been like this. We talked equal parts and made eye contact that lasted the entire meal. All I had wanted was next to me, with a year between that moment gone and still I had to wait. The vigilante was not who I was anymore, maybe he never had been. The beating I was good at, with investigating still a skill needing improvement. Just because something comes easy doesn't mean you should do it.

Finally, Candice left the table for the women's room in the back. Alysa showed natural skill and timed it so she left her stool as Candice disappeared down the hall for the restrooms. Igo kept eyes on her while I kept mine on him.

He was slow to get up, adjusted his scarf, and then excused himself from the other two co-eds at the table. Just as he took a long stride towards the hallway, he glanced over at me. The straight and narrowed hawkish expression rounded and drooped as he eyed me slipping off my stool.

His pace picked up as his stride grew longer. Candice, then Alysa disappeared down the hall. So did Igo. I charged forward. Level five Thai Chi or not, he was not going to lay a hand on Alysa. She was tough but keeping her safe was my responsibility.

I rounded the corner on the hallway in time to catch the women's room door close on his pointed nose. He balled a fist but did nothing with it. He put his back against the wall and exhaled.

"This is starting to resemble harassment." Igo said, looking up at the sagging and yellowed ceiling tiles. A neon beer sign threw soft lime colored light down, filing his pasty face with color.

"I was just headed for the men's room, but I guess you're choosing to wait for the women's room." I said and stepped slowly towards Igo as he remained against the wall between the women's and men's room doors. I wanted him to get angry, to lash out, and strike.

"You're a pig!" Igo growled as his face flushed and his jaw clenched so tight his head began to tremor. My peripheral vison caught his fists. He might have it in him after all.

"Oink, oink." I replied slowly.

He took a deep breath and let it out, then softly in as he began a rhythmic breathing exercise, no doubt a part of his level five ancient teachings.

"Your day is coming caveman. Soon you will go the way of Neanderthal and disappear."

I stepped in close and grunted.

Candice opened the bathroom door and stood watching us toe to toe. With her head down, she hurried past Igo. Alysa came out after her. She took one look at my face and knew what was coming.

Igo called after Candice and reached for her. Alysa stepped between them. Igo's hand swung, giving Alysa a shove.

Red. It was hard to see past it.

Alysa was quick, she spun, deflecting Igo's reach and then grabbing his wrist, she twisted. He winced. She shoved him back.

Igo recovered and squared off. He was breathing heavy as he stared Alysa down then he saw I was right behind her. His eyes rounded out as he began to control his breathing though his jaw remained clenched.

The door clinked shut reminding us all we were there for Candice. She had run out the back in the chaos. We stood between Igo and the exit. The fury built in his eyes as he brushed frazzled hair from his face. He was a man seldom denied what he wanted. What he didn't get with his superior brain he leveraged with his size. Now in the hallway of a bar, he was bested by a woman bartender and a caveman. He needed revenge.

I made a presence of force known to Igo. This Neanderthal was not going to let him touch Alysa again. As much as Igo disliked primal senses refusing his brain the power to control his bodily movements he understood in this jungle fight he would lose.

A gentle touch to my arm and a voice, "C'mon Grimes. He isn't worth it."

Then she turned to Igo, "At least not yet."

Her strength impressed me and broke my focus on Igo. The beast within was denied blood lust. The smile from the one side of her mouth and the tips of her fingers down my arm took me to a place I would rather be, not this bar, not some fight either. I felt her hand slip into mine. It was a secure grip, not to force me to move but letting me know it was alright to go. Together we walked out the door.

Out in the parking lot, the neon of the beer signs faded, she let go of my hand and jumped up and down.

"Yes," she exclaimed. "That was awesome!"

Her energy transformed my face into something that felt good. My smile was big and bright and dumb because I had no idea what she was going to say.

"Glad you liked it. You're impressive, but first let's find Candice and celebrate later." I said and scanned the full parking lot for movement.

Alysa restrained her excitement and put on a professional face, "I know where she's going."

"Your car or mine?" I smiled.

She pulled her keys and jingled them. "I'll drive."

# **Chapter 14**

Alysa knew just when to shift for maximum RPM's of the Subaru's boxer motor, swinging us around corners and pushing us back in our seats shooting up straightaways.

"You know I'm not a cop, right? A private investigator doesn't get to speed." I said gripping the door handle as we passed under a light going from yellow to red.

"I'm not speeding. This is how I always drive." Alysa snickered, a tiny chink in her hot girl armor that only made me crazier about her. Suddenly a gut punch of shame for not snatching her up long ago, sloshed the beer in my stomach. But I was here now, sitting next to her. There was still time.

She down shifted and the motor whined. We coasted to a stop along Granada Avenue. Across the street was a freshly power-washed brick wall bordering tall glass windows covered in vinyl wrapped images of copper pipes and gears. The outside to a gastro pub, *The Pump House*. It was the latest hot spot in town. New drinking attractions no longer interested me and besides Alysa hadn't worked there so naturally I avoided the place. Supposedly the food was good, custom one-off dishes, with a much-advertised craft beer selection.

As we approached, I could hear the live band playing in the back of the place. I hesitated by the door.

"What?" Alysa asked reaching out for the handle.

I grumbled then said, "I hate this place."

"So do I." She smiled and opened the door.

Inside the brick motif continued along with the copper pipping and gears. The booths were red leather with black trim and the tables made from copper and steel. I couldn't hear the music from outside any longer. All the tables were taken with groups eating and drinking. Though crowded, voices were low and subdued. Soft jazz pushed down from hidden speakers above. We found enough space at the bar to order.

The bar tender was tall and lean with a dark scraggily beard. He had on a faded denim shirt with a big square pocket on the left breast. His hair was slicked back in a dark oily sheen, giving the cut an old time 1920's feel that went with the rest of the décor.

He tossed a drink list down and said he'd be right back. The drink list was not considered. Neither of us wanted anymore alcohol. When he finally came back, we ordered a couple of waters. His cold dead stare was enough to push us away from the bar.

We moved over to the corner of the room.

"I would have tipped him had he not been a dick." Alysa sneered.

"And that's why I hate this place." I said sipping my water and casually looking around the room for Candice. Neither of us came up with her so we moved on.

Through a hallway of servers and bussers hustling and cooks shouting from a side doorway we made our way out the back and into a courtyard with a beachy theme. This back bar held double the crowd. A band played pop covers on a small stage to our right as we waded through middle class drunks out for a good time on our way to the bar.

Again, we picked a corner to the side of this open-air bar to observe the crowd and find Candice. Skunked again and our waters gone, Alysa said she would go to the bar, it was time for a beer.

I watched her walk off. As she leaned against the bar a guy started up a conversation. She smiled and shook her head no and waved over the bar tender. The bar tender was a young brunette wearing a trucker ball cap and heavy eyeliner. She smiled at Alysa and they stretched over the bar to hug one another. Chit-chat ensued as I stood in the corner with empty hands.

Alysa bounced over with a couple of beers and a grin that would not quit.

I smiled not knowing why.

"So, that was my friend Kaylee." Alysa said slowly. "She comes to my Tuesday Cross-Fit class. Anyway, she thinks you're pretty cute. I could set you up." She looked at me with those green eyes over the beer bottle as her lips pressed together to sip.

I looked over to the fit frame of bar tender as she slung drinks from toned arm covered in tattoos. I could see the guys lined up to order drinks only from her and studied the never ceasing hope on the faces of the guys unwilling to leave their barstools for one more drink order. Yes, she was the *it* girl for this time and place. "I'll pass."

Alysa shook her head, "You're an enigma Grimes."

I didn't bother to unpack the accusation and instead refocused on the case. Candice was still nowhere to be found.

"You sure about Candice being here?"

"Oh, yeah she's here. Kaylee saw her go upstairs." Alysa pointed to a couple of windows that belonged to apartments that were above the bar. They appeared to be old garage apartments back when a house stood on this lot, before it became a bar.

"Let's go."

"Wait." Alysa threw out a hand to stop my forward momentum. "It's best she to talk to me, me alone. I don't think she trusts you."

"What did I do?" I smiled.

Alysa shrugged.

"Okay. Make sure you find out who was feeding April her inside info." I chugged on the beer.

"And?"

"What?"

"And who she thinks the vigilante is?"

The one question I did not want Alysa finding out. April suspected it was me leaving the chance Candice did as well.

"Yeah," I said.

She smiled and handed me her beer, then told me to wish her luck. I nodded back. She had to go alone to get the answers I needed. There were indeed places I could not go. Alysa was better equipped to handle a scared twenty-one-year-old woman. Her soft smile and sparkling eyes could calm any soul. It worked wonders on mine.

From above the bar a yellow light slipped through vertical blinds. I waited and watched. The light stayed on, as I counted the seconds for Alysa to return.

There was still half left in the beer Alysa gave me when I heard the rumble broadcasting from a group of motorcycles pulling into the parking lot behind me. I leaned against the wooden railing in the corner of the patio and watched Addison and the rest of the Dead Ends cruise past the valet pointing them towards the motorcycle parking.

The whole gang was there, even Lexi. I turned my back and slowly melted into the crowd.

This was not the kind of place bikers wearing real cuts came for drinks. The gastropub might get the occasional group on a poker run for some local charity to swing in on their Harleys and pound a few until hitting the road again. This was no poker run.

The crowd of sloppy people in expensive clothes quieted as the motley crew of flannel and leather riders made their way to the bar. A bar that was three people deep, parted like the red see for Denny and Wino to order drinks. The rest of the Dead Ends took a table that was abandoned by women in long dresses.

The shock of the bikers wore off quickly for this crowd as the chatter picked back up. Denny and Wino joined their mates at the table and passed around beers as they sat.

I approached the table from an angle I could still see the bedroom window up in the apartment. As if triggered by some hunter instinct, Wino cocked his head and caught sight of me.

"There he is." Wino's words rumbled like the exhaust on his hog. We shook hands, he still wore thick leather gloves. All but Denny said hello.

All the seats at the table were taken so I had to stand which I preferred.

"What brings you guys out to a trendy bar like this?" I asked the group.

"About to ask you the same thing." Addison replied first.

I looked over my shoulder at a black Maserati rolling in.

"Just seeing what's on the market." I said to which they all chuckled. "I'll see you guys later." I said and turned. Wino called me back.

"Come hang out man. Maybe we got another try out for you." He was smiling.

"Yeah, c'mon man," Lexi said leaning so far over the table she was nearly out of her seat.

"Sure, but I need a gig that pays. No more volunteer stuff."

"You help us tonight and you'll get a cut." Wino said.

"Your cut of the ten G's." Addison added.

"You mean your march didn't catch the ghostly vigilante?" I laughed at the thought of their signs and marching would catch this crypto vigilante. No one laughed back.

"What does this guy look like?" I finally asked.

Addison looked to each of his crew. "White guy, shaved head."

"That isn't much of a description." I fought a nervous smile from showing and left my face blank. I needed to be empty inside, totally blank of thought. I had to convince them I thought of myself last as the possible vigilante.

"You got a picture? Your description doesn't narrow it down much." I said pushing back. If they were playing some kind of game, I would call them on it now and get this inevitable fight going.

"No." Denny said from behind Addison.

"Spoke described him. He says he wants to be the one that brings him in." Hitch said while looking down at his phone, flipping through some social media app.

The laughed caught in my throat, nearly choking me. The head of a weak millennial biker gang wants to be the one to catch the vigilante.

After catching everyone's frown, Wino said, "Don't underestimate Spoke. Dude's got a plan and knows what he's doing."

"Like sending you to a trendy bar like this to find the vigilante?" I shook my head knowing the true vigilante would never come here. Except there I was with a beer, but this was work.

We got a lot of looks from the crowd, some good, some bad, many were indifferent. A short brunette in tall heels took her time excusing herself as she brushed against me wiggling through the crowd. She was cute, done-up nicely. She held my gaze with a hungry look in her eye. When I broke the gaze and came back around once more, she was smiling at some curly haired guy with a toothy grin of his own. Just another cute girl who was not my type.

"This place is packed. You think he's here somewhere?" I said to no one in particular.

"He's here somewhere." Denny grumbled as his head swiveled scanning the crowd.

The light in the window went off.

"I don't see anyone matching that description." I said. They all looked at me. "Maybe we should try inside."

No one said a word. They were looking into the crowd for a man that looked too much like me. I wanted them out of here for when Alysa came back down those steps. She was sharp, if she saw me with this crew, she would get Candice someplace safe. The only thing I knew about Candice was that she liked to run. If she spotted me with these clowns she might freak.

I pulled my phone thinking I would text Alysa a warning, but Lexi scooted up next to me. She smiled and took my beer and wrapped her lips around the mouth of it. Addison's cherub cheeks turned red as she handed the bottle back. I took a drink and when I was done, I looked in Addison's two slits for eyes and I knew he wanted me dead. I enjoyed that.

He tilted the green bottle of beer straight up and chugged through to the bottom. When he came up for air he said, "Lexi I'll get you one." Then he walked off for the bar, disappearing into a crowd waiting for a drink of their own.

I leaned against the railing keeping one eye out for Alysa and the other on the gang. Everyone else stood around as well. Denny grumbled at Hitch to stay off his phone, reminding him we were looking for someone. Lexi nestled in next to me, saying something about being cold. I smiled.

I leaned down to Lexi's ear, "Are you seriously out after the vigilante?"

"Scary right? I hope these bone heads don't get to the vigilante before I do. I want a crack at him." She pouted at the thought of not getting to plunge an imaginary knife into a man's chest. With sudden spunk she said, "Can't wait."

"You sure? The guy sounds tough."

Lexi opened her phone and pulled up a video. She held it up as it played, "We've been practicing."

The video went on to show a frail thin man in an extra-large, stain covered tee shirt getting pushed around by the gang until one of them threw a punch knocking the man to the ground. He barely held his hands up as the rest stomped and kicked and laughed and played. A chill pushed tiny bubbles of sweat over my body. I could chew lead and spit bullets into each of their heads.

"What'd this guy do?" I said holding my cool.

Lexi shrugged, "Wrong place, wrong time." She giggled.

The Dead Ends had struck again. Where was I, the white male, shaved headed vigilante? Drinking with what I thought were friends. The laughing, talking about cars was gone and so was the peace that came with not having to be violent. Now I knew for certain, we would be facing off. There was no more making excuses for these immature wannabe outlaws. My vacation with them was over.

Addison slithered his way out of the packed bar with two fresh beers. He smiled at Lexi who gave a weak smirk back. His smile faded as he looked at me. I don't know what was on my face, but whatever it was it wiped the cherub off his and left him wide eyed and pale white. The learned behavior was taking over. Triggered, it would be difficult to control. Excitement nor adrenaline filled me, that big black hole was opened, the killer inside was clawing his way out. This had to come to an end.

Movement just over Addison's left shoulder caught in my peripheral vision cracking the whip on the beast within, sending it back down in its hole. Alysa and Candice came around the corner.

Alysa was talking and stopped cold when she spotted me flanked on either side by bikers. Our eyes locked. I had told myself not to let that happen, but something overrode the electrical impulses in my brain controlling those muscles in my eyes and neck. It was too late. Lexi looked up at me then as if following a laser to Alysa. She pinched her eyes into slits as her upper lip curled at the corners. This created a chain reaction. Addison turned to look over his shoulder just as Hitch sensed the movement and looked up from his cell phone.

"It's her!" Hitch jumped from his chair as if it had become electrified.

Everyone froze. Then as if the starting gun fired, we were all off.

Alysa grabbed Candice by the wrist and dragged her back the way they came. Addison started running towards me at first then dropped the beer and cut left down the wooden walkway and out into the parking lot. Heavy motorcycle boots clopped down as the rest of the Dead Ends followed nearly falling over each other to get after them.

I cut back and split the crowd of partiers, nearly toppling a few as I made my way to a side gate in the bamboo fence that ran along the north side of the Tiki bar. The latched flipped back and I stepped out into a shadowy alleyway.

Alysa's eyes shown bright as two moons as she came to a halt. I waved her and Candice on, nearly shoving them down the alley. The clopping biker boots neared.

I spun on my heels just as Alysa and Candice rounded the corner for the street. The Dead Ends slowed at the other end of the alley. Denny shouted.

"They didn't come this way." I shouted back.

A car in the parking lot across the street started up. The gang ran towards the running engine.

I caught up just as Denny pulled out the driver, a young guy in a shiny button up shirt. His hands were up. A woman screamed. Denny let the guy go.

"Damn it." Addison shouted as the chaotic chase started attracting attention of the bar patrons coming and going.

"Let's ride." Wino grumbled in defeat.

Lexi slipped up next to me, "Wanna ride bitch?"

I smirked, "I have wheels tonight."

"See you back at the clubhouse, you're in this now Georgie." She winked. I felt Addison's sour face burning on my back. I nodded to him. He turned and hustled off with the rest of the group.

I walked around to the front of the Pumphouse and on down the street to the bridge then made my way behind a bait shop near the boat ramps. I text Alysa and she text back her and Candice were safe. Then I text Billy to come pick me up.

"Could you give me a ride to Jaffy's?" I asked.

Billy said, "Sure, but what's wrong with the truck?"

"The Dead Ends know it."

# **Chapter 15**

I left Jaffy's in a 2010 VW Golf GTI. Jaffy wasn't happy about my choice and even less happy when I told him I was only leaving a deposit. His tone got tough then I got tougher.

There was a text from Camp and a missed called. The call worried me. I called her back from the confines of the GTI.

"Where are you?" Detective Camp asked answering the phone. Her tone had an edge to it.

"Just left a bar." I said, leaving it vague.

"Meet me under the west side of the Sea Breeze Bridge in ten minutes?"

"I can be there in twenty."

The large bridge split into two bridges expanding east and west over the Halifax River. Under the base of the bridge was a small parking lot with fifteen empty spaces. It was night out and even darker in the shadows of the bridge making it a favorite for homeless to sleep it off. This night the place looked deserted; the cold must have driven them to shelters until morning. At the water's edge, a wooden pier went out over the Halifax and ended in a T shape. On the north end of the T was an elderly couple seated in folding chairs with several rods spread out along the railing. Lights above cast yellow cones down on the dock. Water lapped at the sea wall as I walked halfway down the dock then leaned forward on the rail to look down at the water.

Headlights sparkled in the falling mist as I watched a Chevy sedan pull into a parking spot. Detective Camp got out and I made my way off the pier to meet her. Her black hair was pulled back tight against her scalp. A tight-fitting suit wrapped around her rounded frame.

We stood in the shadow of a large concrete pillar supporting the bridge above our heads. The *clap-clap* of the cars driving above echoed off the concrete as tiny waves lapped against coquina rocks and pockets of sandy shore. A breeze wafted off the river and penetrated through my coat. I shoved my hands in the front pockets and tried shaking out the cold.

"Have you kept up with the news?" Camp said.

I shook my head, no, but I knew what she would be getting at.

"They marched for the victims of the vigilante, calling it race motivated and that's why the police won't catch him or them. Then while all that's going on, a low-level crack dealer was beaten off First Street earlier today adding fuel to the fire."

"Copycats."

She nodded, "I agree, but some of them are damn close to the vigilante. Same locations, same style." Her eyes went to the white coquina asphalt. "Someone has the vigilante dialed in."

"They're copycats, Camp. Amateurs out looking for kicks."

"I looked over the crime scene, ran the background on the victim. Didn't strike me as someone the vigilante would go after. I told my captain this wasn't the work of the vigilante. He didn't like it; the mayor didn't like it." Camp slid both her thumbs along her waist, pulling her sport coat open.

She went on to say, "The constant bad press is really bringing the pressure down on the department. Patrols are stepped up around the clock. Now there's a reward by the newspaper and its supporters are just creating more vigilantes out chasing the vigilante. No one is safe. Every person on a street corner is a suspect. Even police officers are being confronted by angry crowds. Some officers are turning on each other and pointing fingers. You would think this ten thousand dollars was ten million the way these fools are going about. This is no way to handle it." She shook her head and wiped a palm across a furrowed brow.

"I know who is behind the copycats, a couple of them anyway. A biker gang, calling themselves Dead Ends."

"Yeah, I looked into the Dead Ends. There isn't anything on them. They aren't on any law enforcement radar. So far, they're clean."

My shoulder pressed into the white concrete of the pillar. "They're behind this. I saw it on one of their cellphones."

"You have the evidence?"

I shook my head, "A member named Lexi, it's on her phone. They beat a guy and took video trophies."

"To death, he died today in the hospital."

Heat built around my neck. I was breathing through a dry mouth, my tongue stuck to my teeth as I tried to lick my lips.

Camp was head of the task force that was failing the city. Feelings of responsibility bore down but I pushed them back. She was a veteran officer, it was her career, and she took the promotions that came in the wake of the violent justice of the vigilante. This time it was her own detective skills that lead her to a true conclusion, the vigilante did not kill that crack dealer. There was a copycat out there with a press pass.

"Now what?" I said.

"Shelter in place."

"This isn't a hurricane."

"No, but it sure as hell feels like one is coming. Stick close to that lawyer you're always working for."

I nodded. It was good advice. Sanford made a solid alibi. We had been doing it for years.

A man in a long coat walked by carrying a bedroll and backpack. This was a common hangout for the homeless in town. A silent part of my brain kept my eyes on him as he circled the parking lot.

Camp had an eye on him as well, just being a trained observer. She took a breath. Her left hand went up and cupped her forehead.

"I should have just arrested you way back when." Camp said, her voice unsteady.

"You never had anything on me." I smiled in the dark.

"I could take you in now. At least you'd have a lock tight alibi for the next attack." Camp said through a smile of her own.

"A locked *up* alibi, you mean. No thanks, I'm better out here."

Then she went for her pistol. Reflex took over as I went for mine, though my thoughts were conflicted. In the milliseconds between drawing the pistol and taking aim, my trigger finger fought back and stayed off the trigger.

She was fast on the draw, saying, "Down." And then fired.

I ducked as her Glock went off. The forty-caliber round exploded over my head. She fired three rounds that came out as fast as the semi action could cycle them.

I spun on one knee, turning from Camp, I saw a man in a hoodie level a pump action shotgun.

The hooded man reeled back, the shotgun, pointed at the under belly of the bridge, going off in a fiery orange burst.

Camp spun around as I spun the opposite direction checking her six for any other threats. After all clear, I ran over, kicked his gun away and flipped him over. He was gasping for air. His eyes were large and looking up past me. My hands searched his pockets and found nothing, no ID, no cellphone, nothing to tell me who he was.

Camp called out to not touch anything. I responded he was still alive, but barely.

The elderly couple on the pier stood and watched.

By the time Camp ran over, the man was dead.

"Grimes, I know this guy." Camp said. Her pistol dangled loosely by her side ready to be freed under its own sheer weight.

"He used to be a cop," Camp said and quickly holstered her pistol. "He resigned a few months ago."

"Did he give a reason?"

"I don't think it was his choice."

The guy must have been dirty, somehow, some way.

I stared at his face as the color faded white around an open mouth that would never utter another word. It was a face I had seen before. There was a fresh yellow bruise over his left eye. That was familiar too. I put it there. The specifics weren't important enough to be clear to me, but I knew I left the mark.

"I gave him that bruise over his eye." I said over my shoulder as Camp came up behind me.

"What'd he do?"

"I can't remember. There's something familiar about his face and me punching it." I had worked to mentally pixelate all the faces I smashed. A practice I started back when Sanford first got me into this, back when I saw what real evil was capable of. Then it became a habit I applied to any face that disagreed with me.

"Let us protect you." Camp as she got out her cell to call it in.

"A former cop tried to kill me, and you want me to go down to a police station filled with 'em. You've done more to protect me than I could have asked for." I started for my car, but stopped and turned back to Camp, "Its better I go my own way."

I left.

Blue and red lights popped down every other block. A fire truck, red and screaming, raced the other direction. More black and whites sped past like I was standing still. The closer I got to the shop, the more cop cars. An unmarked police car swerved around a car and ran me up the curb spinning over some St. Augustine grass. Three helicopters circled above shining spotlights down. I didn't dare take a breath for fear the electricity in the air would burn my nose hairs.

I rode heavy, weighted down by a city on the brink. Another face of a dead man was ever present in my mind. The reasons for those bruises trickled in like flashes of police lights off in the distance. It was a stalking case, one of the legit cases Sanford had me do now and then to keep up appearances. Easy enough, I sat and waited, watching the perv leer into the window of a young woman. On the third night, I pulled him from his car, and we scuffled. He was good, I hadn't expected that. He managed to get away and never came back. Until now.

Someone had turned the tables on me, someone capable of hunting me down, but instead was making a game of it all. Why go through the trouble of luring me out? Why not kill me then? I called ahead to Billy.

"What the hell is going on out there?" Billy said. I could tell he was two tall boys in for the night.

"The city is losing its mind over the *vigilante*."

"Aw shit man. I knew this would happen. Haven't you seen those movies? It always ends bad, man. And you know who gets it right?" Billy went on to string cuss words together.

"It will be okay. Just keep your head low."

"The sidekick, that's who gets it. Damn it, well I'm the hero in my story."

"You're not the sidekick. Just to be safe, maybe tell Jose not to come in tomorrow."

"Hell, I ain't worried about some gangbangers showing up here. I'm pissed 'cause you're gonna ride out and take them all on alone."

"You want to ride shotgun?"

"Hell yes!"

"So, like my sidekick."

"Aw shut up and get your ass back to the shop."

Billy hung up on me, but I knew he was smiling on the inside. I called Sanford. He didn't answer then he called me right back.

"Someone has figured us out." Sanford said through heavy breathing.

"I know" I said.

"When were you going to call me?" He snapped.

"I'm calling you now."

Sanford took a deep breath. I braced for a verbal barrage, but he just let it out again. "We need to meet, but not yet. I think it's time for you to go home." Sanford hung up. I looked at the black screen of the cellphone and fought the rising urge to get offended by his casualness. Reminding myself how hard the man works kept my emotions in check. He was in this past his elbows with me and he would do all he could to keep me safe. I would do the same for him. If it comes down to it, I'll confess and admit I was a lone wolf. Sanford would protest. Detective Camp, Billy and even Monique would stand up with me, but I would deny them all.

# **Chapter 16**

Billy sneaked a look out the small window in the office door as I pulled into the shop's parking lot.

Inside Billy sat tapping his boot. I could tell he was out of smokes and the beers that he had drank were wearing off.

I nodded and hurried past him for the stairs up to my room.

While I was up there packing, Billy called out. "We got visitors."

*Shit*. The bikers were on me faster than I expected. Without a window facing the parking lot, I grabbed an extra two nine round magazines for my Glock 30SF and shoved it in my KYDEX waistband mag holder.

I came into a dark office. From the stairwell, I whispered how many. He pulled back his long black hair and peered through the tiny window once more.

Without turning he said, "Looks like two people in a Subaru. Who brings a Subaru to a fuckin' gunfight?"

I let out breath I should not have been holding, it was just trapped there in my throat. My cell dinged with a text. Alysa let me know she was here.

Alysa came in with Candice in tow. A white streetlight spilled in behind them. The pair eyed the shadowy office as if looking for traps from the dark corners. Billy flipped on the light as we all squinted until our pupils adjusted. Alysa, seeing Billy, smiled having recognized him from our past nights at Coopers.

Billy smiled to Alysa then with a hand on his chest he introduced himself to Candice.

"Do you think you were followed?" I asked getting a little closer to Alysa.

"The way I drive?" She laughed light and free. It put me at ease even though I did not want to be.

With a look to Billy I said, "Candice here has information I need on April Ward."

"Good, but is it what you need to clear you?"

The whites of Candice's eyes popped like flash bulbs.

"You said you were taking me to the cops." Candice's voice creaked like loose floorboards, unstable and worn.

"This is better than going to the cops, right Grimes?" Alysa assured Candice.

"We'll go to the cops, but first I need to know what April was after, what it was she knew and where she got her information."

Candice's shoes scraped over the concrete floor as she backed up. Her fear charged the room, she was going to make a break for it.

"Candice, you're safe here." Alysa said sensing Candice's movements as well.

"That's what you said at the apartment and look what happened, they chased us, those bikers, those killers." Candice had her hands up to her sides. She was a frightened rabbit about to be eaten.

"It's time to go home." I said.

# **Chapter 17**

*Home* was a safe house Sanford had set up as a place to escape to if and when we needed. It belonged to Monique's grandmother. When she was put into a retirement facility, the house went to Monique, but never put in her name. Sanford managed to bury true ownership of the home to avoid any connections.

"Maybe you should come with us." I said to Billy. He shook his head and ran a hand down his long braid.

"These pussy bikers don't scare me none."

"I never thought they did, but this is about more than them. Daytona is about to explode with everyone gunning for the vigilante. Whoever is on to me, may find you. I'd rather you were at my side."

Billy looked at the three of us and then paced around the office like he was looking for a misplaced receipt instead of contemplating what I just said.

"Tell me where it is, and I'll be there shortly." Billy fussed with some paperwork and jingled some car keys. He mumbled about finishing up some work.

"Great man, it'll be fun." I grinned and he grinned then a helicopter flew overhead, and we all remembered this wasn't summer camp. Trouble was brewing outside, swirling like an oncoming hurricane. People were racing to empty the shelves, but it was not canned food or ice they were after, it was bullets and guns.

The three of us took Alysa's car, she drove. I sat in the back wearing my Daytona Tortugas ball cap pulled low. Candice sat up front wearing a hooded sweatshirt pulled up over her head. We drove on as more blue and red lights raced by as more and more people took to the streets in protests that descended into riots. The town Willis Sanford loved so dear was about to go up in gun smoke and it was all because he wanted to make the streets safer. I was on board easily enough. Busting heads hoping to one day see Sanford's bigger picture.

Candice wanted to stop by her place to get clothes, but Alysa talked her out of it better than I could have. She was dead silent for a while then out of nowhere crying hysterically. All the questions we asked were refused then she went silent again to think, to reason how she got there. Yesterday she was just a college kid writing articles for the school paper. Tonight, she was wanted dead, same as me, for doing what she thought was right. With every move I felt less in control. Any question I had for the girl resulted in more tears. Alysa's calm words and smart ideas kept us above water.

Alysa was off anyone's radar, so we swung by her apartment before heading to the safe house. I waited in the backseat as her and Candice went up to the second-floor apartment. They were not long and came out with only two bags a piece. It seemed reasonable until I realized none of the bags held guns.

# **Chapter 18**

Alysa kept the RPM's high in the boxer motor all the way down to the end of Nova Road, where it dumps out at US 1 in an area called Harbor Oaks. Then a couple of turn right, turn left directions from me through a small neighborhood of mid-century single-story block and red brick houses. Finally, we stopped at a house with red brick and brown wooden trim. A typical three-bedroom, two-bathroom ranch house but the best part was the view of the Halifax River in the back. I knew there were two fishing poles in the garage.

I left them in the car as I made my way to the porch. I punched the code into the electric lock and went in. The air was stagnant with a musty weight. The bare terrazzo floors echoed each of my steps as I walked the rest of the house; three bedrooms, kitchen then into the garage, to make sure I was alone. A layer of dust and general mustiness of the place convinced me no one had been in the house since I stayed there sometime last year. The last thing to do was draw back the drapes and open the windows facing the river. A breeze pushed through the house and took the musty air back out over the water.

I opened the garage door and Alysa pulled in.

We settled into our new home, with its sparse outdated furniture and lack of TV or internet would ensure things were quiet. Once we all dropped our bags and picked out our beds, we gathered back in the living room.

"I think you made the right decision coming with us." I said to Candice who had curled up on the long square couch.

Candice shrugged, "This is all so crazy. First April is dead and now a biker gang is after me."

"We're safe here. No one knows about this place. Tell me what April knew, what was it that got her killed?" I said taking a seat in a square burnt orange

Candice wiped away tears bubbling from her eyes. She sucked in a deep breath that only fed the grief. The weight of it all was tumbling down, something I had felt before, the first time you realize you can actually die. I was about Candice's age the first-time mortality struck me. Smitty had paid for Billy and me to go through corporate security training. It was two weeks of learning how to protect clients and assets. At the end we went on a real detail. They fitted us for our suits. I came out of the dressing room in a baggy dress shirt. A white-haired lady in bifocals said to me, "That extra room is for your body armor."

It hit me then that people would be trying to kill me. I wish it had sunk in deeper, maybe I could have avoided the last decade of people trying to kill me. The next time I wore a vest was during bank robberies to protect myself and no one else. The tables had turned now, I was here risking my life to safeguard someone I didn't know.

Alysa was quick to sit beside her and offer some comfort in ways I was not capable of.

"I know its hard Candice. April's killer is trying to frame me for this and there are people out there trying to kill me."

Candice slowed her breathing, "Wait, so you're not the vigilante?"

"No, I'm just an unlucky private investigator tangled up in this." As the words fell from my lips it was too close to call who looked first, but there we were, our eyes locked. Alysa broke eye contact and let go of Candice's hand, folding her own two hands in her lap. Convincing words that assured her I was not the vigilante scrambled in my mouth, but I kept them in knowing they were all a lie. Instead of talking I watched her get up and go into the kitchen. We had never talked about all that I do. There was no doubt she had her suspicions, my ups and downs, black and blue bruises. If she never asked, I never had to lie.

I didn't like lying to Candice either. I had not won her confidence and she had not won mine.

"April was so sure she found him." Candice said, the worry leaving her body as her mind focused on what April knew. "She told me the night she—" the tears rolled down from the corners of her soft brown eyes. She rubbed them hard, but they kept coming.

"Who put her on to the vigilante?" I asked not letting up.

Alysa came out of the kitchen with three juice glasses. Each one held about two shots of a golden amber liquid. She didn't look at me as I took mine and sniffed bourbon. A stash for medicinal purposes was always kept in the house.

"This will help." Alysa handed Candice a glass. She found a place on the other end of the couch.

Candice sipped the bourbon, coughed a little then said, "She was writing for the school paper, like I do. Dr. Igo, he works at the city paper as well as teaches, he offered to publish an article of hers in the paper. A real paying gig." She sipped some more, coughed again then continued, "Dr. Igo had been doing a piece on how unfair the criminal justice system is, how blacks are stopped more by police and have hire conviction rates. Things like that. Similarly, with poor whites. Then this vigilante started attacking the poor."

I shifted in my seat and sipped my bourbon. The twist to the portrayal was all wrong. Igo never looked into the watery eyes of a rape victim or mother holding her dead son because a heroin cooker mixed a bad batch. These people weren't getting the justice they deserved either.

"Well, I work closely with Detective Camp, she heads up the vigilante task force. Maybe April got my name from her somehow." I said leading suspicion once again away from me.

"The night April died, she was at Coopers, watching Grimes. I saw her from the other end of the bar eyeing him, but they never spoke." Alysa said tucking her feet under her thighs as she sipped her bourbon. There was no wince or cough when she was done. A beautiful, fit blonde that could drink bourbon. If this was my last night before getting caught, what a way to spend it.

"No, we never said a word." I jumped in. "I blacked out in a dune alone. How she got there, only her killer knows."

Candice's teary eyes thinned as the trust me-trust me not wheel spun in her head. "But why was she killed?" she said uncurling from the corner of the couch as the bourbon warmed her insides.

"Whoever killed her and put her next to me, took my truck, but not my wallet or keys."

"If you ask me," Alysa said, "That creepy Dr. Igo killed her."

"What? Why, why would he do that?" Candice began sobbing again.

I shot Alysa a look and she gave me a sarcastic dirty look back.

"He didn't do it." I said trying to comfort Candice.

"How do you know?" Alysa said.

"Because, he doesn't have what it takes. I can see it in his eyes." I said before she questioned me on that too. The eyes of a wrong doer, a killer, child molester, those that are heartless, had become something I came to recognize as I punched, choked, stabbed, or shot them to death. It's an absence, a vacancy of the soul the lights normal people's eyes.

"Igo definitely wanted to talk to you at Coopers." Alysa said to Candice.

All the tense muscles pinching Candice's shoulders together eased. Her face a blank slate as she stared off into something neither Alysa nor I could see.

"If April did find the vigilante, Dr. Igo must think I know who he is too." Candice slowly turned towards me, her face soft and careless.

Harley-Davidson pipes roared towards the safe house popping off the hollowed interior. I flipped off the light and slipped my gun out. Alysa reached out a hand and led Candice towards the kitchen.

I took a position at the kitchen entry which let me see the large sliding glass door to the backyard as well as an easy look to the front door. We waited, holding breaths we desperately needed as the roar went past the house and faded down the twisty road.

"It was a single bike." I stuck the pistol in my waist holster. "I don't think it was a Dead End." I turned to see Alysa holding a long kitchen knife. I smiled. She shrugged and put it back in the knife block.

We locked the windows down and set the alarm. The rest of the night was spent in the dark in the living room. Eventually Candice fell asleep, then Alysa. At some point I decided it was okay and nodded off.

My eyelids fluttered and finally opened to a pink sky filling the gap in the curtains. Candice was stretched out on the couch, quietly purring while wrapped in a green and white blanket I did not give her. I walked the silent home, checking every corner. Both Alysa's bags were here, but the garage was empty.

Sitting left me with an uncontrollable tapping foot. Pacing did little to ease my mind. Every car that passed brought me to the window like a nosey neighbor. Finally, she returned, and I was ready to lay into her like a teenager home past curfew.

"There's one more bag in the car." Alysa smiled with an arm full of groceries. Her morning hair was pulled back tight with a sheen of oil from not showering. Any makeup from the night before was gone, just leaving her green eyes to sparkle free from distraction.

I went out and came back with the last bag. She was unpacking the food.

"I really appreciate this." I said and sifted through the frozen pizzas and bottle of soda.

"7-11 didn't have many healthy options, but it will get us through a couple of days."

"Thanks, but I meant just being here, helping out with Candice last night was, I couldn't have done what you did."

She popped her hip to one side and caught it with her hand, "Don't sweat it. That's what partners are for."

"Oh, so you're my partner now and not just an employee?"

She opened cupboards until she found the one pan in the house. "Bacon and eggs?"

"I'll put some coffee on." I spun in a 360. "Did you buy coffee?"

She smiled and flashed me the emeralds I loved so much and pointed to one of the plastic bags.

"How about I handle the kitchen since I've worked in them most of my life and you find something else to do?" She swatted at my ass but missed. Her hand came up and touched my arm.

"I can do that." I said standing there without moving.

"Well?"

I saluted and backed out of the kitchen.

In the living room, Candice was still asleep. There was no TV and no books to read. Sitting did not last long. I paced for a few minutes, checking locked windows and doors. Then I grabbed the rod and reel I had stashed last time and went out to the dock.

A bright yellow sun greeted me with a warm hug allowing me to shed my hoodie and spread out in the red painted Adirondack chair. The freezer burned shrimp took a few minutes to thaw until I could run a circle hook through. Then I cast it out with no expectations beyond a channel cat or small mangrove snapper. A beaming sun on my face was enough to escape the world for a while.

Light pushed down on my closed eyes, turning the back of my lids red. Images fluttered through my mind as a cool breeze rolled off my skin.

A passing boat sent a small wake slapping against the dock pilings. In those moments I could forget the hot Florida summers and remember why I live here. The rest of the country under ice and snow and here I sit in a t-shirt, fishing.

A couple of birds called out to each other and not being an Audubon Society member, I could not identify them. The calls took me back to a few mornings ago. It was another sunny morning on the water when I heard the gulls arguing and opened my eyes to see April's face. Cold and still, she looked at me, saying nothing, revealing not a clue. Her silence filled me with an uneasiness I had not experienced with the other dead men I saw in these last few months. Their stories didn't matter to me, they were molesters, serial rapists, and killers, that was all I needed to know. She was different, I wanted to know more, I wanted her to open her mouth and tell me things, the kind of things she would tell on a second date. The only things I've learned have been the facts; name, age and what she studied in school. There was so much more I would never know and no one else would forever more.

I checked my line, and the dead shrimp was gone. I never noticed the bite. After rebaiting the hook, I checked my phone. Nothing. The urge to text the outside world was strong. What was going on with Camp? What was it Sanford knew to send me home? Was Billy safe? The questions circled like the seagulls above.

I put the phone away. Laying back in the chair with a wet line as my priority. The tide started to shift, going from a slack high tide to finding its way out. That meant the bite should pick up.

Just a nibble at first then the hit and I pulled back setting the hook. As the rod bent and the tip bounced, I knew I had something sizable. The reel zinged as line zipped out. I tightened down the drag and cranked. The water broke, the tail splashed. White silver streaked across the top of the brown water. I had something good, something I could eat.

Reeling in, I saw it was a speckled trout. Judging by its size I could keep it. I pulled the fish over the railing and gazed on my catch. It had been a while since I caught a good eatable fish, mindless excitement built, like hitting it off with a beautiful woman after several duds, this was mine. I checked the size and took a picture to send to Billy.

I caught my reflection in the fish's bulging eye. This beautiful creature was waiting for me to do something. It knew the laws of nature better than I did, it ate the little fish and escaped the jaws of the larger ones. Now I held it at the end of my line, hooked through the lip, awaiting my judgment. Food or freedom. I could not stomach any more death, even to survive I could not kill it. With a splash the trout was free once more.

With fresh bait, I cast out. There was nothing to do but wait and think. April was a college student with her life ahead of her, no criminal record. In an innocent way, she was a nonviolent version of myself. She found something that I couldn't. For all the dead faces I pixilated in my mind, hers was the one I could not let go. She was me, dishing out justice, exposing the guilty, and passing judgement. Her court was that of public opinion, a mix of words on the printed page she triumphed justice for those with no voice. I sought justice through brass knuckles and a loaded gun.

We were the same. That meant someone was feeding us, nurturing that sense of right and wrong and supporting us when it was too much, when the story got too deep, or the body count piled up.

Someone was there and it was not a leap to guess who was there for her.

I needed facetime with Doctor Igo again.

Somewhere between the sun and the breeze, I dozed off in the slanted wooden chair. I popped awake with a shutter and looked around. Thick pewter clouds began bumbling in, shutting off the Vitamin D filled rays. I needed sustenance.

Bouncy steps on the wooden dock brought my head around. Muscular tan legs ended in bare feet.

"Catch us fish to go with the eggs?" Alysa said taking a seat in the other chair.

"No."

"Been out here a while."

I rubbed my eyes, "Sorry, I guess I fell asleep."

She looked around at the river, the birds, and a boat cruising, leaving a small wake. "I can see how, sure is peaceful."

A lousy attempt at a smile broke my lips apart. Alysa saw it and smiled back. There was no controlling it.

"Did I miss breakfast?"

"I saved you a plate." She smiled and leaned against the railing, looking out at the water.

"Thanks for your help."

She shrugged, "You thanked me already."

My smile left my face, "I mean it. This isn't over yet."

Another shrug, "If it means keeping Candice safe and busting these assholes, I can handle it."

I packed up the tacklebox and we went into the house to wash up.

Alysa had the food plated and waiting at the small circular dinette. Candice was up now blowing on heavily creamed coffee before sipping it.

They joined me at the table as I ate. Alysa and Candice chatted about the weather and how they were going to fix up the house to make it homey. My thoughts were on April. Her life over, never going to do another damn thing with it.

I dropped my fork on the plate. "This isn't summer camp; we are hiding for our lives."

Alysa snarled, "Ugh, said the guy who just came in from fishing."

I looked at them and took a breath. "I'm sorry. I don't know how long we'll be here."

"You said a few days. I already called out of work."

"What'd you tell them?" Candice asked thinking she would have to do the same.

"I told them my brother wrecked his motorcycle and I needed to go help him out for a few days."

"You have a brother?" I went back to eating the eggs.

She laughed, "No. Wayne said the same thing. Then he said to please be back by Friday."

"What's today?"

"Sunday." The two women said in unison.

After breakfast we went back into the living room. There was more to April than any of us knew and it all needed to come out.

"Candice, you said Igo got April investigating the vigilante, right?"

She nodded I was correct.

"Was the vigilante a natural curiosity to April? All her previous articles were fluff. What made Igo think she would even want to investigate this, *killer?*" That last part was hard to get out, but it was true.

Candice pushed back on the sofa cushions as she began, "Her dad died in prison. He had sworn he was innocent, and April believed him. It was something she was passionate about." Candice sipped at her coffee. "I mean she wasn't wrong. Her last article, the one that hasn't been published, showed how the vigilante was unfairly targeting minorities and immigrants. Look at the neighborhoods he strikes. I never hear he was up at some gated golf community."

"You read this article?" Alysa came in with a question while I was fighting inside with conflicting thoughts.

"Yeah, she gave it to me to read." Candice dug through her phone. "Here." She handed me the phone opened to a word doc.

Not only was the vigilante described as a racist and xenophobe, but then went on to hypothesize that the cops had failed to apprehend whoever was behind the killings on purpose, implying they were too. Her statistics were not wrong, I had been in poor neighborhoods. There was no mention of my first act as this vigilante. I was behind the biggest shake up to hit the state of Florida. Sanford and I broke up a sex trafficking ring that took down lobbyists, politicians, and law enforcement officers, those in gated communities. What the article did not detail, nor anyone even know, was my agenda was not my own. Willis Sanford had his agenda and being a black man from a poor black neighborhood, he sent me there first. Together, our justice blindfolds were on, and we were balancing the scales, looking after those who had been looked over.

The article wrapped up with her take on what justice was and should be with no mention of her father's prison sentence, but she expressed doubts about due process and punishments fitting the crimes.

I gave Candice back the phone and went into the room I picked out. Agitated by having to cut my little isolation trip short, I went through the gear I brought. Guns, knives, knuckles, and a Kevlar vest topped the list. The rest were just clothes. Preparedness put me at ease.

A text came in from Sheela asking about Terrence. I hadn't heard from him, so I ignored it. I laid on the couch and listened to the tick tock of the wall clock above the kitchen sink. A steady rain began to fall then the heat kicked on, that smell of burning oil filled my nostrils and made me think of Christmas when I was a kid. Just glimpses and flashes of smiling faces, aroma of food in the oven and new toys in a pile of torn up wrapping paper waiting for their turn to be played with.

Alysa sat at the other end of the couch. She tapped my leg then handed me her phone. There were two headlines. To the left, *Death by Vigilante* written by April Ward and the other, *College Reporters Last Article* written by Dr. Igo.

My eyes skimmed it. It was similar to the article Candice had given me, but with a harsher take on the vigilante. As I continued to read my hand began shaking, scrambling the words on the screen, as I tried to read without bias. Bias, what a joke. The piece started out the same but quickly diverged in tone. Hard on the attack, sighting none of the victims of extreme violence was tried in court, the vigilante was labeled a serial killer. Only one line mentioned anything about priors and suspects to crimes, made these men saints. The article claimed the vigilante struck fear into the economically oppressed neighborhoods forcing innocent residents to look over their shoulders and double lock their doors. I knew for a fact the opposite to be true. Sanford was a pillar in that community, he talked firsthand with the folks who felt safer knowing someone other than the police was looking out for them. He had the stats. Drug use down, crime down. We were winning.

A few paragraphs down described the case I had months back. Fredrick Jones was found dead, beaten to death in his home. Never mind the fact he was peddling child pornography and was just released on parole after being found guilty of child molestation for the third time. He pled down for lesser charges and only served three years. The tip on Jones came to Sanford by way of the District Attorney's office. Willis set up my alibi and I took Jones out. The article conveniently left out the nauseating filth I found on him when I got there or how I gave him the option to turn himself in. He refused so he died quickly. He can suffer in Hell, not in my hands.

The cops of course would not comment on an open investigation. The facts were so cherry picked I could mix it in my coke and splash some bourbon over it.

A text from Terrence came in and I skipped that one too. Now wasn't the time to deal with him.

The rest of the article was calling on people to step forward and not live in fear. A hashtag, *injustice*, was created to get tips on the vigilante. Lastly the article called out the mayor and police for incompetence on this vigilante. Below the article was a little public opinion piece with tiny square photos of the people. Three of the five called for a man hunt to capture the vigilante, one was for the vigilante, and another had no opinion. A quick run of the names through a mug shot website would show why the first three wanted the vigilante caught, but I had better things to do.

Dr. Igo's shared headline was even worse. It read like it would be about April's fight for justice, instead it was purely an opinion piece with no facts to support his opinion other than that I was violating victims' civil rights. Not in a sense that I was judge and executioner, but that I was using race bias to pick my targets. He laid the implication out nicely at a third-grade level, the vigilante was responsible, directly, or indirectly, it did not matter. I forced myself to read his drabble twice to make sure I did not miss anything. Then without a doubt I was dreaming of the time when I could meet Igo face to face.

I handed Alysa's phone over to Candice, "Looks like she polished the article before submitting it."

Candice began to read the lies I just swallowed.

After pacing for several moments, I went to the refrigerator and grabbed a beer. My phone dinged with more texts from Terrence. I didn't bother reading them, all I wanted to do was go down and punch the professor in the face, but it wouldn't do me any good. His mind was made up and facts no longer mattered. There was a better chance with Detective Camp. She didn't know about some of the crimes they alleged were the work of the copycats. Camp had always warned me if evidence ever pointed my way, she would have no choice but to come after me.

"These aren't her words, it's not her style. Someone else doctored this article."

"Just like a good little editor." Alysa said.

Candice and Alysa held blank expressions as they waited for me to stop pacing. Each time I paced the room it took fewer and fewer steps. The walls grew closer and closer until they were six by six. The clank of bar doors locking filled my ears as paranoia churned my guts. I could spit acid. The calm collected thief I used to be was gone, buried under years of burning pure animal instinct and running on a red line of adrenaline.

I made a dash to the bathroom and splashed cold water on my face. Pinching my eyes shut did little to soften the electrical zaps in my brain or loosen the tight rope around my chest. My brain was on fire from withdrawal. In the mirror, dripping with sweat and tap water was the hollowed-out face of a man on the edge. My hands came into reflective view. Scared and veined they now had a slight tremor like a soft breeze on a leafy branch. Down my wrists I traced over arms that were thinner than they had been. The softball bicep that used to stretch the limits of my t-shirts were gone. Now the only bulge from under my shirt was the pudge around my waist.

I did it to myself. For the past year there was nothing in my refrigerator that was not in a bottle. Day and night had run together as the hands on the clock spun, landing on numbers with no significance. When my head cleared enough to think about food, I was too tired to cook. Microwaved chicken nuggets were the best protein I could get. The processed food showed in the dark bags under my eyes, large enough to check on an airplane. My hair, once jet black, now sparkled with specks of silver.

In being so mission focused on getting bad guys, I had gotten sloppy. Tunnel vision had left my peripherals a blur. Sloppy enough to let my Scout be stolen. Sloppy enough to wake up next to a dead girl. So sloppy that I was back in a cell, this time without bars but none the less locked up. This was a fight for my life and not one I could win with my fists.

The ding of a text filled my ears. Gripping the phone, I wanted to smash it on the counter. With a fresh breath I sat on the edge of the tub and finally read Terrence's texts.

They weren't bearers of good news. People were sending him screenshots of social media posts of death threats from the thugs in his former gang. Something had got them wound up, maybe it was the extra police presence in their neighborhood or maybe it was rioting in the street, either way they were feeding on the negative energy in the city, and it was being directed at Terrence.

I called Billy and asked him to bring me the VW.

I left the house telling them I had one more fire to put out.

I had walked two blocks when I saw Billy swing in. I dropped him back at the shop and asked him to check in on the safe house. I called Terrence from the car. He was upset and said he knew this would happen. I assured him I was on my way. He had already called Ben. I was glad I wouldn't be alone on this.

The GTi zipped through the streets. As I neared Terrence's house, I saw Ben's blacked out Dodge Charger. The two of them were standing in the door talking. Ben was dressed in a black turtleneck tucked into jeans. Terry was in basketball shorts and a hoodie.

Now with two cars in front of the house I felt the eyes of neighbors on us. Though no one looked directly at us, but they were there.

I walked past the broken bird bath and stood at the porch.

"Where's your Auntie?" I said.

"She ain't here, went to visit her sister." Terry said. I could see the small block edge of a pistol butt in his waist band.

"Good, let's get out of here." I said waving them off the porch.

"I ain't going." Terry said, puffing up his chest.

"There's bigger things going on right now and I don't have the time." I shot back.

"He needs to face them." Ben said catching me off guard. He had been in counterintelligence and always flew under the radar. Now in the midst of the city about to ignite, he wants open warfare.

I threw up my hands. "I don't have time for this. What if they don't show until after we leave? I can't rush over here every time they threaten you."

Terry didn't have to answer the question. He looked down the street at a white Chrysler 300 with tinted windows roll towards us and pull into the driveway.

Terry stepped off the porch, but I stopped him from approaching the car. I didn't know if these guys were serious and if they were, they would simply shoot us in the front yard.

The rear window behind the driver went down. Smoke plumed out then a man with a shaved head and a gold tooth said, "Yo, Terry get in, we got bid'ness."

"Get the hell outta my yard." Terry shouted. He started to sway.

The window rolled up then all four doors opened. I waited for the gun barrels but only saw four men get out. One was tall and skinny in a white long-sleeve shirt and sagging jeans. The guy from the rear seat was in a red track suit and on the other side both men wore hoodies and sagging black denim jeans.

Ben was three feet to my left and Terry over my right shoulder.

"What'ch you got bodyguards now?" said the leader with the gold tooth. "Y'all crackers better bounce." He smiled.

"It is you who should go." Ben replied.

The tall one from the passenger side stepped up snarling into Ben's face. "Fuck you old man—"

His voice was cut short when Ben chopped him in the throat. He staggered back then fell on his ass, holding his neck. The other three stood still for a moment then the fight was on.

The driver was closer to me, so I went after him first. He danced around a little and took a wide hammer swing. I blocked it and stepped in swinging a fist of my own into his gut. He buckled. I heard a swear word and caught site of a fist coming my way. It caught me in the side of the head. I turned to throw a left jab, but saw Terry was already there.

He grabbed the gold tooth leader and tossed him to the ground. I glanced over at Ben who had already taken the other passenger down, tied him in an arm bar, then SNAP! Ben was on his feet before the man could scream.

A crowd gathered; kids, a white-haired lady clutching her purse and a couple of middle-aged women watched as the fight echoed through their neighborhood.

Terry and the gold tooth were tangled up, each struggling to get the upper hand, swinging fists and sometimes locking up. Before I intervened, a shout came from the driveway across the street.

A bald man in a blue button work shirt with a name patch on it was climbing out of a plumber's van, "Hey stop it. Damn it, I said stop it right now!" He marched over carrying a short pipe. He was breathing heavy but looked to be in good shape and about forty years old.

I let go of the driver, letting him fall once more to the ground. Ben came to my side, we kept six feet apart. Terry and gold tooth were still tangle. The bald plumber grabbed Terry and pushed him back then he pointed the pipe at the gold tooth ringleader, jabbing him in the chest.

"I said enough." He was breathing heavy with spit bubbling in the corners of his mouth. "What the hell is going on?"

The white-haired lady stepped up, "That one there is Sheela's nephew. He lives there."

The plumber looked Terry over and nodded then he turned to Ben and me, the two that stood out in this crowd.

"We're here to help Terry." I said. Terry nodded as he checked the blood seeping from his lip.

The plumber turned to gold tooth, "I've seen you around."

"Better watch it with that pipe broth 'a." Gold tooth said as he backed up. His two friends picked up the third with the broken arm. With his three friends behind him he said, "We know where you live now."

"That's right." The plumber smiled. "This is where we all live." He turned and pointed at all the people that had stopped to watch the fight. He jabbed the piped once again into Gold tooth's chest. "Now get the hell out of *our* neighborhood."

The gangster staggered back then yelled a warning. When the plumber lifted the pipe, they all scurried back into the car.

Once the car was gone, the plumber said, "We got enough trouble in town, we don't need it here. If they come back, you just come get me."

Terry thanked the plumber and stuck out his hand to shake. The white-haired lady echoed the plumber's offer to help and shuffled off.

"You want to come back with me?" I said to Terry.

Before he could answer Ben said, "You can come stay at the gym."

"Nah, I think I'll stay right here. They won't be back any time soon."

We said our goodbyes and left. I didn't have the time to stick around and try and convince the kid to leave. He was old enough now to make his own decisions. His fight wasn't over yet but for a time it would be quiet. Now he had allies, neighbors willing to take a risk to keep their neighborhood safe. In some way I wanted to believe the vigilante had something to do with that. The people making the tough choices for themselves, whether out of fear or in spite it.

It left me feeling better about what I had to do.

# **Chapter 19**

Soft laughter came from the open windows as I approached the front door of the safe house. Despite everything we went through and still had ahead of us, laughter managed to persist. That image of myself changed, I was in there somewhere, behind the battered vigilante. If change was going to be exacted, then I would have to make it.

With laughter there was hope. It was something I managed to hang on to. Those jail cell bars had not locked yet; I had a chance of turning this thing around. Since I did not have my computer with me, I was limited on the electronic snooping I could do.

I sent a text to Monique requesting she dig up Dr. Igo's address and any other information she could find. She didn't reply. I called Sanford but he didn't answer. Then I got a text from him, *hold tight*, which told me he was busy doing lawyer things. Probably covering my ass and here I am texting him.

Back in the living room, I went over everything with Candice once more. Her story was the same, nothing extra or helpful. Hiding out, total isolation, no social media and a couple of strangers with nothing much in common was taking a toll on Candice's patience. Boredom was over taking her fear and she wanted out. She kept checking her phone, looking at the time and opening apps she could look at offline. She played a game on her phone but without internet it did not take long for her to put the phone down. Then go right back to it.

The boredom was catching. Alysa went through every room. When she didn't come out of the master bedroom for a while, I went in. She was on the floor with a box. The lid was off, and a photo album spread wide on the white Berber carpet.

She looked up, "This is great stuff." She handed over a black and white photo of a man in a fedora holding a cigar with his foot on the running board of a car. His smile was proud, and his fingers were spread on the door sill like he just bought the car.

"Must be Monique's great grandfather."

"Is that who owns this house?"

"Yeah, she works for Sanford." I knelt beside Alysa and took a stack of loose photographs. Family, friends, gatherings, and high points in a life lived.

"Hey, this is on Beach Street." Alysa said flipping the photo over for me to see. It was just a random street shot. All the stores gone now. New business occupied the fronts.

"I think they all are from around Daytona." I said. Monique's family, like Sanford's, had gone back a long way in this mostly transient town. Not too many native Floridians and even less Daytona born residents left. I was born here but didn't grow up here. The Merchant Marines had shipped my old man around. My mother and I followed. My mother was from here, sort of, as far as I knew. Ideas of how my life would have turned out differently if we had never come back to Daytona were never far.

"You from here?" I asked the beautiful blond sitting with her legs crossed and open album in her lap.

"Sorta, I was born in Illinois, but my parents are from here. We moved back when I was in elementary school, and I've pretty much been here ever since."

"Kinda the same here. I was born here, left as a baby came back a teenager."

"Something about this town, just can't seem to leave it." She worked a crooked smile across her face.

"You think you will?"

"What, ever get out?" Alysa shrugged, "I think about it, but sometimes it's nice be in your hometown."

I smiled. I thought about it all the time. Suddenly I didn't want to tell her that. This had been the first time spent outside a bar together. I didn't want it to end even if the circumstances that brought us here were life threatening. We couldn't playhouse forever. There was still danger out in the street waiting to meet me. Running away from this swirling black hole would have to wait. Maybe when that time comes, Alysa will be ready to join me then too.

We sat smiling at one another. Then we went back to the sifting through images of someone else's life. The choices they made and lives they lived were there in black and white. There were choices for me to make and sitting around waiting for the inevitable to find me wasn't buying any time worth using up.

I got up and went into the bathroom. Under the sink were a set of hair clippers. The fresh black sprouts of hair tumbled into the seashell pink sink. The clippers went over what little growth of beard I had and turned it back to a shadow. The hot shower washed away any traces of the job.

Wrapped in a towel, still with beads of water on my shoulders, I passed through the short hall to my room. Suddenly I was pushed from behind, low on my back, forcing my hips forward. The door shut behind me.

"Just what in the hell do you think you're doing?"

I gripped the towel as fear of it falling off gripped my throat. I cleared my throat and said, "Shit you scared me. I could of—"

"Could what?" Alysa said, one hand on a hip with the opposite leg jutted out to the side. Her foot tapped.

"Who said I was going anywhere." I looked for fresh clothes and moved slowly in that direction. Alysa cut me off.

"You cut your hair and you have that look in your eye."

"So what?"

"I've known you for a while now Grimes. All the times you sat at my bar, nursing a beer for hours then coming back later and slamming shots. Now that you've nursed your beer here with us for a couple days, you're ready. You're ready to leave us here and go out and find those bikers alone." Alysa clenched her fists and moved towards me. I braced for the swing. It didn't come.

"I need to do something. Sitting in this cell isn't going to stop the violence. Innocent people are losing their lives over this insanity." I brushed past her to my duffle bag where I knew clean clothes waited. There was a plan forming in my head to get out of here and get to the bottom of Igo and the Dead Ends. It was time to stop running and stop hiding. Alysa was the one that had said this was our hometown, for good or bad and it was on fire. My actions had been the kindling. The Dead Ends were adding fuel and Igo, with his articles, was fanning the flame.

She grabbed my arm and spun me around, the towel swirled like a ballroom gown. I thought I might lose it. Her eyes did not budge from mine. Towel or no towel, she did not come in my room to catch me compromised. Her message was clear.

"I was there last time you got that look, remember? This is more than some porn king and his minions. These are gangs and murders and don't forget about trigger happy cops all after that vigilante. What if they mistake you for him?"

"I know what I'm doing." I said as a lie.

"Damn you Grimes." She said confirming the lie and let go of my arm. She stepped back as her eyes relaxed. They rolled over my bare skin, over the puffy scar tissue of a bullet wound, pink lines from knife wounds and other puckered scars my chest and back.

"What the hell?" Alysa whispered gently. Her hand went out, but she never touched me.

There was no hiding the evidence. Months of being the vigilante had left a scrap book of scars on my body and hidden ones in my mind. The two of us under one roof, away from the whole world had been a dream. It was a fairytale that could not last.

"I know what I'm doing." I said again reassuring her as much as myself.

"I'm not sure you do." She said then left the room without looking back.

After I dressed, I was in the kitchen finishing a glass of water. Candice had a mini melt-down when I said I was heading out. Alysa did the job she took on and calmed the college girl. She said nothing to me as I made my way to the door. I was better out there on the street, being holed up was not in my blood. As bad as I needed a little break, some fishing, and a bourbon to forget the world, was not the answer to this problem.

Before I got to the door, it opened. Looking down the barrel of my Glock was the perfectly put together Monique. She did not flinch or stutter. "You better contact Sanford."

I holstered the pistol and took her suitcase. Judging by the weight she came for the long haul. I walked her to the living room where Alysa was standing while Candice sat on the couch.

I dropped the suite case and turned to Monique who stood in silence at the additional house guests.

"I'll head up to his office." I said.

She shook her head, "He isn't there. Better call him." She looked at the other two with less interest in an introduction and more of wondering why they were here.

"This is Alysa, and that is Candice." I said pointing rather coldly.

Monique nodded while Alysa and Candice both said hello.

"Grimes, this place isn't your secret clubhouse." Monique looked Alysa up and down. Alysa crossed her arms. Two beautiful alpha females squared off.

My hand cupped her shoulder then waved her down the hall so we could have a little privacy though I knew Alysa and Candice would hear it all. The terrazzo floors and bare walls made for a perfect echo chamber.

We went into a back bedroom. Monique wouldn't look me in the eye. Though this house was an established safe house and I had stayed a few times, bringing guests, female guests, was a violation of trust. This home was a tomb, a dedication to her family and the success they had achieved.

"Look," I said running a hand over the bristles of my freshly shaved head, "I had to bring them here. Candice knows what April Ward was working on and is probably the only person who believes I did not kill her."

"Fine." She finally looked me in the eye. "I didn't want to come here anyway, Willis made me."

My ears tingled and my brow pushed together. "Why?"

"I was followed this morning. I thought maybe it was a cop. Checked in with a source at the station and there's no official tail on me, or any of us."

"Get a good look at him?" I reached in my pocket and pulled my phone.

"White guy, late thirties, early forties."

Sanford's call vibrated in my hand, "Time to meet." He said before I could speak.

# **Chapter 20**

Sanford's superhero speeches had begun to sink in over these couple of years. Daytona Beach was my home as much as his. If busting skulls and crippling drug and sex trafficking rings were to mean anything than maintaining it had to mean something too. Hiding would be letting them undo what we all had worked for, safer streets. Changes had been made. My criminal justice system was not a revolving door, I gave criminals a reason to look over their shoulder and something to fear. As much as Dr. Igo and his newspaper wanted to condemn my actions denying the violence had worked. It was time to deliver a little more.

I left the house on foot and walked along the residential street lined with large brick homes, to the corner of an empty lot where a gas station used to be. Billy was sitting there in the Ford. We decided it was best he didn't come straight to the house. We crossed over the river and drove north along A1A until we got to a mostly deserted parking garage. I jumped out and he pulled around to watch from a distance in case of trouble.

My phone told me I had been there thirteen minutes, pacing, waiting for Sanford to get there. As my feet slapped down on the descending concrete floor of the parking garage, a silver Ford Taurus swung the corner in a hurry. I stepped back and let my muscle memory slide my open palm over my Glock. The car slowed; the dark tinted windows showed me just what I looked like today. My fingers slipped under my shirt at my waist, anticipating locking down on the grip like a gator on a thirsty wild boar. I struggled to calm my racing mind, the words, and images of what was in that car waiting to dole out revenge, retribution or just hate against me. The Dead Ends?

The passenger window went down and instantly I was relieved. A pair of redden brown eyes wrapped in familiar metal frames looked up at me.

"Get in." His eyes pulled away, straight then to his left.

I slid into the grey fabric seat and Sanford hit the gas before I had the door fully closed. He checked all three of his mirrors several times as we circled down the garage eventually making our way to the street.

I remained silent for a few blocks. He sped up and slowed, taking corners fast, and he checked his mirrors a lot. I sucked in air to say something, and he held a finger to his lips. I shrugged and exhaled.

A few miles down US 1 we pulled into a park alongside the river. Sanford popped his head to the side, and we got out.

"I always pictured you a Cadillac man." I said patting the hood of the Ford.

Sanford wrinkled his brow, "Why, because I'm a wealthy black man?"

I shrugged and looked away feeling a little embarrassed.

Laughter broke out of Sanford's never tired mouth. "Aw of course I own a Cadillac. Two, actually. I borrowed this car. Thought it best not be out and about in my own car." The weight of his words dulled the humor.

We walked out onto an aluminum pier with concrete pilings covered in barnacles. He waited until we were to the end before he spoke,

Sanford grabbed the metal dock railing. Then resting his elbows on the railing, he took off his glasses and rubbed tired eyes, eyes that had been watching the candle burn at both ends for too long.

"I was followed home last night."

I looked over at him but said nothing. He should have called me.

"I know, I should have called you, but you got so much going on right now. And now Monique was followed too!" Sanford ran his long fingers down the sides of his face.

"I'll keep Monique close to me and you should – "

"Someone has pegged us for the vigilante."

I took a hard swallow and gulped some air. This was bad, this was the day I stopped thinking about every son of a bitch I killed. All the drug pushers, pimps, and child pornographers I buried under my fists were rising from their shallow graves and burned-out dens to come for me. I had hung around too long, spent too many nights in the shadows watching the evil men do and then confronting them with their own sins before sending them to hell. It had become my second nature, no it *was* my nature. I had become a well-mannered animal but an animal all the same.

"I don't think you heard me. Someone has pegged us, Grimes, you and me. They are on to *us*."

We stood in silence as the breeze lifted from the river. The water was calm, the sun out, it was all around a nice day if we weren't in this jam. A bounty on my head and cops breathing down our throats.

"Us?"

"There's a video, of you. It was sent to me, directly."

Sanford was looking at me, waiting for me to speak, say anything so he didn't have to.

"Doing what?"

He took a deep breath, "A week ago I gave you a racketeer case."

I gripped the railing and would have pulled it out if I could. My biceps stung as they exceeded their limits. I let go and watched the blood return to my fingers.

"I remember." I said. I had been wrong about which case I had met the dead man under the bridge. The face of the gangster returned to my mind's eye and as I superimposed it over the bruised face of the dead hitman Detective Camp shot, they matched. Deceiving myself by hiding the faces of my victims had worked too well. Only a couple weeks ago I beat a guy for trying to extort money out of a small business and in that time had blocked out his face. My protective mechanisms were working against me.

Sanford took out his cell phone. It was in a small clear plastic bag. He punched something on the screen using the bag as a shield for prints.

"The whole thing stinks of a set up." Sanford said and handed over the phone. The video was at night. A car parked under a streetlamp. One man in the driver's seat. His window down. I remembered the rest from first person point of view. I had followed the man in the car for several hours that night. He settled out front of the newly opened Mexican restaurant. He had escalated things by going after employees, making them afraid to come to work. He called the owner a few times letting her know he was waiting. He didn't know I was waiting for him.

I pulled him out of the car window. A few gut punches got him to his knees. My plan was to scare him, he was all about scaring the owner, I would scare him and hopefully he'd stop. He showed resolve when he stood up. His swing was fast, but I managed to dodge it. He grabbed me and we tussled in the street. It was more than I expected from him and caught me off guard. I rallied and got the upper hand landing a few blows to his face.

A car came around the corner and nearly hit us both, forcing us to separate. He made a break for it and I lost him somewhere in the shadows of the downtown city streets. By the time I back tracked to find his car was gone. Later research revealed the car was stolen. The owner was never bothered again, so I marked it in the win column. Until I saw him dead under the bridge.

"If this guy is the one who sent it, he' dead." I said handing the phone back to Sanford.

"By way of you?"

"No, Camp shot him. He pulled a shotgun on us as we were meeting under the Seabreeze Bridge. I knew I recognized his face."

"Grimes, it came with a warning. The video is going to be posted to the vigilante tracker website." Sanford pulled his own cell and started searching the web for it.

"I've seen it."

"This doesn't make any sense. We're changing this city for the best." Sanford put the phone away.

"Not everyone agrees with our methods." I said, having heard it from Dr. Igo and someone much closer to me, Alysa.

Sanford nodded, "Hubris."

"We haven't fallen yet, but it gets worse. The guy in that video was a cop, he resigned recently.

There's no doubt the video was a set up. Who sent you the lead on this guy?"

"That's what I've been trying to figure out." Sanford sighed again. I didn't know anything about his contacts or how I got my leads. Each case was different, leads came from different places. We still had our *List*, those that had been tied to Gregg Hines and his poker games. The names were dwindling, leaving just those at the top. They were public figures, politicians, people I couldn't reach in the middle of night without drawing a lot of attention.

Sanford dropped other leads in my lap with a place and time as well. Those took a little longer, more foot work. This had been one of them.

"Usually we do our research, look in the papers for crimes and suspects then you go after them. It's not the most efficient way but it eliminates a trail. Sometimes we get tips, we have people out there keeping an ear to the street.

"Ti'Neesha. She's one of our informants and sometime prostitute. Anyway, she messages Monique tips that usually don't go anywhere but we pay her for them." Sanford's voice trailed off. He didn't like saying it as much as I didn't like hearing it.

"Where do I find her?"

"She's dead. Overdosed on heroin." Sanford said.

Sanford wasn't done yet, "To make matters worse, the cops haven't stopped calling. This Detective Waycross always has another question about your whereabouts on different nights. I keep providing fake cases you were working but I'm running out here. They're on a shared calendar so I suggest you memorize it quick. I'm not sure those cases will hold up under much scrutiny. They'll find a way around my roadblocks." Sanford pushed off the railing. His hands went in his pockets then out then on the railing. I'd never seen him this frayed.

Someone was out there watching all of us. Their eyes giving me a chill that comes with being naked.

"Why are they giving us the phone with the video? Why not just turn it over to the police and be done with us?" I said trying to pick this whole tangled mess apart.

Sanford shrugged, "They hate us. They hate what we are doing for this city and want to see us sweat."

"Like we've been making them sweat."

"Yeah, but who?"

"Any number of the criminals we've gone after."

We stood in silence, each with a list from the past.

I looked out over the river, "Whoever this is, isn't the only one that knows. April figured me out the night she died."

"Are you sure?" Sanford asked, knowing full well I was.

I nodded, "A reporter was on to me."

"I read the article." Sanford processed the news as I did. "No good deed and now we got it coming from all sides. There has been a silent civil war in the FDLE. Some of those powerful people we embarrassed when we took down that sex ring are putting pressure on state law enforcement to find out who was responsible. We really got them good." His smile was a lie.

"You think they traced Gregg Hines back to you?" I had been looking at this from the wrong shore. It wasn't do-good cops or valiant reporters trying to expose me, it was someone whose life had been turned upside down by me and Sanford going back to our first case, a big case.

"We have our story; you were hired to find his daughter and it led you to the sex ring only you never saw who did all the killing."

I nodded. We had gone over the events of those days forward and back. I had become the narrator in my own story, claiming I showed up just after it all went down.

"Grimes," Sanford patted me on the shoulder. "This is my battle, off the streets and in the high rises. Some place is a criminal we overlooked, someone who didn't like their little pedo-ring dismantled. I'll find him."

I believed Sanford. He withdrew his hand and grasp the railing once more.

"I talked to Terrence. That gang won't be bothering him." I said hoping it would cheer Sanford up a little.

Sanford's eyes twitched. He folded his arms and a certain professionalism returned to his demeanor as he stood a little straighter.

"I heard. He seems to be doing better. I appreciate you taking that on. I know you have your plate full. So, tell me what's going on, catch me up."

"I've just been digging myself out of quicksand."

Sanford nodded, he wanted more. I had to fill him in. "There's a biker gang involved."

"Bikers?"

I leaned against the railing, "This isn't a normal motorcycle club. They're all young, younger than me and mixed races, even have lady riders. It's like," I struggled for a way to describe how different the Dead Ends were from real clubs like the Outlaws. "A new kind of club. Something for millennials."

"Millennials? Did they Snap Chat their crimes? Maybe check their Tik Toc."

I laughed; Sanford was up on the young crowd was doing these days more so than Billy who had trouble pronouncing the word. My previous criminal life was void of social media. It just leads to capture.

"Yeah, they were on their phones a lot. I got the impression they are not very experienced criminals, but they're learning fast."

"So, we call it in? Maybe it will get the cops off our backs if we turn them over."

"Not yet. If they are responsible for killing April, I need to figure out why." I said. The wind off the river picked up and blew through my mechanic's cut jacket.

"So, we can't call it in, there's no proof." Sanford shook his head. "I'm sorry Grimes. I should be way ahead of this. We're smarter than this." Sanford shook his head as his chin dipped into his chest. He was tired and this made him more tired.

Sanford looked out over the brown chop forming as the wind grew stronger. Along the other side of the river sat large houses. Each one surrounded by tall palms and had swimming pools protected by concrete seawalls. Living the dream while we were living a nightmare. The worst scenario was presenting itself before us. Someone was on to us. They were stalking us, following our every move, and keeping track of our wrongs. Suddenly walls were closing in and soon it would be cell bars. I wasn't going back to prison.

"I'm not going to let them beat us. I'm going to find who killed April and get whoever is coming after us." I said.

Light returned to Sanford's dim recessed eyes. He was up on the balls of his feet, and he began talking with his hands. The bell had rung, and he was ready for another round. He was on fire, he wanted to get in a gym and start punching something. That fighter was back, and it wanted to brawl.

"Alright, my man. Go cut'em down Grimes." Sanford slapped me on the shoulder, and we headed back to the car.

"Billy will give me a ride back." I said and pointed to the white Ford parked across the street. Sanford shook his head. He had never spotted Billy's tail.

I told him Billy would head over to his office and scan for bugs or any other devices. Sanford agreed. I watched him walk back to his car and leave. I walked to the street and Billy rolled up in the truck.

"How'd it go?" Billy said as I climbed in the truck.

I shook my head.

"That bad? Well, not to pile it on but you all had a tail alright. But don't worry, I lost them for you."

"How'd you manage that?"

"Blocked 'em in when you guys turned off, they missed it. I circled back and found you." Billy lit a smoke.

"Drop me back at the house and then if you can keep doing me favors, bring some tech over to Sanford's office and check for bugs or anything else." It was indeed a big favor. For Billy, that uneasy tension of having betrayed a friend lingered still after more than a year. I had moved on, no one died, well at least neither of us died because of it. As badly as I needed Billy to do this for me, there was also the hope of him helping Sanford would break that tension and we could all be in the same room together eventually.

# **Chapter 21**

A text to Alysa and Monique gave them a heads up I was coming back. Inside the safe house, the three women were all in separate rooms. Alysa was in the living room watching a laptop stream nonstop news coverage of a city on fire. People were sending in videos of beatings and roving groups of other vigilantes out looking for the original vigilante. Vigils were held for victims, real or imagined. Most reports were about feelings and not facts. Helicopters still circled overhead, four or five at a time. Tip lines were flooded with calls of a violent march that positioned cops on every corner in riot gear holding shotguns or AR's. A zombie apocalypse had come to Daytona Beach, one with me as patient zero. People roamed the streets searching for a reward and others armed themselves and hunkered down behind boarded up windows like a hurricane was coming. Indeed, a storm was brewing. I had to get to the eye of it to find who was responsible.

"Hi," Alysa said. "Monique turned on a Wi-Fi hotspot."

I nodded but said nothing as I sat on the other end of the couch. We watched the coverage in silence. A plan was forming in my mind. There were two major players close to my secret and they both wanted it out. One was a millennial biker gang more interested in how their selfies looked on social media than committing crimes. The other was a shadow, methodical in its moves, tracking me. Whoever it was, would get their chance for real evidence on me.

"This is awful," Alysa said without taking her eyes from the television.

I nodded without speaking. I expected her to ask questions or lecture me on the risks I was taking. She did neither.

"They might call in the National Guard." She turned to get a response. I nodded.

"Hey," She said, "About earlier, I shouldn't tell you your business."

I smiled. We sat there in silence. My mind shifted from worrying about Alysa to solving this case without going to prison for the rest of my life.

I got up and walked into the spare room. Candice was laying on a bed in the corner. Earbuds in and her foot tapping. I could hear pitchy squeaks of the tunes emanating from her ears. She popped one out.

"Hey,"

"Hi. I think it's time we went to the cops."

She sat up and turned off the music. "Are you sure about that?"

I nodded, "You can be honest with them. It's better that you are."

Candice kept her eyes on the floor, "April thought you were the vigilante." Candice had to make that clear before I turned her over to the cops. "I was suspicious of you too, but well if you wanted to kill me, I'd be dead."

I nodded, "April sent you her article, but did she keep a notebook or anything that may lead to something?"

Candice leaned her head back against the cool white plaster of the wall. Her eyes went up to the ceiling as her brain looked for a connection. She went to her bag and pulled a laptop. Clicking away she said, "I just thought of something."

I waited patiently for her to finish that thought, but all she did was click around on the internet. Realizing she was lost in the process; she patted the bed next to her and I took a seat so we could share the screen.

"Yes," she turned the computer slightly more towards me, "April suspected Professor Igo or someone else of hacking into her computer at the paper and reading her notes so she asked to keep stuff on my cloud. I have all her files." Her smile was bright, and her shoulders rolled as a rhythmic celebration dance came out.

Candice started looking through the names of the word files. She paused, "You sure you want me to search this? I mean, she was on to you for a reason."

"Go ahead, I think whatever led her to me, killed her, and we both know it wasn't me."

Candice went through each file in each folder. April was a prolific writer from fan fiction to blog posts to her news articles. Many articles were not finished or never published. Finally, she came to what we wanted.

"Here's her notes. I'm not sure how she has it organized." Candice turned the computer over to me. My palms were beginning to sweat and the dexterity in my fingers seemed to diminish as I tapped at the wrong keys try to navigate the word document. The rough draft article started off with unsubstantiated claims and rumors around town about who the vigilante could be, but quickly petered out. Then thoughts took shape, a conclusion formed tracing its way back to the beginning. An original vigilante, one that went after much harder targets, like sex traffickers. She discounted the police account of the pool hall shootout two years ago being gang warfare. She recognized it as the start of the vigilante.

At the bottom of the second page was an outline with ideas. A suspect description list of the supposed copycats. A name stood out. The news reporter had done her homework. I was impressed and saddened all at once. Such a promising life cut short to hide a dirty secret that I was the vigilante. She had figured it all out, just a little too late. To do this right, I had to meet with Detective Camp once more.

"Hey," Alysa came in and plopped down on the bed next to me. She leaned in to get more screen time with the computer. I tried to block her, to shut the computer but she was quick and locked on. Her lips moved as she silently read the article. I handed the laptop over and stood up.

"She makes a good case for you Grimes." She said looking up with a grin, not believing what she was reading. My face was stone, my head was currently buried under a ton of bricks with sharp corners. I had no response.

She continued reading. A crease formed between her eyebrows as she gripped the laptop with both hands. When she was done, she looked up at me then back at the screen.

"Is this some kind of joke? Seriously what the hell?" Alysa pushed the computer away from her like it was full of cockroaches. She stood up, her green eyes to my blue. Before I could say or do anything, she slowly backed towards the door.

"C'mon Grimes, I mean, it isn't true. Tell me she's wrong. You're not some killer, I mean, there's no way, I was there...when you, you had to, they were going to kill us. But not this," Her tan skin erupted with tiny goose bumps. Her teeth started to chatter. She heaved, sucking in breath like coming up for air, drowning under flooded eyes. Fingers ran up over her face as she wouldn't allow herself to look at me any longer.

"It makes sense now, it, it just, there was that missing piece, that reason you've kept me away. And oh *GAWD!*" A slight stumble as she rounded the door for the hall.

I heard the bathroom door slam shut. Sickly heaves echoed off the pink tile. Each retch tightened the lasso that had been synched around my chest for days. Breathing was something I had to force. The one thing I had ever wanted in this life was repulsed by my existence. Suddenly I hated all the victims, the people who couldn't be as strong as me and had their lives cheated by useless criminals. I hated all of them, the thugs, gangsters, and the easy people they preyed on. Damn them, let the wolves eat the sheep. I no longer wanted to protect strangers when I couldn't protect the ones I loved.

My fists clenched tight. I wanted to pound someone's face but the only person in the room deserving of such punishment was me.

Monique came running in from the other room. We were in the hall outside the bathroom as Alysa heaved. The shower started.

"It's time to deliver Candice to Detective Camp, no matter the cost." I said to Monique.

She stood looking at the young face of Candice, a girl caught up in something she never wanted.

"We've done the best we could do, Grimes. I always believed in what we were doing." Monique said accepting this could start the house of cards we so carefully built tumbling down on us.

I agreed. We went over a quick plan and decided our fates were worth protecting Candice. We gathered everything and went to the front door.

"I'm going too." Alysa said emerging from the bathroom. She walked past the two of us and headed for the kitchen. I heard the cap to the Jack Daniels spin off then the golden Whiskey sloshed in the bottle.

"You don't have to go with them. You've done enough." I said loudly.

She came through from the kitchen with the square bourbon bottle in hand. Two gulps and she pulled it from her lips.

"I was talking about going with *you*." Alysa said pointing at me with the bottle. She knew that I was off, headed for trouble, tying up loose ends. She wanted to go with me. I took her aside.

"Listen, we never discussed what happened last year." I had trouble looking her in the eye as we spoke.

"Grimes, it doesn't matter. When I was in there puking my guts out, I realized I made it, you made it. I'm stronger now. Getting kidnapped made me go after the things in life I always put on the back burner and one of those is taking more risks. You know why we didn't see each other for so long? I took time off to travel and when I got back, I opened my own gym and I'm adding parkour. I'm doing what I want to do." She finished speaking with her hand holding mine. She looked down and clasped her other hand over both of ours.

"I can't ever let what happened to you, happen again," I said. She hadn't seen who I had become since then and what was left for me to do, but she knew what I was scared to keep doing. In her eyes I had been a rescuer, someone to save the day.

I didn't know if she believed I was the vigilante or not, but there were things left for me to do I didn't want her to see. Retribution is not always delivered in the heat of the action. It's planned out, catching them when they are most vulnerable, sometimes it's catching them asleep.  The process was about to repeat itself. The vigilante was going out again. This time was different. My anticipation was building not for the fight, but to get out of one. I, Roger Grimes, PI, was heading out to expose the truth and find April Ward's killer. If my investigation skills were half as good as my killing skills, I could come out of the shadows and finish this one in the light.

"I'll always protect you. And doing it this way, I will be able to do just that."

She protested. I shook my head. She let go of my hand. I left.

# **Chapter 22**

I sent a text to Detective Camp. It was time to air my dirty laundry. She had been understanding to a point this past year, but I did not know what would tip her to eventually arrest me. If I revealed too much, she would have no choice but to take me in.

Camp met me at a small park in the center of town. It was new, set up in what was just an empty lot filled with overgrown Florida jungle and junk tires and mattresses. A councilman who lived nearby rushed the approval through. Put a park near your house with a jungle gym for kids and it's a sure way to keep registered sex offenders from living near-by. I ought to know, I kept an active list of them.

I got their early and watched Camp pull up in a gold Crown Vic. She got out with two cups of coffee on a brown cardboard tray. Dressed in her detective suit, a tight-fitting grey pantsuit with navy blue blouse. Her badge was clipped to her waist and bulging out from under the jacket was her pistol.

Camp spotted me quickly, sitting facing out on a picnic table bench.

"Thanks." I said with a slight smile as she handed me a steaming cup of joe.

"Not sure how you take it." She said taking a seat next to me.

"You know I take it how I take my women." I tried to stop a smile as I sipped the steaming java.

"Don't you dare say black, Grimes." A grin broke her familiar stern cop frown, brightening her face into something attractive.

I popped my eyebrows a couple times then said, "I was going to say hot."

"Let's just get through this meeting without shooting anyone." Camp said and sat facing out alongside me.

"Right,"

"The only reason I'm not on mandatory leave after the other night is how fucking crazy this city has become."

We sat sipping hot coffee for a moment. There were heavy words on their way out with no need to rush.

"Is this conversation off the record, or you use your PI badge and dug up something?"

"Off the record." I said, and Detective Camp lost what little pleasantries our meeting held in her face.

"Everyone with a badge from the dog catcher to the chief is out looking for the vigilante and here I am sitting calmly next to you as if we were waiting for a bus together." She looked up at an afternoon sky mixed grey and blue. The specifics of what I've done or how I could be labeled were not mentioned. I never took her for stupid. She knew what I was.

"It's a nice day to be outside."

"You called me down here to talk weather?"

I took a breath and held it until I spoke, "These news articles are making it difficult for me to do my job. I am becoming more myth than reality."

"Public opinion is waning; body counts are racking up and all the blood in the water will attract sharks." She sipped her coffee, "April Ward was one of those sharks. She wanted justice for the victims."

"Victims? You mean the meth cookers, child pornographers and all the other sludge I've scraped out of the gutter in this town?" I stood up; my blood was pumping. Caffeine had been a bad idea.

"According to her articles, the vigilante isn't qualified to be judge, jury and executioner. I actually agree." Camp said ignoring my self-incrimination.

"Crime is down. If there wasn't a need for the vigilante, then he wouldn't be out there roaming the streets at night, keeping the sickos and deviants away." I was going off Sanford's stats. I truly didn't know, I hadn't followed my exploits in the news, and I was not keeping tally with notches in a pistol grip either.

"Some pot dealer was beat unconscious early this morning. Press has video and claiming it's the vigilante. Maybe it's time the vigilante retires, there's little evidence on who he is, only the bodies he leaves behind. Just that he's over six feet, white and likes to punch people. I bet if he goes back to his day job, something he enjoys more than beating people or killing, it will eventually go away. It can't be good for the soul." Camp shifted and crossed her taught thighs.

"There is a vigilante out there, but not all the crimes were committed by him. There's copycats and April found one of them."

The bulldog frown returned to her smooth mocha face as she formed her own conclusions. Camp had been lead-detective chasing the vigilante and knew better than anyone that not all the crimes were done by the same person. "That cop I shot, ex-cop. IA had a file on him. It seems FDLE interviewed him in connection to that child trafficking case you were mixed up in."

"What was his role?"

"No formal accusations, but in the notes, he was suspected of running protection or interference for these scumbags to operate. Can you believe that?"

"So what happened?"

"Well not too long later he was caught roughing up a drug dealer and taking his cash."

"I'd say that's a copycat enough," I said. An ex-Officer was under pressure for covering for the trafficking ring then goes out and shakes down drug dealers to make up for his lost wages when I bust the ring up.

"What about a partner?"

"No partner, at least not while on duty. He was just off rookie probation and finally on his own patrol."

"What's his name?"

"Jacob Florence."

My eyes went to the sandy soil beneath my feet. April knew the copycat was a cop. She had DBPD and Florence listed in her notes. Florence had followed my lead, took notes, and copied my playbook. His big failing came when he broke the oath, he took, to uphold the constitutional rights of the citizens. My lips never uttered such an oath, I was free beyond the confines of laws of men and only restricted by the laws of nature. That is why Dr. Igo hated me, why he wanted to turn the people against me. But I did it because no one else could.

"What do you know Grimes?"

"April was on to him. I got a look at her notes. She had Florence at the top of the vigilante list and you guys missed it."

"Hold on a second. Don't you think cops were the first people we looked at? Everyone on the force hates us, we got no support in the department or out on the street. Patrolmen aren't reporting anything."

Camp wrinkled her brow and shook her head. Steam was about to burst from her eyes as her brain caught fire with anger.

"You said it yourself, he was dirty. You need help outside the department and I'm going to start helping you Camp, from here on out. I'm going to hand over Candice Burke. She needs your protection. She has all of April's notes, all about Florence and other vigilante suspects."

"All of them?" Camp vented some of that steam as she cooled to operating temperatures.

I nodded I was in there as well. It was ending. The flame of vengeance and crimes that followed. The late nights and no sleep. A way out lit the black tunnel I had wandered through. Soon I would be free, no more looking over my shoulder for both cop and criminal.

Camp leaned back against the edge of the table, her hand went out and touched my knee as she began to speak, "When I think of my life, my day-to-day life, all I see is a tightrope before me. My career has skyrocketed in the last eighteen months. Went from patrol to corporal to detective real fast. Some on the force didn't like it, that's okay, I don't wear a badge for them. I wear it to help people, like a fifteen-year-old runaway who got caught up in the sex trade and was just longing for a way out.

"I think of that, and the tight rope gets wider and wider, and I can walk with my head up instead of always looking down for my next step. And that's good, I can get through my day. Until I close my eyes at night and see the faces of four women who traded money for their lives and got neither. I wake up and that tightrope has shrunk again. In ten years on the force, it was the only shooting I was ever in, and I killed four women. Justice for all?" She shook her head uncertain of an answer to her own question.

She had killed four conniving women who had set me up. To appropriate justice meant losing a piece of her own sense of the word. She didn't want to kill them, she wasn't there to shoot anyone, but she had to in order to stop more violence.

In a short time, we had gone through a lot together. I felt my head get heavy, my neck could no longer support it and my chin tucked. I stared at my feet. The vigilante was affecting more than just the criminals. It was hurting the good guys too. My own fat gut was evidence of that, but now Monique was followed, and someone had video of me in a street fight. We were all just trying to dig our way out of quicksand.

"I'm becoming less Batman and more Joker."

"Try dusting off that P.I. badge the state gave you and go back to what drove you to earn it in the first place."

Camp was right. I needed to stop the violence and start investigating, observing, and reporting on wrongdoing rather than getting in the middle of it.

A white Ford F-150 pulled into the small parking lot. Camp was quick to assess the vehicle. She watched the three occupants get out. A man with a braid and two young women.

I waved them over.

"Camp, I want you to meet Candice Burke. She's going to need your protection."

The three, Billy, Candice and Monique, all met us at the bench. Billy waved awkwardly, still nervous around police officers.

"This is Candice Burke, Monique, Willis Sanford's secretary and—"

Monique reached out her hand taking a lead in front of Candice, "Monique Sanford, I will be accompanying Ms. Burke as her attorney." Monique turned to watch my jaw drop.

My knees went weak and as embarrassment twisted my guts. I had no idea all this time Monique was related to Sanford and even less of a clue she was a lawyer. Some investigator I was.

"Detective Rhashonda Camp." Camp said while I was still trying to just my hanging jaw.

Once I found my bearings after being knocked over with Monique's revelation, I filled Camp in on Candice and let the college girl do the rest of the talking. Candice recounted her knowledge of April's notes and theories, leaving me out of it. I mentioned the Dead Ends chasing her out of the bar the other night.

"What do you know about the Dead Ends?"

Camp thought for a moment then said, "Never heard of them, I'd have to ask the gang unit. Why?"

"They're some kinda new motorcycle club in town. I think they are the ones who stole my truck, but the cops aren't even looking at them for it. I took it upon myself to meet most of them. Young mixed group, not like the other clubs in town. A couple even ride café racers. They're connected somehow, with orders to grab Candice. They're led by a guy named Spoke. I haven't met him yet. When the time is right, I'll tip you the car theft ring they are orchestrating."

"Car thieves are the worst, huh?" Camp's sly smile told me she knew I had been into stealing cars and the irony of my pride and joy having been stolen.

"Yep." I smiled.

"Don't worry, I'll keep you safe." Camp said to Candice. "You two can ride with me back to the station. You coming too, Billy?"

Billy tugged on his long braid, "Not me, no thanks." A weird chuckle unnerved us all.

I pulled Camp aside as Monique and Candice walked towards her car.

"I reviewed the notes April had. I think Florence had a partner in the department. So, watch your back."

Camp nodded. Her eyes told me she already knew that, but without being sure she wasn't going to say it out loud.

There was a lot of work ahead to do and parting ways was the start. Detective Camp would go off to fulfill her duties and that oath she made when he received her badge. I was not restricted in that way; it made me more effective when I had to be. It's what made me popular with those polled in the newspaper. That was before Igo took over and his smear campaign to rid the city of the way I fought crime.

"I've got an in with the biker gang I can exploit. Once I find out Spoke's connection in all this, I'll wrap it up and put a bow on it for you."

"A bow? I'm not sure I can take another promotion Grimes."

She started for her car and paused, "You really should have been a cop."

"Nah, I don't like donuts." I smiled and caught Monique getting in the front seat of the car. My hand came up in a half-attempted wave. She smiled. That was more than I expected.

Billy was waiting in the truck.

"What now?" Billy asked when I got in.

"There's something else I need you to do."

Billy nodded.

"I need you to dig around the Dead Ends and tell me what is really going on there. I can't wrap my head around them being able to ride free and clear and not get gutted every time they leave the clubhouse."

"I got a couple of old timers I can call. Did you hear?"

"Probably not."

"Some nineteen-year-old kid got beat to death. He was known to sell drugs. The news is calling it an attack by the vigilante. The mayor is supposed to hold a news conference just in time for the five o'clock news."

"Shit, I did hear about it actually."

"Shit is right. You got a price on your head brother, and it's not just coming from the cops. They're organizing neighborhood watches. And these protests are getting out of hand. It was supposed to remember April and victims of, well, the other people. Now it's just about rioting and violence against cops. They want the vigilante, Public enemy number one." Billy pointed his cell phone at me.

On screen the tiny screen were photos of people and maps of town. Zooming in I read captions letting me know they were victims of the vigilante with dates and times. A couple I recognized; someone had done their homework. The others, including this new nineteen-year-old, were not by my hands, but the silhouetted vigilante was getting the blame.

A timer in the corner was counting down to a post, hinting at more information on the silhouette.

"A new clue to his identity is going to drop tonight." Billy said taking the phone back.

Though Billy was true to what he said, I didn't want to hear it or even acknowledge it. The numbers on the clock meant something now, stacked up and counting down. I felt the walls closing in again. The next attack could come for anywhere or anyone. I had no idea who had real proof of me or didn't. Had my picture begun to circulate? Disgraced police officer Jacob Florence had a bullet with my name on it. Or was Detective Camp getting close to the copycats?

There was one more person I had to speak with before I confronted the Dead Ends. Now that I had read all of April's notes, it was time for Dr. Igo to come clean about the vigilante man hunt he was conducting through his newspaper. His editorials had dusted up a fervor against what I had been doing to criminals in this town. If he knew it was me, why had he not exposed me or trapped me in the act?

The little VW hopped along uneven coquina crushed asphalt as I made my way to the newspaper building. The loud muffler drew looks but just from other tuners. The car was quick and had a sport tuned suspension that took the turns well. Though I didn't check it out myself, I figured the motor had the usual upgrades getting a little extra horsepower.

The newspaper building sat back off a busy road. A three-story red brick building tucked behind a tropical jungle of palms, wide-faced green plants and hanging vines. The parking lot was small, visitors were not welcomed. I parked where I could and headed for the door.

Security was not something I expected. A man with a black mustache and gold badge sat on a stool just on the other side of a metal detector. I went back to the car and unloaded my pockets of a gun, knuckles and pocketknife, the standard operating cache.

The small rectangle entry way was poorly lit and smelled musty from damp a/c units needing filter changes. The linoleum floors had a lime tint either by design or age and needed to be replaced decades ago. The guard handed me a clipboard to sign and asked who I was there to see.

"Blaine Igo."

"Not sure he's in." he said and flipped a rolodex looking for the extension to Igo's office. As I waited, I wondered had I entered a less used side entrance or a time machine.

Chatter came from the receiver on the phone. The guard nodded and then wrote out a visitor sticker for me to slap on my chest. I got directions to Igo's office and headed on my way to the elevator.

On the third floor the doors opened. The newsroom was filled with a maze of empty cubicles. As I passed, a few here and there held remnants of being occupied, but most were cleaned out, not even a desk chair. I stopped at the back wall with two office doors. One was open.

Igo's long legs were stretched out up onto a desk stacked high with newspapers, file folders and empty bottles of Star Bucks cold brew coffee.

"Ah," He looked up over his glasses at me and pulled the pencil he chewed from his teeth, sticking it behind his ear.

I stood silently in the doorway. Igo waited for me to start the conversation, a negotiation of what each knew, a tell, one way or the other, to find out who held the upper hand.

"Okay," He said looking down at the papers before him. He plucked the pencil from behind his ear and started chewing it as he tapped away furiously on an old desktop computer. Mumbles whispered from his thin lips.

There was nowhere to sit. So, I stood in front of the mess on his desk.

"I want to know—" I was cut off as he held a long finger in the air, then more typing. Finally, he stood up in a rush. My right leg dropped back as I lowered my stance. But he wasn't getting up to fight.

"There." He looked me in the eyes, "That will be it. Now I can send it to print." He came around the desk to remind me of the height difference, something that made me want to take him to the ground all the more.

"Another article attacking the vigilante, getting the mobs rallied for more night patrols and more cops shot at?" My question got him to frown.

"I am simply raising the people's consciousness. Empowering them to take back their city from the archaic socio-economic structure put in place by our *oppressing* forefathers."

I shrugged, using indifference to check his enthusiasm. "Your articles are getting good people hurt and risking a lot of lives over nothing."

"Of course, *you* would take that stance, Roger. You are part of the oppression. Oh, maybe not consciously. It's in your actions, thoughts, in your very being." He crossed his arms and leaned back against his desk.

"You can leave me out of it."

"Can I?"

"Yes, I'm here for April. What you have against the vigilante is your problem. I've read through some of her unpublished articles and research. Articles you changed with your own words before publishing. I want to know what else you did with her."

Igo's finger came out once more as he pressed it against his lips not to silence me but to delay his response. I had something he did not, Candice and her information on April. The ice beneath his feet suddenly became thin and if he went too far, he might find it easily broken.

"Once April decided to turn on your vigilante theory you couldn't stand it."

"You don't know what you're talking about. April was my protégé, my carbon copy."

"She wasn't anything like you, she still believed in integrity and reporting facts, not opinion-soaked articles to push an agenda!" I shouted inches from the tall man's face.

He stepped back.

I pressed him some more, "So when she figured out you were just a hack and really did no investigating on the vigilante, she wanted out, she wanted to write her own article, in her own words, but you couldn't let that happen."

"Enough!" His eyes were pressed against his glasses ready to explode.

"Is that why you didn't let Candice out of your sight the other night? To find out if April had confided in her, told her your dirty little secret. Someone as smart as you should be two steps ahead of all that. You should have this vigilante dangling from a light pole or whatever it is you want done to him, but you haven't." I looked around the small office, at the awards on the wall, the bookshelf with books on writing and great people of history he either drew inspiration from or desired to be.

"April was very special to me, and we worked very intimately." Igo adjusted his glasses, "I was interested in Candice to pick up the torch, to carry on what April was doing. As you know, she declined the offer."

"There's a biker gang after Candice, did you know about that?"

"What she does with her off time is her business." He spun around his desk and took a relaxed pose in the chair. His legs apart as he leaned back. The pencil came out from behind his ear, and he tapped it on the edge of the desk. The formal education from a top tier university, got him started in life, separate from the rest of us. I didn't know where he grew up or if his father had to work two jobs to make ends meet so little Blaine could go to college. Judging by the way he idealized the poor yet used them to sell papers while doing nothing to support them led me to think he never was poor.

"You published one of April's articles, but not her last."

"Yes Roger, what I have of them, the other articles weren't completed." Igo bit down on the already chewed middle of the pencil.

Igo did need Candice, just as I needed Candice. April's tone was changing in her last article. The rage and rally cry were absent, it was levelheaded and sought a real solution instead of more protests against the police. Solutions to problems don't sell papers, only bigger problems do.

"April was changing her tone… her direction. She didn't like the vigilante, but she understood why he existed, and you didn't like that did you? She was out there beating the pavement digging into who the vigilante is and more importantly why. That didn't fit with your narrative."

Igo's curly hair draped along the sides of his narrow face. Despite his age he had the complexion of a teenager. He took his glasses off and pinched his eyes. With them back on he looked at me then looked inside me, trying to figure out my inner workings. The gears in my brain that turned this way and that moved information and ideas like an assembly line, and he wanted to get to the end and destroy my finished product.

"So, you weren't bluffing. You did read her last article and maybe more." Igo smiled and tapped the pencil once more.

"Yeah, she made a list of names and whoever killed her is on that list. It's only a matter of time before I scratch each one off myself." My teeth clenched; my forehead was damp as my guts began to tingle with anticipation. Pressure from all sides was building around me, state level operatives spying on Sanford, a biker gang after Candice and Detective Camp wanting me to go straight. I was about to burst and all the while this lanky wannabe elite was stirring the pot of anarchy making it difficult for me to do what I had been doing.

"Oh, Roger, tough guy bravado will not last you forever. Times are changing. You will be left behind."

"I keep hearing that but remember there will always be a need for men like me, to do the work that frightens you."

That got him to his feet. He had bravado of his own and I just stepped on it. We weren't too dissimilar; he was surprised by who he was while I set out to define who I am. Perhaps definitions were changing for me, but my goals never changed.

"I am taking on the vigilante, something no one seems to be doing." Igo brought up his right arm across his chest as if he were holding shield.

"No, you're making a hundred more. April knew that. She saw the chaos publicizing the vigilante was creating."

"You underestimate the people, Roger."

"No," I said raising a finger of my own and pointing it in his face, "You do. There are copycats out there, spurred on by your rhetoric and your articles. Things were changing."

"The people will win when the vigilante is eliminated."

"The people were winning, Igo. If you spent any time in the neighborhoods you honor with your articles and tweets, maybe you would have seen that. Violent crime was down, people felt safer at night."

"You talk as if you actually believed that. I determine the facts; I tell them what to think about the vigilante."

"Those copycats have killed and it's you with blood on your hands now."

Thin lips parted, curling into a smile, flashing polished white teeth behind them. Pleasure didn't begin to describe what he was feeling. His arms and legs swung and bounced as if her were about to jump up and dance a jig. Manicured fingers tapped on the keys then he swung his laptop around. On the screen was the same website Billy had shown me earlier. The map, the victims, and the ticking clock. Closer now to zero than it had been.

Igo lowered his glasses to get a good look into my eyes. My jaw clenched before I could hold a poker face. His smile was wet, "April did a wonderful job, and I will forever remain grateful so will the people of this town. Once the mask is pulled off."

Reaching over the monitor, his finger hit a key. The screen was filled with an artist composite sketch of the vigilante. I was looking at a black and white sketch of my face.

"Look familiar?" Igo snorted as he laughed.

Fight or flight was building pressure in my skull. My eyes wanted to burst out of their sockets and take my scalp with it. Fighting Igo was not the answer nor was running out of there for South America. I had to fight; I just couldn't do it the only way I knew how, with my fists.

"So you're the one behind the vigilante tracker."

His smile was full of large white teeth. His body shook with laughter. That big brain of his was exploding with pleasure.

"Very clever. Using the tracker as a source for your articles against the vigilante."

"A valuable tool for getting the public involved. Each new bread crumb dropped on the site excites the fan base. The amount of traffic grows by the hour and the latest post is about to drop. Wonder what will be next. Something tells me you already know." He sat back in his chair, placing both hands behind his curly hair.

"With out April to uncover the next clue for you, I doubt it will be much." I said calling his bluff. He had the video of me and Florence in a street fight, I wanted him to prove it.

Igo's eyes narrowed. He sat up, bringing his hands out in front of him. He stood slowly, puffing out his chest. "What are you going to do about it, kill me?"

"No. I'm going to fight like hell to hold this city together."

"It must all be destroyed before it can be rebuilt Roger. There cannot be any remnant of the old guard. Don't you see? Tonight-we-are-taking-it-back!" Igo's chest was rising and falling rapidly as slight wheeze leaked from his windpipe. Large bug eyes made larger behind thick lenses shot out at me.

I slammed the laptop shut, "Through lawlessness and anarchy? That's regression, not progress." I said, tensing my shoulders. "You don't give a damn about April. Your star pupil is dead and now you need the city to feed your ego. You make me sick."

He made a fist as his chest began rising and falling. I pressed on.

"You might play real tough with your Thai-chi correspondence black belt, but like your words, it's only on paper. There was a time I thought you killed April, now I see your problem is your fear and you wear it on your sleeve."

"I'm not afraid." He lifted his fists in the air, nearly touching the ceiling tiles then let out an ear-piercing shriek, "Heeeeeeee!"

He spun and pounded both fists down on the desk with a thud then repeatedly pounded the hard wood surface much like the caveman he so despised.

"Real tough." I said. "Desks don't fight back, but April did. She fought hard and so am I."

With his back bent away from me as he leaned over the front of the desk, "Get out, just get out of here." He whimpered.

He repeated his statement in a shout after me, but I never turned around. I had what I wanted.

# **Chapter 23**

Dr. Igo was a pompous ass filled with fear, but it wasn't of me or the vigilante. Instead, it was channeled into hate and directed at me. What did I do to him? Once that picture went out tonight it would be obvious to so many around me that I was the black silhouette, the one causing a city to turn on itself. The truth would no longer stay hidden from Alysa. Waycross would bring more pressure. This wasn't just about my own neck. Camp's career was on the line would implode. Sanford and Monique would go down with me. Igo would destroy everything I was building, including this town.

I needed more answers to questions I never asked. Someone brought me into this when they dumped April's lifeless body next to me on the beach trying to set me up. The Dead Ends had been after Candice at the same time I was. Someone was directing them. It was time I met Spoke.

I swung into the shop parking lot and saw all the bay doors were closed. Billy said nothing as I passed through the office headed for my upstairs apartment. He saw the look on my face. It had led me down a dark path before. Back to the old ways, just for one more night. I needed to get ready if I was going to take on a biker gang, even if it was just a bunch of wannabes.

I dragged an old duffle bag full of weapons over to the couch. Objects used to kill were pulled out and laid on the cushion next to me. All my Glocks had fresh barrels. Sanford kept me so busy this past year I was running out of suppliers of arms, so things got more physical. My brass was used more and more.

The darkness in me had nearly been extinguished. Over a year of wrestling with death and life, I had managed to suppress the rage of the beast, but I could not kill the beast. It lived in me even when I spared lives. Coerced, brainwashed, and groomed, the beast it fed on the diet it was given. A past in stolen cars and robbed banks led down a twisted path of killing the worst of the worst. Each time their faces were pushed down, eaten by the beast. As it fed it grew. Now I've lost sight of where it ends, and I begin.

The safe house with its fishing dock and salty air eased my tensions and gave me a glimpse of what life could be like. It wasn't home, wasn't real life, just a dream. I was with people who didn't know who I had been, nor would they have approved. The couple of days I spent with the Dead Ends was different, it was playful, and it was life lived, not in the dark, behind a mask. My past wasn't hidden there, it was relished. Hitch and James loved my stories of stealing cars and robbing banks. Addison hated me because his crush was crushing on me. It was all so ego boosting without having to play hero or rescuer. Now all of that had come to an end and I was the one that must end it.

Scattered pieces struggled to line up, but that didn't let the Dead Ends off the hook. Going after Candice confirmed their involvement. Becoming a copycat vigilante brought them even deeper, killing a man for no reason other than to be part of the bigger action turned my stomach. I thought I had found a place that I could be me, and it turns out I can. I can be the *me* that seeks vengeance for the victims, and justice for the innocent. The Dead Ends will see the real me.

With the duffle bag over my shoulder, I stood in the doorway to the office. Billy stood up, his .357 tucked in his waist. He cleared his throat. "I got rid of Detective Waycross for you."

"What?" I never heard him while I was upstairs."

"Thought you'd a heard us but guess not. Yeah, he came around asking if I'd seen you." Billy lit a cigarette. Through a smoky exhale he continued, "Told him you rode off on a motorcycle."

"Thanks. Wonder what he's got on me now."

He shook his head.

"Dr. Igo showed me the new drop tonight on the website. It's a composite sketch of my face."

"Shit, once that's out..."

"Yeah, so listen, take precautions."

Billy nodded knowingly. *Precautions* was code when we were thieves. Any trace of our friendship would have to be erased. It also meant we were on our own and that we may never see each other again.

We shook hands and I could see the questions for me behind his eyes. None of them he could know the answer to. I started for the door.

"Can I come?" he asked, already knowing my response.

"Best if you didn't."

***

Due to the proximity of Billy's shop to the protests and vigilante watch groups, I had to double back and take a long route to Tomoka Farms Road.

The sun was beginning its dive into the west and the sky was ablaze in orange and red.

Detective Camp called just as I was pulling up on the clubhouse. I swung a U-turn and parked with the hatchback facing the clubhouse. I had a good look at the gate in the side mirror.

"I guess they haven't picked you up yet." She said quietly, probably from her office.

"No, why would they want to?"

"They found a hair in your truck. A long blond hair."

Visions of a breeze off the lapping ocean lifting April's hair like blowing on a dandy lion into my truck crossed my mind. There was no way I could make a case for that carrying it all the way to my truck.

"And it was a match to April." My chest went tight, it was hard to get the words out or the air in to make new words.

"Maybe if—"

"No, you're not walking me in to get ahead of this. I have something to check out and then when that is done, if I have no other choice, I'll call you."

"If they catch you, I'll have to give them the facts."

"All you know is that I'm a confidential informant with a tip on a biker gang and went out to investigate on my own."

"The Dead Ends, huh?"

"Yeah, did that gang unit ever get back to you?"

"Kinda, Detective Waycross—"

"Waycross?"

"Shit, Grimes stop interrupting me, as I was saying, before the April murder, Waycross worked in the gang unit. Decent cop, we used to do some narc cases together. Anyway, he said they were on the radar but so far just seemed like wannabes who watch too many biker TV shows. Also, he had a whole lotta questions about you being a CI. He's tried to get into your file."

I stayed quiet, listening to my heart thump in my chest.

"He doesn't have access, but he's requested it from the Chief. Just lay low, Grimes."

"I can't do that."

"Grimes, Detective Waycross totally dismissed them. He agrees with you, total amateurs. Don't risk going out there and making this worse for you."

"He also thinks I'm April's killer. What he doesn't know is, the gang has cellphone video of beating a guy to death remember?"

"Oh, so that's all you need to…" She stopped what she was saying.

"All I need to investigate them. Like a PI framed for murder would." I said finally giving myself a title.

"Well, finally taking my advice."

"Yeah, and asking favors. Did you ever find any other officers that hung out with Florence?"

"Shit Grimes, just don't, please don't say anything that gets me looking into the department for the vigilante. Internal Affairs is so tightly woven into our vigilante task force that there is no way, just no way."

"Take your blue blinders off for a second, Camp. Did it ever occur to you, I wasn't the target? We both were standing down barrel of that shotgun."

"Grimes, damn it." Camp was quiet for a few seconds, just heavy breathing, then she said, "I'll pull his file and run his name back through internal affairs."

"Put a rush on it and get back to me."

She had a lot to say about that, but I didn't have time to listen and gave her a quick goodbye. There was something I needed to do before I entered the clubhouse. I stared into the side mirror mentally preparing each step, what the yard looked like, what the inside looked like and where everyone might be positioned. My Kevlar vest was snug due to the recent girth around my belly. With the tee-shirt on and heavy flannel, I hoped it was hard to notice.

A flood light popped on and shown all the motorcycles in a row parked on the gravel. A trashcan fire was smoldering, but no flames reached out. I wanted to be sitting at that bench sipping PBR and laughing with the gang, not sitting across the street anticipating killing them.

A procession off the wooden porch was led by Denny, Addison, Wino and Lexi. In the back was someone new. At this distance and with a helmet and amber glasses on, I couldn't make out a face. He wore a black and red flannel covered over with a denim vest that had a Dead Ends patch on the back.

This had to be Spoke, the man of the hour, the one I had been waiting to see. I was too late. He slapped hands with everyone then straddled a Harley-Davidson Street Bob and fired it up. He pulled a bandana up, over his face and cranked back on the throttle, revving the cold motor like a real amateur. That's the wrong way to warm up a modern motorcycle, but he liked the music of the loud pipes and so did those standing around him.

Slouched low in the seat, I waited until I heard the motor rumble past, then down the highway. I peeked out to watch the taillights begin to fade. The GTi fired up and I fought the urge to peel out after him. Instead went slowly as not to alert anyone still in the yard.

Luck was on my side as I slowed to a stop at the only traffic light on the road for ten miles in either direction. There, one car ahead of me was Spoke on his hog. The light changed and he cut right quickly while halfway through the intersection and accelerated hard. I kept things under control and took the turn slow but eased down on the gas to get the VW up to speed.

The road ahead was dark and there was no car between me and the one small red taillight. We traveled east and he maintained the speed limit. I kept my distance without drifting too far under the limit to upset the drivers behind me and cause them to pass.

Soon we reached civilization and all the lights associated with it. The intersection just before the highway was a busy one. Spoke slowed for the yellow light, I didn't, anticipating him to then gun through it. He stopped. I stopped. He looked around but never behind. Then he did something unexpected. He took off the vest, rolled it up and shoved it into a saddle bag. The light changed and he took off.

We wound through the city going east then north then he turned off into a storage unit facility. I drove by and pulled over just beyond, into an appliance store parking lot. Circling the lot, I made it to the furthest corner so I could watch the gate. Not long later a silver late model Chevy Impala came out. The windows were tinted so I couldn't see the driver.

Was it Spoke? I put the VW in gear but didn't pursue. There was no way to tell, it was only about eight o'clock, that car could have already been in there. I watched the car turn right at the next intersection, but my foot never let off the clutch to follow it. I shut the car off and jumped out. Running to the fence, I scaled it and landed to look up and see the camera watching me.

I ran up and down the four rows of storage lockers, but none were open and there was no sight or sound of a Harley. I raced back to the VW and sped off down after the Impala. After a couple more intersections there was no way to tell which way he went.

I pulled into a gas station and went in for an energy drink then pumped some gas. Inside the car lit with the soft blue light of an incoming call on my cell.

The missed call was Sanford. I called him back.

"Grimes." Sanford rarely called me Grimes. His tone was calm, but I knew him well enough to hear the suppressed anger.

"I've—"

"My office, now."

"I really can't right now, I have a lead on—"

"No." Sanford interrupted me once more, "Now it's time to do as I say. Please Roger."

A soft electric wave washed over me, igniting nerves in every part of my body. This was it, the beginning of the end of the vigilante and the life at night where I stalked criminals and made them pay for their crimes. We both knew it would end one day, either with me dead or in cuffs, but my plan was neither. I was not going to prison.

"Thirty minutes." I hung up. There was something I needed to do first.

All my gear and personal possessions were always in a state of half packed. The longest I had ever stayed in one place was a duplex I had on the beachside. That didn't end so well. Turned out the landlord had an unhealthy crush on me along with some other problems. After that I shared an apartment, but that burned down, and I lived in my office until I was kicked out. To put down roots took on a responsibility my night job would not allow.

The time had come to leave it all behind. Sanford's cryptic call told me all I needed to know. The jig was up. Now I was the hunted. The cops or the bad guys or both would start to hunt me. All the signs were there for some time. I knew it in my gut, Sanford saw it in my face and busted body, Detective Camp was all too familiar with occupational burnout. The only thing to do would be to leave Daytona Beach, the town I fought for in the night could no longer be my home. Just when I saw a life of normalcy within reach, it pulled back and reminded me of who I am. It's summertime in South America. Maybe I can finally get a dog.

The apartment was wiped down, my cache of weapons, guns and anything that may have DNA (mine or others) was disposed of in the shop with a hot torch. The left-over metal was tossed in the scrap pile of bumpers and other broken auto parts Jose would drop off to the recycler in the morning.

I wouldn't leave myself completely unarmed. I still had a Glock with two magazines filled. It was clean for now. I also had new identification, a credit card matching the I.D. and cash tucked away in a locker down at the marina. All that was left would be to ditch the car and take a taxi to the airport. Fly away and never come back. Billy was home wondering about me. Alysa had text me a few times already and I let them go. If I ran, I'd never see them again. I could never come home because they would never want me to.

I parked the VW along the street outside the CBR building and looked up at the only yellow light on the black facade. Up on the seventh floor Sanford was probably pacing around or drumming his fingers against the heavy mahogany desk. My gut was twisted much as it had been that night after being in a shootout and wounded. I sat in my car then thinking whether to kill Sanford. Now I consider him one of my closest friends, something I only had two of before him, and I received a warm smile out of Monique this week.

The unmarked sedan was easy to spot in the empty parking lot. A salty breeze carried in the air reminded me the marina was only a few blocks away. A new ID and money to get me to Uruguay was waiting there. Sanford's tone and use of my name tipped me to trouble, but he didn't use the words we had laid out for me to skip town. Trust had been built over this past year and I had to rely on that. He was a good lawyer, always steps ahead, he wouldn't fail me now.

The curly permed security guard waddled over with a familiar grin when I tapped on the glass. She swiped her key card and let me in.

"Howdy, forgot your card?" She said turning to return to the large desk to the right of the entry.

"Sorry, won't happen again."

"You said that last time." Her cackle laugh was enough to bring a smile to my face. Nerves, excitement, or just impending doom got a soft chuckle from my throat.

I opened the office door and looked around. Monique was not at her desk. The bustle of files being destroyed had to go on through the heavy wooden double doors to Sanford's office. With my ear pressed against the door, I listened. Murmurers of voices vibrated through the wood, but they were too muddled to understand. I tested the knob, unlocked.

With my weight behind me, I pushed the door wide. Standing at the left wall in his silver vest and rolled up white sleeves was Sanford. He took one look at me and went back to pulling files from a locked cabinet. The other two men stood perfectly still. Both white and about fifty years of age. Both dressed in suits and both with receding hair lines. The taller of the two and with short hair, had his hand on his waist, just under his sport coat. He was the cop. The other parted his sport coat and placed his hands on his hips. He was the lawyer.

"This is State's Attorney Newsome and FDLE Special Agent Gibson."

"That's New-*strom*," he said looking back at Sanford. Sanford winked at me as Newstrom turned back to me. He approached with his hand out, "You must be Roger Grimes."

We shook hands. Agent Gibson relaxed his hand from his holster and nodded at me but did not offer to shake my hand.

Sanford shut the file cabinet drawer and stood behind his desk. He dropped the files saying, "Yes, that is *the* Roger Grimes. The reason for all this…" He parted his hands, welcoming Newstrom and Gibson to pick up the files.

"What do you need me for?" I asked, getting to the point. Sanford was a talker and could communicate on these guys' level. Not me. I wanted out of there. Either arrest me or don't, my business wasn't finished out on the street.

"You fellas are tough to get a hold of. I've been requesting Sanford share these files on the sex trafficking case with our office in Tallahassee for some time. I'm no longer asking." Newstrom said. I followed his eyes to the desk and the warrant that lay on top of it. Again, this was all part of Sanford's world. He kept files on who was guilty. I just received the file and went out and did my business, the business of busting skulls and putting criminals on the straight and narrow. I knew he kept double files. Some stuffed with fluff jobs, the simple work of an attorney and a PI. We needed those jobs for just this occasion.

"It seems my paranoia was getting the best of me." Sanford said as he separated the files and then restacked them. "These boys were getting suspicious when I refused to cooperate, I mean get around to organizing Monique's peculiar filing system."

"We didn't appreciate the hold up." Gibson finally spoke.

"So, you *surveilled* us all?" I said. It was his job to sit outside Monique's house and tail Sanford. The Special Agent was playing secret agent.

Newstrom casually stepped between me and the cop. "We're gathering a case and going to start handing down indictments. This case has roots, deep roots from Miami to Tallahassee."

"It wasn't all based on our suspicions of you." Gibson said. "While I was watching Sanford, someone else was too. You two started a shit storm for some very powerful Floridians and they will want revenge."

"That's why I was playing it close to the vest." Sanford said handing over the files. "We didn't know who to trust. The further I ran down the names Grimes uncovered, the deeper the rabbit hole went. I appreciate you contacting me through back channels, through people I trust, but I would have liked a little more notice." Sanford looked to me. I had been so wrapped up with April Ward's death and the city hunt for the vigilante that I had lost sight of my job, to investigate for Willis Sanford. Just because I killed a few bad guys responsible, the case wasn't closed.

Newstrom slipped the files into a briefcase. He thanked Sanford and I for our work last year and said he would be in touch if there was anything more, he needed.

Gibson nodded his goodbye. He paused before getting to the door and turned back.

"This is no joke. Someone with training is watching you. I don't know who or what, but they are good. When you decide you want our help, call me." Gibson pulled a card from his shirt pocket and walked it back to the desk.

Once they left, we were free to catch up.

"Where the hell have you been man?" Sanford went first in our exchange of information.

At the wet bar I pulled a bottle of water from the refrigerator. After drinking down half I came up for air and said, "Trying to find out who killed April Ward, so the cops don't arrest me for the murder."

"As your attorney, I've reviewed the evidence, and they don't have squat. If you bothered to check in with me, you'd know."

"What about the blond hair they found in my Scout?" I paced around; stress was eating away at my insides. I hadn't taken a Xanax in days and my brain was still zapping, neurons firing on overload. My mood was steady, my thoughts were searching without going in circles, so on the surface I was holding it together. Inside, deep inside, my body synched tightly with fear as my mind refused to accept the trouble, I was in.

"Turns out they were bluffing, just trying to rattle us. The results haven't come back yet."

"Good." I took a seat. "April started changing her mind about the vigilante. She figured out there were copycats out there rolling the low-level thugs. She had her finger on the man we want and was killed for it." I picked at the rubber sole of my shoe. "Have you heard from Monique?"

"She's still at the station with Candice. Candice wants to stick with us instead of going into police protection."

"Good. Something stinks at that department."

"Gibson smelled it too." Sanford sat back in his stuffed leather chair. "We've got to start watching our backs."

"A disgraced cop becomes a fake vigilante for his own profit then tries to kill me and Detective Camp. There is no way he is on his own. Take Monique home and I'll meet you there when I can. I'd loan you a gun, but I melted them all down before I came here."

"I love how cautious you are, it helps me sleep at night." Sanford smiled.

# **Chapter 24**

The few blocks drive back to the shop were frenzied as two cruisers raced by with just lights on. The protest march had started over on Beach Street just northeast of where the CBR building sat. For three nights in a row there was more than just humidity in the air. Every siren brought on the twitch of that little nerve in the back of your head, the one that flops around reminding you that the mother of all storms is coming. Like when you have been watching the weather reports for days, all the hurricane trackers with red, blue, yellow, and green squiggly lines making landfall predictions and all of them run through your town at some point. That twitching nerve is telling you it's time to stock up, get the canned food, water, and batteries, but you defy common sense and instead you watch others wait in line at stores because you've been through this before, your house is still standing. Sanford and I were working as a team now. He took my direction when it came to protecting Monique and Candice and I listened to his legal advice and ability to navigate government officials. We needed each other, and I wasn't going to let him down.

We had been under surveillance by the state. That still didn't explain the quick-change artist from the Dead End's club house. There was another player making his own rules and setting up a nice game of cat and mouse. I was the cat, he the mouse, but more of a rat. There was something dangerous about this rat, like it had rabies, so even when I catch him, I'm a goner.

Back at the shop I caught Billy as he climbed into his pickup. He rolled the window down as I parked the car alongside.

"I didn't expect you back. Thought maybe you finally took that slow boat to South America." He said without getting out of the truck.

I walked up to the driver's side door.

"Yeah, I blew it. I was on the Dead Ends President and lost him."

"Rookie," Billy laughed.

"Sure. He gave me the slip when he switched up from his hog to a silver Impala."

Billy looked surprised and a little impressed. Whoever Spoke was, the guy knew what he was doing, even if he didn't know I was following him, he was being cautious with everything he did.

"The weirdest part was, at a traffic light, he took off his cut and stuck it under his saddle bag."

Billy didn't say anything. He started up the truck and pulled into the first bay. He was sticking this one out with me.

Back in the office we sat around with cold beers in our hands. He didn't say anything when I slipped off my Kevlar vest and put my t-shirt back on.

"So, he gave *you* the fuckin' slip." Billy laughed. I wasn't going to live that down anytime soon.

"Hey, you wouldn't have followed him in there either. How was I to know he'd switch cars?"

Billy leaned back in his office chair, letting it squeal out as he looked up at the yellowed ceiling tiles.

"You remember that old Impala I had? The one we took out to run down those dope dealers?"

"Yeah," I slurped some beer.

"What'd you say when we got in?"

"That cruising through those neighborhoods we'd look like cops." I almost choked on the little bit of suds still running down my throat. I got out my phone and sent a text to Monique, asking what color car had followed her. When she didn't reply within a few seconds I texted Sanford the same thing.

"Did you get a look at the tag?"

"No. I was focused on trying to see the driver." I said, as I was now focused on my cell. Sanford hadn't replied and neither had Monique. My next call went out to Alysa.

"Hey, you." She said sounding upbeat.

"Hey yourself. How's everything?"

"Good." This time her throat tightened a little as her voice got higher. Then she let out a little chuckle, a fake laugh, one she used with customers at the bar when they told her stories she didn't want to hear. Chatter picked up wherever she was along with the commotion of some busy place.

"What's so funny? Where are you anyway?"

"Oh, you know around." A casualness to her voice brought images of her in bed about to go to sleep. Then something scratched in my ear and she began to whisper, "I'm at the police station. There's a cop here looking for you. Detective Camp called me down for a statement about the other night at the bar and Candice and that motorcycle gang."

"Good, I haven't been able to get a hold of Monique or Camp. Is she with Candice?"

She continued to whisper, "Yeah, they're talking with Detective Waycross."

"Waycross? Why?"

"Don't know. I guess because—Oh my god." That scraping sound came over the phone once more. "Igo just walked in. I don't want him to see me."

"What's he want?" There was no reply to my question, the line was still open with the noise of a busy police station coming through until she replied.

"I don't think he saw me. I had to get around the corner."

"What's he doing?"

"He just talked to the desk cop and now he's waiting. He looks mad."

"He must be there to talk to Candice. I had a little conversation with him and may have tipped my hand about April's unpublished article." I swore inside but maintained a clear head. There was no going down to the station, this was out of my hands.

"Uh, oh…"

"What?!"

"Detective Waycross just came out and waved Igo over. They're walking down a hall, buy wait…"

"Dammit!"

"Jeez, calm down, I'm watching. They're talking really close, like whispering."

"Go find Monique and tell her not to let Igo anywhere near Candice."

"I don't know where she is. Oh, he's coming this way." Another round of scratching then I could hear her grunt and cuss.

"Hello Investigator Grimes."

"You forgot the Private part, Igo." I said controlling my rage, knowing in the polices station Alysa was safe, for now.

"No not after tonight."

"Igo you—"

"Careful here Grimes or you might wake up next to another pretty blond or maybe you'd prefer someone with a little more *color*."

A spear separated my chest and ripped through my heart. A racing blur of images too real crossed my mind. I was shaking. Billy stood and gripped the counter, resisting the urge to shout questions.

The line went dead. I shouted the cussed then set the phone down like it was burning my hand.

Billy rushed to the door and held it, waiting for me. I shook my head and struggled to slow my breathing. The blackness of my phone lit up with Alysa's picture. I snatched it.

"Hello!"

"Easy, I'm okay." Alysa said. "Take a breather."

I did as I was told. On the exhale, Billy did the same and shut the door taking his seat.

"What a prick," She began, "Igo just left. I'm going to follow him."

"What? No, please, you stay put."

"Ah you really care." She laughed. "I'll call you from the road." Alysa hung up on me as I shouted not to leave once more.

My knee was bouncing, and my chest tightened. I scrolled through my phone to call Camp.

Billy stood up, "What can I do?"

I held up a finger to give me a second as the line rang.

"What is it Grimes?" Camp said nearly out of breath.

"Go arrest Alysa or something, anything, make her stay at the station."

"Grimes, what on earth?"

"Dr. Igo just made threats against Alysa, go arrest him then."

"Dr. Who? You're not making any sense here and I got my job to do."

"Then you need to stay with Candice."

"Not my problem right now."

"But—"

"But nothing, I'm trying to squeeze my *butt* back in a patrol uniform I ain't worn in over a year. Anyway, Waycross smells what we got going on. He's got more to talk about. I suggest you get with your lawyer friend and have a chat." She exhaled then took a deep breath. "I gotta hit the gym."

"You gotta keep him off my ass. Dr. Igo just threatened Alysa. That son-of -a-bitch has more to do with April's death than I expected. Alysa's out tailing him, and I've got to meet with Sanford before Detective Waycross arrests me." My hand was rubbing over the bristles of my shaved head.

"Grimes, after I get these damn pants on, I have riot gear to put on. There's bigger shit happening than you talking with the *poe-leese!* There's a *Justice for April* march tonight down on Beach Street. I've got to go but listen here, they don't have enough to arrest you. The hair hasn't been positively identified as April's. Alysa made a statement she saw you leave Cooper's alone that night and Candice is vouching for your character, saving her from the gang. So, I'd say you're okay for now."

"Yeah, for *now*. Shit." Frustration grew out of my chest and into my arms. She didn't know about the website and what was coming. I got up and started pacing.

"You're innocent and you have a good lawyer. You'll be okay."

"Thanks, Camp. Be safe out there." I hung up. Billy was looking at me, ready to get out there and do something. I plopped down in the chair, my knee still bouncing. Why was Detective Waycross talking to Igo at the station? The pieces were out there, floating. Waycross's mustched face floated in the air above all of this, looking down distastefully. The connection wasn't coming to me and the more I tried to focus the greater the pain in my head became.

Billy sat down. He held up a business card with a shield embossed on it. "I hate cops." He looked up at me, "That Camp is a cool lady, but damn it."

I got up and took the card from him. As I stared at a cell number, I decided to make him work for it. If Camp couldn't protect Alysa, I'd find her and handcuff her to me or lock her up or something. I tried Alysa again, but it went to voicemail. I looked at my phone, there was Sanford's number. It was time to make the call and get the legal ball rolling. Before I could tap the screen a call from Alysa came up.

"Hey," I said loaded with anticipation.

"So, I'm on Tomoka Farms Road headed south."

"Pull over, don't go any further."

"Why? He doesn't know I'm following him. I'm doing a good job."

"He knows. You have to pull over, we aren't doing this again!" I was being overly protective. I had got her into danger before and I would do anything to prevent it from happening again. The spark of innocence went out with that night of terror. The experience had changed her, it had brought her a new look on life. She handled it well enough, choosing to get tough so she would never be a victim again. Instead of running from danger, she like me, now ran towards it. And I was that danger.

She started to argue and ask questions. At the worst possible time, a call from Sanford finally came in.

"Look, I'm serious."

"Don't worry Grimes. I got this."

"There's a gas station on the left just before the clubhouse, wait for me there, please."

"Fine." She hung up.

Billy was back on his feet, already heading for the door.

"We'll take my car, but you drive." I said and tossed him the keys then picked up the vest.

"Yee-haw!"

# **<u>Chapter 25</u>**

Billy pushed the GTI through its gears and chirped the tires a time or two coming off a light, but otherwise kept his speed just above the limit. We were able to avoid any blockaded roads for the impending march. The night air was damp, the dash said it was sixty-eight degrees. The few weeks of winter we had were nearly over. Too humid to drive with the windows down, we ran the A/C. As we cruised in the dark, I texted Lexi to see what the gang was up too. If they were at a rally or march, my plans would have to wait. They could be out beating people to death as well. She got back to me instantly and said they were *chilling* at the clubhouse. I said it was a quiet night and asked could I stop by. When her invite never came, I knew something was up at the clubhouse I didn't want to miss.

Bright white lights lit up the front of the gas station. Dodging potholes in the stained concrete parking lot, we pulled in next to Alysa's Subaru. Her window was down, and her left arm hung out the window. She pulled it in and brought it back out with a cold can of Monster Energy. I grabbed it.

"Sorry, Billy, I can go get you one too." She said from her car.

Billy shook it off, "No problem-o."

"So, I followed Igo this far now what?"

"First," I said, "Are you okay?"

Her eyes started to roll, then she stopped and smiled softly, "Yeah, Grimes, I'm fine. He's all threat."

I took a breath and let it out, thinking how I would break the good doctor's neck. "I got a text from one of the gang," I started to say.

"Would it be the little black haired one?" Alysa smiled and sipped from her own Monster can.

I nodded, "Yeah, anyway, she said they're all at the clubhouse. I think something is about to go down and it probably has to do with the March for April tonight."

"Yeah, the police station was abuzz because of it."

"The Dead End's clubhouse is right over there." I pointed to the small building surrounded by chain-link fencing.

"You've got to be kidding. That's where Igo went. I saw him pull in."

"Wait," Billy pipped up, "So the professor is tied in with a biker gang full of millenniums?"

"Millennials." Alysa and I said in unison.

"Let's go ask him." Alysa said sitting up from her relaxed position.

"Gotta case the joint first, little lady." Billy said with excitement building in his veins.

"We're gonna do this as a team, right? I mean, I was the one that followed Igo here." Alysa tugged a hair tie from her wrist and pulled her blond hair back into a bun. After another swig of her Monster the caffeine started to mix with the adrenaline in her system. Her enthusiasm took me back to my early MMA days when loud music and energy drinks would get me ready for a fight. Now, older, and wiser, I use my mind more and my body less when fighting. It was all about anticipating the opponents' moves and often using their momentum against them.

"Let me go in first." I said.

"Ah, come on Grimes. I can take the girls and probably a couple of those skinny dudes."

"I don't doubt it. This isn't about smashing in their faces. There will be time for that. I want to meet their club president. His name is Spoke and he's the one directing everything. I think he will lead us to bigger fish."

"So, then we wait here until he comes out." Billy said then checked his pack of smokes. Satisfied with the nearly full pack, he relaxed a little in the seat, settling in to wait. It was something we had done dozens of times.

"I have an idea." I got out of the car and leaned down so both Billy and Alysa could see me.

"If you hear gunshots come pick me up. I won't be long."

"We'll be here brother." Billy nodded. I nodded back.

Alysa got out of her car. She stood there in front of me, and I felt my arms drift from my sides, my center of gravity shifted, and I leaned forward.

"Be careful." She said and softly punched me in the arm then climbed into the VW with Billy.

Well, that wasn't a good start. At least from inside the car next to my best friend she couldn't see the stupid puzzled look on my face as I stood motionless waiting for an embrace that she never anticipated.

"We'll be waiting." She called to me as I walked away. I looked back and waved then headed off.

The whole 50-yard walk to the clubhouse I tried to shake the foolishness of my attempted hug. There may never have been anything to our flirting. Some girls are just like that. Her bounce back after the news of who I was might be at play too. Her wall was up, the physical contact down. It was for the best, there was too much going on, and feelings would get in the way.

The outer reaches of the bright white lights of the station faded as the sandy soil turned to gravel. I couldn't see past the chain-link fence, so each step was soft and purposeful. The gate was open, and I peered around the corner. The echo of the hollow steel door of the clubhouse held me in my place.

Wino stepped out, paused to light a smoke, and then stepped down onto the gravel yard. He took a seat on the tabletop with his boots on the bench seat. He pulled out his cell phone and scrolled through it. From my angle I couldn't see the screen. His fingers punched the screen then he put the phone away.

Just beyond the bench and row of motorcycles was Igo's shit-box Chevy Volt. Though I had never seen him drive it, the 'coexist' bumper sticker on one side and 'my cat is smarter than your honor roll kid' sticker on the other obliterated any doubt. What doubt began to circulate in my mind was Igo's part in all of this. Had he been Spoke all this time? Or was he here seeking the truth about April's death same as I? Though I didn't like the guy from the start, I had to hold off on judgement until I had proof of his intentions.

It was time to make my move, whatever that was. I had lied to Billy and Alysa when I told them I had a plan. A few things skated through my mind, but nothing really worked out as I stood in the shadow burning seconds towards being discovered.

Wino's phone rang. He got off the table and answered it. His voice was the usual low and gruff making it impossible to know what he was saying. Judging by the way he began to pace; the call was not what he wanted to hear. Every step he made in the crunching gravel, I mirrored, brining me ever closer to him. Still covered in shadow, now crouched behind a couple of oil drums.

Without a plan, in a hornet's nest and now fully exposed. I needed to go back to my roots, bring out a little confidence man, a grifter. As a thief my network was small. Smitty lined up a job, Billy and I cased the place, planned then executed.

Coming around the corner, my shoes chewed gravel as I made my way towards Wino.

He spun and his hand went for his waist. His eyes narrowed beneath bushy brows as he took time to identify me. I walked up slow with my hands out at my sides. Again, his eyes rolled over me. I felt them pick out every sharp corner on my body armor and pistol grip, just as I was picking out the corners of weapons on him. We knew things about each other in that moment, the kind of things neither of us were ready to discuss.

"Hey, George." His gruff voice was soft. He did not bother with a fist bump or any other greeting requiring extending his hand.

"So, what's new?" I tried my best at small talk.

He shook his head as he took a drag, "Nothing." He said full of smoke. His eyes were no longer on me, but I knew he was still watching me.

"Looks like everyone is here." I said pointing at the row of motorcycles, including a Harley-Davidson Street Bob next to the Volt. "Looks like more than everyone."

Wino glanced over his shoulder at the row of bikes and one car, "Club meeting."

"Cool." I said doubting my chances of getting in that door without having to go through him. "I'm still waiting to join."

Wino nodded with a smile, "Sorry bro. I don't think we're taking new members." He took a long drag on his cigarette then blew the smoke from the corner of his mouth so it wouldn't come in my direction. He watched the red ember turn grey then he flicked off the ash.

"Listen man, I think its best you just leave." Wino's voice kept a low tone, nonthreatening, but had potential.

In a moment like that, the next words I chose would have to keep things level. It couldn't go up without trouble and down would be defeat.

"Sure man, but I'm still owed my cut on the Benz."

"It isn't worth it." He took all he could from the cigarette then smashed it out on the side of the trash can.

The door flung open with Dead Ends coming out. Hitch was looking back over his shoulder talking to James and didn't see me. Addison came out after him with Lexi pushing through as my presence bottle necked the exit. Like a backed-up assembly line, they bounced into one another.

"Well *looky* here." Addison said coming down the steps first. He climbed up on the table with his boots on the bench seat.

"What's up George?" Hitch put out his hand. We slapped hands. James said 'hi' and moved to the table.

"So, the cat came back?" Lexi said then let out a feral *meow*. She was wearing tight jeans and a black zip up hoodie with a bright white zipper.

I shrugged, "I like this place." *I'd like to watch it burn.*

She stood with a smile, thinking I meant her specifically, then reached in for a hug. I dropped my arms under hers, so she clasped the back of my neck instead of around my chest. She would have felt the body armor for sure.

"We've been busy too," Addison piped up, bringing Lexi and my hug to an end. "Club business, and since you ain't in the club." He smiled and hitched his thumb towards the road.

"Sure, Wino already told me."

"Fuck off Addy." Wino said to which Addison frowned. "He's still due his cut." Wino turned to me, "Listen man, better go. I'll take it up with Spoke and text you when it's cool to come pick it up, alright?"

Wino was doing his best to get rid of me, the problem was I couldn't leave. One or all of these people were responsible for April's death and the cops had me pegged with some planted hair for evidence. I needed something concrete, like a full confection from the real killers. My timing was off tonight but I couldn't let that stop me now. All the things I should have done passed through my head. There was still a matter of evidence. Beating it out of them wasn't exactly in line with my new law-abiding ways.

I looked around and noticed hot-head Denny wasn't in the group. Neither was his old lady, so I figured they were still inside. If I was going to start looking for evidence, even if it was in their eyes, I needed Denny front and center. Then I remembered the Street Bob was here.

"I think I'll just take my cut now." I went up the two steps for the door. Addison jumped off the bench and grabbed at my arm. I spun and palmed his face pushing him back. He cleared the bottom step and ass planted on the gravel.

"Hey!" Wino grunted. His hands were up but he wasn't coming up the steps after me, he was too smart for that. I had the high ground. I also now had the door to my back and Denny inside. Not a place I wanted to be.

I grabbed the handle and slipped inside.

Denny was walking out of the hall to my right. Carry sprung up from the couch.

"What the fuck." Denny said in a guttural whisper.

I moved to the center of the room trying to get my back against a wall. The hollow metal door banged open as all of the gang piled through with Wino in the lead.

"Damn it, George, now ain't the time for this." Wino said.

"What the hell is he doing here?" Denny shouted moving towards me slowly.

"I want to talk to Spoke." The money ruse was growing old. Igo was here leaving the chances were good they all knew who I really am. The way Wino was trying to get me out of here safely made me think he pegged me for a cop and knew what was coming.

"That can't happen." Wino said. The rest of the group shouted things, but Wino kept a cool head, so cool it was starting to worry me.

All their scowls and frowns were directed at me for disrupting their fun. Along the couch were signs demanding justice and on the bar were black masks and pepper spray keychains. The small table I sat around laughing and telling stories a few days ago was covered with guns. The guns were all old and small caliber pistols. Not enough to kill many people but just enough to scare. They didn't want justice, they wanted chaos. Club business was going down to that march, a march intended to help solve the murder of a beautiful young reporter who had her whole life ahead of her, one of real justice, getting to the truth. She died for the truth.

Now it was this rough and tough millennial biker gang that looked more like an ad for expensive jeans than a real MC, to face justice. Beating up junkies and cripples made them tough, it bruised their knuckles and raised their testosterone from all the soy they ate. I was an emaciated junky.

"Real tough gang. You all don't give a damn about anything but likes on a social media page." I looked around at all of them. I thought my words might bring shame to their conscious, but it only threatened their good time.

"Spoke," I shouted. "If you're here and man enough to come out, I'm waiting."

"Denny, let's get him outta here." Addison shouted. My knees bent slightly, and my arms fell apart. I was ready for Denny and for all of them. This isn't how I wanted it to go down, but I was going to bring it down no matter what.

They all jumped me like angry hornets defending the nest. Their punches and kicks stung like a hornet too. I blocked, swung, blocked, and punched them back. Constantly turning, swaying, and ducking to avoid as many blows as I could. The image the cellphone video raced across my mind, using a victim's pain to build my rage. Man or woman, these new agers were all equal right? They all got equal punishment.

When Lexi kicked me, I grabbed her ankle, pulled her near then pushed her face back sending her to the floor. I made sure to get a solid punch right in Addison's cherub face. The cartilage in his nose could not stand up to the force of my knuckles. Red splattered his face. He sunk into the floorboards. Denny got me good, and I stumbled back, resisting the urge not to go down. Wino shot in and grabbed me; he was strong like I expected but I knew he would go for a toss. I slipped down, grabbed his ankles, and kicked with both legs, sending him back.

Denny was immediately on top of me as Hitch and James cautiously backed up. The two bulls were about to tear up the China shop. His fists were fast and hurt as they landed but I forced him to miss my face and stomach. He squared up and took a wide swing. I shot in and took him to the ground. My arm slipped around his neck, and I squeezed until he stopped moving.

The pack started stomping me again and I now had Denny's unconscious body weighing me down.

"Enough!" Wino growled.

Silence. Everyone stopped immediately. I pushed Denny off me. He started to come to. His ole lady knelt and rubbed his back as he shook his head awake. The room was hot and humidity climbing with every expended breath. I spit a mouth full of heavy pink saliva to the floor.

I finally laid eyes on Wino who had a pistol pointed in my direction. It was enough of a direction to keep me still.

"We have our orders and we're not gonna mess it up." Wino said looking at everyone's exasperated pink cheeks and small bruises I managed to give them. They all nodded in agreement.

I sat up but didn't stand. I was breathing heavy and bleeding from somewhere on my face. The vest did a decent job of protecting my midsection from the blows.

"We're behind schedule, damn it. Tie him up and let's get out of here." Wino put the pistol away.

I heard the metal baton expand but never saw it coming. My brain went on an electrical override as I lost control of my muscles. There was nothing stopping my face from hitting the floor. My left eye was closed under the weight of my face and the unforgiving floor. My right eye, though teary, could still see shapes and colors as two black boots scuffed with grey scratches, stood over me.

"Here I am dipshit." Said the voice hovering overhead.

Wino's boots came up beside me without saying anything. He didn't have to. I knew he was acting guard, not just for Spoke but Denny too. I had avoided thinking he killed April, I tried to blame everyone but these guys and girls. It would have been nice if the rest of them weren't such immature assholes, maybe I could have joined for real. In another life Wino and I could be friends and run our own club and just left it at that, a club not some gang that beats up helpless people. That was not the case. I was the lone vigilante, with no joy and no rewards for what I did to criminals. These people, Wino included, had beat up people for sport. I couldn't let that stand in this town.

There wasn't enough left in me to get up, so I let them have this round. I learned long ago sometimes more is said when you're not talking. So, I lay there as each of the gang spit on me and called me names as they picked up their protest signs, masks, and guns.

The scuffed black boots of Spoke clopped back down the hall. Then they came out again followed by a wide gate pair of loafers and both headed towards the door. I was still not moving. It was kind of nice on the floor.

"Roger Grimes?" The voice was higher in pitch than I remembered.

"An easy two for one." said the scuffed boots of Spoke. The others whispered my name and asked questions I couldn't answer. They had all been looking for Roger Grimes the vigilante and here I lay, someone they were going to let into their club.

My good eye caught sight of small black Chuck Taylors coming my way. The rubber tipped toe sunk into my gut. Then a barrage of kicks and slaps came down on me. I felt spit as name calling from Lexi lashed out.

"Enough, damn you!" The voice was clear now and it belonged to Dr. Igo.

The beating stopped and everyone backed away.

"Do you know who this is?" Denny rasped after the chocking I gave him.

"Of course, I do you imbecilic. Why is he here?" Igo nearly stepped on me as he paced alongside my body laying on the rough wooden floor of the clubhouse.

The hateful group began to murmur but no one spoke up. Igo's pacing stopped, "We had a plan. I realize some of you have been kept in the dark and for good reason."

"Who killed her?" I mumbled as blood seeped from my mouth. My legs were out before me, and my arms locked back keeping me from laying down altogether. My head felt loose on my neck, and it was hard to focus on anyone's face as I asked again, "Who killed her?"

More whispers. Then Denny dropped his boot into my chest, flattening me back out on the floor.

"How am I supposed to unveil the vigilante if he looks half dead? Aren't you worried about the cops?" Igo stood between me and the mob.

"I told you that's under control. Besides, a little *vigilante justice* is in order." Spoke chuckled so did a few of his followers.

"All the planning, all the steps. There's a process here. You think you can just get in the way of all of that?" Igo began to pace, dragging the heels of his loafers past my face.

"The plan was to get rid of the vigilante."

"Step one, we turn up the heat, articles swaying public opinion. Step two, whip the people into hysteria. Step three—"

"Step three the frame up with the dead girl. That wasn't part of the plan, but it happened." Spoke grumbled.

"Yes, yes, I let my emotions run rampant. She," Igo used one of his pregnant pauses, "She had other ideas about the vigilante that did not go along with mine. April threatened to expose the plan. I couldn't let that happen. It all worked out, if you had done your part."

"Looks like your plan is changing again. You wanted to sell papers, Doc. Imagine the headline, 'Our very own reporter killed by the vigilante'" Spoke said.

"This was never about selling papers!" Igo protested.

"This was always about the money. So much of it passes through dirty hands out there on the street and we are taking out cut." Spoke shouted.

"I will expose you! All of you. The power of the press will bring you down."

"Not if we bring you down first." Spoke's boots stopped short of the door. "Denny, take the professor and this shit bag out to the barn and get rid of them."

"Spoke, damn you, I am in control of this, me, not you. It's not what we agreed! Denny, tell him I am in control."

No one spoke. My vision was clearing. Igo stopped pacing. Spoke had his back turned to us. He was headed for the door.

"Looks like I'm in charge now," He said.

"You won't get away with this."

"Sure, I will," Spoke said over his shoulder, "The vigilante did it."

"But,"

"We are the vigilante now!" Spoke shouted. All the other mindless twits chanted along as they headed out the door. *We are the vigilante!*

The pain in my head had not subsided and even facing certain death, I struggled to regain my faculties and get up. The fingers on my right hand crawled inched back to my side. Spoke had to die now even if it cost me my life. The vigilante would have his last kill.

The .45 caliber Glock was heavy in my hand and my draw came out in slow motion. I leveled it with one good eye, the white dot site was fuzzy. The barrel followed the scuffed boots then slowly up his jeans and squared the middle of his red and black checked flannel. Time to die.

A strong grip ripped my wrist back sending the pistol from my hand and halfway across the room. Denny's knee came up and hit me in the head. I was staring up at the ceiling thinking now would be a good time for Billy to show up.

I wasn't giving up yet and there was no way I was dying on my back. My own brain was screaming at me go to sleep and to make matters worse my eyes decided they couldn't handle the light. With a rocking motion, I rolled to my side and pushed with my hand and dragged my knee up to help. Eventually I was sitting up. The door was open. The motorcycles outside fired up, revving loudly.

A wavy red and black figure in the door shouted *Kill him!* Denny raised his pistol. Igo jumped in the way. His hands were up, pleading for Denny to calm down and think about what he was doing. He shoved Igo out of the way.

Wino had a pistol out. He fired. The bullet punched me just to the left of my belly button. I spun and my face once again hit the floor. Denny shouted and Wino shouted louder.

Two more shots went off somewhere over my head. The door shut, the last of the motorcycles roared away. It was quiet. My brain stopped screaming and the throbbing in my stomach slowed. I didn't care any longer about Spoke, the gang or even April Ward. All I wanted was to shut my one good eye and leap into that big blackness ahead, letting it wrap me up so I could float away.

Luck is one of those things I just never understood. It seemed like life would roll on easier if I had just a little of that luck. Instead, I got Billy nudging me with his boot, telling me to get up. My eyes opened to the orange light of a retro antique bulb being chopped by a slow spinning fan on the ceiling. Pain radiated from my side and my head was a sandbag on a rubber neck.

My arms wiggled and slid up to my sides. I pushed up on one arm to see Igo on the floor next to me. His eyes open, blood dribbled from his mouth. He was gut-shot too, difference was, I had my vest on.

Alysa was on her knees beside me, sobbing.

"Grimes." Alysa collapsed on top of me. Her hands ran over my body looking for blood and wounds. With a tremor building in her hands, she pulled them and folded them in her lap. Billy let out a string of cuss words and kicked something, then he pulled Alysa back telling her I was okay.

I was looking up at him when he nudged me with his foot once more. "Get up." He said certain I would. His arm came down and I reached out for it. Together I sat up.

Alysa jumped on me again, nearly taking me back down. I hated to let go of her, but I had to get the vest off.

"Check him," I said and pushed Alysa towards Igo. She checked for a pulse and breathing.

With assistance from Billy, I stood up. All three of us looked down on Dr. Igo. In the light of the clubhouse, we could see the smug arrogance was gone from his face, replaced with a pale empty stare as blood pooled around his long curly hair.

Gunshots this far out did not alert the police and if it had, most were downtown watching the march slowly get out of hand as the Dead Ends mix in the crowd of sincere marchers who wanted justice for April as I did. Here he was, dead from a bullet, but not mine. Igo was another victim of the copycat vigilante I couldn't prevent. The rush to find her killer was just to get me out from under the cops' magnified glass. My rage was mere selfishness, at getting set-up and played by someone who knew I was the vigilante and they hated me for it enough to kill a young girl just to frame me. I hadn't really done any of this for April, it was all for myself.

"Can you ride? We need to get after them before they disappear." Billy said looking back at the door as if he would be able to see their taillights fade away.

"I know where they're going." I said and pointed out into nothing as both Billy and Alysa looked at the wall hoping it would make sense of what I was pointing at. The electrical storm in my brain had not died down yet, making it difficult to tell my legs to work. Billy helped me take off the vest. A white welt was turning a crimson red and soon enough purple. I was alive and still had to scrounge whatever little fight I had left to make sure Spoke didn't get away.

I staggered over to the bar and leaned against it to stay on my feet. Alysa was quick to grab some ice and put it in a bar rag. She took a deep breath and let it out then with a shaky hand, passed me the ice. I whispered, "You're doing great."

She gave me a crooked smiled and took out the bottle of bourbon. Before she poured, she looked around and nodded at the décor of the place "I like it.", then filled three shot glasses with bourbon. She couldn't help but tend bar.

"What a joke." Billy said looking around at the posters and rusted oil company signs hanging on pallet wood walls. "These clowns wouldn't know a real MC clubhouse if it bitch-slapped their Facebook page." He dug in his shirt pocket and pulled a smoke. "This would probably drive those soy boys' nuts." He said then lit a cigarette.

I couldn't decide if the ice should go on my head or my gunshot wound, both needed it. I went with my head. The edge of a cube jutted out and jabbed at the swollen nob on the back of my skull. I pulled the rag away and felt the quarter sized mound. Gently, I covered over the wound.

I had to get a hold of Detective Camp and warn her of the plan the Dead Ends had for the march. Their shouts *'We are the Vigilante!'* echoed through my broken skull. I reached in my pocket and pulled my phone out. The black glass was a spider web of cracks. Sometime between getting beaten by the angry little mob and getting shot, my new phone broke. I could see a text from Sanford, but the glass was too shattered to let me unlock the phone.

Billy blew out a low whistle. "You didn't get the insurance the other day. Gonna be a pretty penny."

His comments to the obvious didn't help. "Someone gimme their phone."

Alysa beat Billy to the draw and slide me her phone over the pallet wood bar. "You got Camp's number in here?"

"Yeah, she's under DC."

I scrolled through a lot of dudes' names until I got to DC and called it. Voice mail. I called it seven times before she answered and when she did, she wasn't happy. I talked her down as I usually do, though what I was saying still didn't make her happy. She was at the march but near the end on a side street. She pressed me hard on the details and my fuzzy brain cleared just enough to make my story sound plausible. A little doubt even crept in, how long was I out.

Camp said she would run the message up, but she couldn't leave the street corner where she was posted. Now my head really hurt, coordinating with other officers would take too long. I knew it was going down tonight. This was the big show for these copycat vigilantes who wanted nothing but to watch the city burn. Balancing the scales for the helpless victims of the violent tyrants that exact their power on the streets was what Sanford and I made the vigilante for, not to get our kicks.

"Here," Alysa said and handed me a shot, this time the tremor was gone. All three of us knocked it back. The warm Kentucky Straight made its way down my throat and into my stomach where it warmed over my entire body. My pain lessened. I took another shot.

"They're all gathering for the April Ward march downtown. They left with signs, masks and guns." I said and poked at the purple circle on my side. Yep, still hurt.

"Guns?" Alysa said.

"I don't get it." Billy added.

"Whoever this Spoke is, justice is not on his mind." I moved the ice from my head to my side, "I don't get it either." My Glock was on the floor near the couch. I walked over and picked it up. I put it on the bar.

"You remember how to use it?" I asked Alysa.

"I've got my own now." She pulled out a Kimber Micro nine-millimeter and laid it next to my Glock.

"You keep surprising me." The smile hurt the back of my head, but I held it any way.

"Okay, we got a killer to get after." Billy said bringing us back on task.

"Right, I still don't know who he is. Alysa watch the door. Billy and I are going to see what's in the office."

Alysa stuck her tongue out and blew, making a fart sound, "Fine." She said and looked behind the bar. "I'll mix myself a good drink."

The office was small, about nine by nine. A desk, a cabinet, and some shelves with overstock for the bar and random motorcycle parts. The office looked forgotten about, like it came with the building before it was a clubhouse. The walls were old wood paneling and the floor beige linoleum. The chair behind the desk was a folding chair and I took a seat then started going through the drawers. Billy went through the cabinet. It took all of ten seconds.

"Empty."

"Same here." I said. There was nothing but paperclips, pens, and little white circles from where a hole puncher tipped over.

"This guy is a ghost." I said growing frustrated. The blood pumped and my head began to throb again.

"He's good, no doubt about that." Billy leaned against the cabinet. "Did the ole' professor say anything before he died?"

I jumped out of my seat and shouted, "Alysa," as I turned down the hall and went back out to the main room. Billy was quickly on my heels.

"Yeah," she said shaking a mixer.

"Did you hear anything Igo said to Detective Waycross at the station?"

"No," she said. "But Igo looked more frustrated than Waycross."

"That makes sense." I mulled it over and over in my head. Igo went down to find out what the cops knew about April's last article and what evidence she had on the vigilante. It sure made Igo look guilty in my eyes and easy for the cops to then peg him as suspect number one now that I was looking to be in the clear.

Billy's eyes shifted down at my tapping foot. "Get this boy another drink."

Alysa started to pour but I waved it off. It would only break my concentration. The days of getting half drunk and busting my way through an investigation were over. I needed a clear head to arrange the pieces and make them all fit. When it was over, like with the other jobs, I would take a drink but this time to celebrate instead of suppressing the pain.

Igo killed April because she discovered the copy-cat vigilante. Florence was dirty and had been working with Igo to carry out the violence needed to spark the blaze in this town against the vigilante. Whom recruited whom? Florence had a reason to hate the vigilante. Igo didn't.

A text alert dinged from my cracked phone. It was Sanford. I tried to swipe the shards of glass, but it wouldn't unlock. Sanford's number I knew so I didn't have to scroll through all the men's names in Alysa's phone again. He didn't answer. I sent a text letting him know it was me calling. He called right back.

"Grimes, how's it going?"

"Oh, pretty good."

"That sounded sarcastic, dammit Grimes don't play with me. It's been a rough day." He breathed heavy in the phone. The work he does always goes unnoticed and underappreciated. The bruises, scars and blood come with my end of the job but is the one keeping my butt safe at night.

"It's all going down tonight. The Dead Ends are planning an attack at the Justice for April march. I couldn't stop them."

Sanford only breathed through the phone.

"What?" I said.

"Monique took Candice to the march. She's supposed to give a speech."

Now we all were running out of time.

# Chapter 26

Every bump in the GTI's lowered racing suspension rattled the loose pieces in my skull. Billy was doing the best he could, dodging potholes while also pushing the car at top speeds where he could, around bends and off traffic lights. Alysa was doing a good job of keeping up behind us in her Subaru. A couple times, even passing us.

The march brought people from all over the county to Daytona Beach. The parking lot behind Cooper's was full so we had to park off Palmetto Avenue, a block away. Subgroups that had nothing to with a local murder passed by with signs for things like; women's rights groups, living wage protesters and anti-president slogans. Everyone had to have their say these days as if their online voices weren't enough.

Sanford stood waving at us. He was dressed down in a black polo tucked into straight leg jeans and a sweatshirt tied around his waist. It was the most casual I had ever seen him dressed. We met on a small grassy island in the middle of the parking lot. Then made our way past the buildings to the sidewalk where the march would pass. The march had just started five blocks north and would end a block south of our location. People started to gather along the street to watch what was going on. They had no opinion one way or the other, they were probably just out for a drink or dinner.

Detective Camp was across Beach Street in her green county sheriff uniform and helmet. I waved to her, and she motioned for us to stay put, then she crossed the street.

"I told the commander and he has sent out a few deputies to scan the crowd, but without IDs on these people there isn't much to do but wait and see what happens." Camp pulled a handkerchief, wiped her brow.

"Then shut down the whole march." Alysa chimed in from behind me.

"Not gonna happen."

"What if we call in a bomb threat?" Alysa challenged.

Camp ignored her and turned to Sanford, "Is Candice still planning on speaking?"

"I'm afraid so."

"There's police up there with her, so I'm sure it will be okay."

"I haven't been able to reach Monique or Candice since we got here." Sanford said.

An itch was spreading under my skin, I desperately wanted to hear back from Monique or Candice and checking my phone, making sure the volume was up and vibrate was on had not brought their response any quicker. I could see that same itch in Sanford's red worried eyes.

"It's noisy down that way. I'm sure they just can't hear the ring." Camp said then turned her attention towards my face and over all beaten exterior.

"Don't ask," I said. She nodded and went back across the street.

"We've got to do something." Alysa said. None of us had a plan. I proposed we spread out and mix among the marchers until we can spot some of the gang. Alysa had a partial recollection of what a couple of them looked like and Sanford said he would focus on finding Monique. Billy said he wasn't leaving my side again.

Billy and I started our way north first with Sanford staying a dozen yards or so behind. Alysa stayed near the finishing point of the march in case the two girls slipped past us. Red and blue lights flashed at every intersection, with road barricades ready for the marchers to pass without worrying about traffic. The night air stayed the same temperature with only the humidity rising.

Within a block of the starting point, we saw the marchers coming our way. The front of the group held candles and remained quiet. Behind them signs bobbed as different chants murmured through the street. There were more people with cameras and cellphones out along the sides recording the march than actual participants. As they drew near, we could make the usual cadence of chants. Some wanted justice other wanted cops to hang. My eyes scanned the shouting faces, the Dead Ends would be the loud ones.

Billy and I blended in as did Sanford behind us. When the group neared police, boos and hissing could be heard. I hated it; it was my fault the police were catching such flak. If you do something repeatedly as I did taking-out scumbags, you wear a path. That path made the cops look bad. The cops stood watching and waiting for something to happen. So far it was peaceful.

We marched along with the rest of the crowd all the way to the end at the intersection of Beach Street and Orange. We caught sight of Candice. Billy pointed to her and then said that was Detective Waycross standing next to her. He wore a vest with reflective yellow stripes as all the police had on. It was when I squinted my eyes to get a better look, his edges blurred, and his shape took on an all too familiar one. Under the vest he wore a black and red checkered flannel. My heart lept into my throat before my brain fully understood what I was looking at. Spoke. He was standing right there and had been this whole time.

I started bouncing trying to get Monique's attention. She wasn't looking my way. I turned and saw Sanford watching me, his head fanning side to side to see around the people ahead of him. I pulled Billy aside and leaned into his ear, "Detective Waycross is Spoke!"

Billy swore and tried to get a better look at him.

"Get Sanford, I'm going up there."

Billy nodded and started parting the sea of marchers.

I shoved my way forward with many people hurling insults back as they bumped shoulders. I could feel the eyes of a few officers on me but the only ones I wanted were that of Waycross. One look at me and it would force his hand, make him do something ahead of schedule. It might be just enough to throw off the whole plan. Then it came.

It wasn't Waycross that spotted me but Denny. He shouted and all the rest of the Dead Ends turned my way. They pulled up their black bandanas over their faces and pulled out guns. There was no way to tell who fired first as half a dozen pops went up into the air. The crowd screeched as one but moved like ants with water pouring into their tunnels. The rough ocean current of the crowd tossed me about. I hopped up to keep track of Waycross. He was crouched now with his own pistol out and moving his head side to side looking for the shooters.

In the commotion I stopped as if watching a movie on the big screen, captivated by the bewilderment as Waycross shot Hitch dead. A hole in the crowd opened as Hitch went down. On the edge of it was Lexi, her gun held by her side. Our eyes locked, but the moment was interrupted by more gunfire. A bullet slammed into her small frame and knocked her to the ground. She rolled and began to crawl. I started to run toward her when a marcher slammed into me. I caught the woman as she fell, my hands filling with sticky warm fluid as I laid her gently to the city street. Her stare glazed over as the light in her eyes dissipated.

Protesters bounded about like bees around a hive. Bumped and checked, I staggered to Lexi. She lay curled in the fetal position gripping her stomach. A protester knelt down beside her blocking my view of her face. All I could see was that black and white panda face tattooed on her ankle looking back at me.

Someone's shout pierced my ear and I immediately crouched. Then I saw Denny with his pistol pointed at me. His eyes wide with freight of what he just did. Then he fired again; I sprang. He missed. I charged.

We collided in the street. I took him to the ground and began pummeling his face until it resembled a bowl of spaghetti. All his toughness drained out with his blood into the street. I paused the assault as Denny coughed up blood and teeth. Then April's face appeared, warm and pinkish now, no longer that dismal grey. I looked back down at the club's enforcer and dropped my knee into his face.

Over my shoulder was Addison charging my way. I still was on all fours over Denny, heaving like a wild beast and covered in others' blood. He stopped, his eyes wide, then slowly began to back up.

Addison was going to get it next. The round cherub turned and bolted into the chaotic crowd.

Before I could give chase, I was sidelined by what felt like a Mac Truck.

Wino bulldozed me. We rolled together until I hit the cement curb. Breathing heavy and fighting the spins, I got on my hands and knees. A hand snatched me by the collar, and I felt much lighter, enough to be on my feet with no effort.

"Move!" Wino shouted in my ear loud enough to block out any more pops. I scrambled for a hedge line just before the riverbank. A couple of thuds spouted dirt as I fell behind the hedge row. Wino was nearly on top of me.

His palms were up, weaponless. "Easy," He said. I listened. "Spoke is trying to kill you."

"I got that feeling."

"This is all so fucked up, man. I don't know how I let it get so far." Wino looked up over the hedge. When he looked back, I had my Glock winking at him.

"Shit," he said in the low grumble I was familiar with.

"What the hell is going on?"

"Spoke and Igo set this whole thing up. It's outta control." Wino wiped the sweat off his forehead.

"You knew Spoke was a cop this whole time, didn't you?"

He opened his mouth to speak when a bullet nipped him in the shoulder. He fell back with a grunt. I didn't wait to check him, instead I scrambled the opposite direction for better cover. With the crowd as dispersed as it was, I decided not to shoot over my shoulder as I moved.

Two helicopters overhead beamed bright white light all around. People continued to scream, as what sounded like fourth of July exploded in the city street. The shooting slowed to one last pop and a banshee scream brought the street to a quiet pause.

I was propped against a tall palm tree peering out as sirens began to whale. I lost sight of Wino. Waycross stood in the middle of the street. In the gutter was a lump and kneeling next to it was the ever-stoic Monique. Blood was running down her perfectly manicured fingers. Her mouth hung open but didn't make a sound. Monique cradled Candice as blood seeped out.

Waycross leveled his pistol, he had taken this to the extreme, but wasn't finished.

My finger squeezed before my pistol was level. The bullet missed. Sparks and shattering concrete did not deter Waycross. I started to squeeze once more but was impacted by two hundred pounds of police officer as I was tackled and then dog piled to the ground.

Through the legs and arms of the officers I could still see Waycross in the street. Then swift moving feet, floated on air to meet him. Willis Sanford speared Waycross and they fell to the ground. Both men were up quickly. Waycross looked around for his pistol, but it was lost. He turned to Sanford and squared his shoulders. Sanford's feet tapped lightly on the asphalt, the old-time boxer returning to the ring for one more round. Waycross charged, Sanford side stepped and swung a left hitting Waycross near the temple. The dirty cop turned and put up his fists. I thought I might have seen the glint of Sanford's white teeth as his hands started to move in a blur. Even at half of Sanford's age, Waycross couldn't match the old man's speed and certainly not his determination.

Sanford closed the distance and made quick work of Waycross, sending him to the asphalt.

More police rushed in and Sanford, with his hands up jogged over to Monique. That was the last I saw as a knee came down on my face and I floated away into darkness.

# **Chapter 27**

Billy was chatting up the female desk officer as the electric lock on the door buzzed me to freedom. Billy was showing her a large Florida Pompano he caught last summer on his boat. I leaned on the desk with him completely unaware I had been released.

The officer with her chestnut brown hair pulled tight into a bun, round face and sparkling brown eyes held a shy grin with a hint of pleasure behind it. She was a little rounder than I preferred, but Billy had told me with time he'd come to appreciate a little more softness for his tired old bones, and I would too. She was just his type, so I didn't want to ruin anything for him.

"I do love to fish." She said handing him back his phone.

"Well, good. I know this sandy little island down near Mosquito Lagoon you can only get to by boat and—"

"Hey brother," I said knowing where this next fish tale was going. It was Billy's little private nudist resort where he would go natural and dance around a fire, 'like his ancestors did', is how he put it.

Billy turned and ran a hand down his long braid, "Freedom." He said mimicking a famous Scott.

"I'll meet you outside," I said and slapped him on the shoulder.

He turned back to the officer, "Now, about this island…"

Outside the police station the bright white light of the noonday sun blinded me. I pinched my eyes as tears formed in the corners. The rays felt great on my skin. The middle of December and it had to be eighty degrees out. Two days in a windowless cell had already taken a toll. Naturally, the police had a lot of questions about my involvement. As my story began to line up with Sanford, Candice and Monique's stories, the cops started to go a little easier on me. None but Camp trusted me and investigating one of their own didn't help to bridge anything. Early this morning something broke in the investigation that got them looking in another direction and things eased up on me. Still, they kept a close watch on me during my thirty-six hour stay in solitary confinement. Though I knew I'd be out quickly, coming that close to life in prison was enough to drive home my need to put the vigilante to death. I was done. So far, I had got away with it and it was time to leave it that way.

As my pupils shrunk to tiny black seeds and my eyelids opened, I saw a familiar shape, one I had observed a thousand times from over a bar. Alysa was all smiles as she suppressed a jog and finally a leap towards me with her arms wrapping around my neck. Her feet dangled for a few seconds before she touched down again.

"Hello partner." She said pulling back to get a look at me. Her hand came up and scraped against the extended growth of my whiskers.

I scratched it myself, "They wouldn't let me shave."

"Looks good. You should grow it out."

"Too many beards these days and not enough men to wear them."

"Did they tell you when we're getting it?" She said looking up at me with a new seriousness.

"Get what? They didn't let me ask a lot of questions between all their questions."

"The reward. We caught the vigilante." She bounced and I liked it.

"We did?" I was so confused. The quick time in lock-up, away from the world, felt like ten years. A while back I was in county jail for nine months, but I still had TV, internet, and other inmates to talk to. This time around they kept the lights on and the questions coming around the clock.

"Camp said they found a bunch of evidence that Waycross and another ex-cop had been going out at night and beating up criminals."

"Camp? Are you guys BBF's now?" I felt the scab on the back of my head where Waycross sapped me and wondered if there was a long-term side effect of the blow.

"No, Monique actually told me that she talked to Camp. She and I have been talking a lot since shit went nuts." She started walking towards the parking lot.

I turned as Billy finally came out the station doors. He cupped his hand over his eyes to shield them from the sun and then hustled over to us.

"Sanford wants to see you before we do anything, like get drunk." Billy said.

Sanford's office was a block from the station, so we walked.

We all entered the top floor office. The heavy office doors were open, and Monique was seated across the desk from Sanford. She had a laptop out and was typing, filling in blank spaces on a document. A stack of file folders was beside her and one on top was open. She stopped typing and looked over shoulder and gave me that ice-melting smile that reached deep in my gut and gave it a spin. I smiled back so big it hurt my face.

She got out of the chair and reached out her arms. The ice queen had truly melted and soon I would get to feel her skin to see if she had thoroughly thawed. As my arms went up, Alysa brushed past me.

"Hey girl." She said as her and Monique hugged.

"Hi Grimes." Monique said as the two women separated.

"That explains a lot." I said and sat in the chair kept warm by Monique. It was my chair, the one I had bled on that night I became the vigilante. Though it was reupholstered, buried in the wood grains was my DNA that no amount of sanding and staining would get rid of.

"Oh, stop it." Alysa said and swiped at my arm. "This girl and I went through some rough stuff the other day."

"You mean while I was hog tied by police and hauled off?" I sat thinking about the time I saved Alysa's life and all I got for it was ghosted.

"Stop being a grouch. Want me to get you another prescription?" Monique smiled but she was serious. I wanted to say yes but my head was already shaking no. I was over the anti-anxiety meds because the vigilante was dead.

Monique smiled again and closed the computer down. She moved the files and sat on the edge of the desk. She was dressed in tight, expensive jeans and a designer t-shirt, so her usual dressed down work attire.

Alysa grinned and took the other seat.

Billy stood between us. "Where's my hug? I was there too."

Monique didn't move.

"After you were arrested, Alysa and I tag teamed CPR on Candice." Monique said nodding to Alysa. "She's still in ICU but looking good."

Candice made it, we had all made it too. Candice surviving was one bit of information the police didn't let me know. Instead, they used it as leverage to get me to confess. She was a bloody mess last I saw her, and I didn't think she would make it. A slight smile on my face felt warm.

The wood paneling split as Sanford came out of the hidden executive bathroom. He smiled, "Roger." He was dressed in a green Stetson University t-shirt tucked into straight leg jeans and brown leather belt.

We shook hands, we never shook hands. I don't think I had touched this many people without trying to kill them in a long time. My place at the table had been set and it was across from Sanford. Alysa now had a place as did Billy. Monique was not just a paralegal, but a lawyer in her own right and judging by the stack of files, had a client list of her own.

Sanford went to the wet bar and grabbed a glass for me but paused before setting it down on the black marble countertop. He reached below to the mini fridge. His hand came back with two golden cans of beer. He handed me one then Billy.

"Billy filled me in on your traditions." Sanford said and went back to the mini fridge for three more beers, handing one to Monique then Alysa. He studied the can like he was looking for instructions on how to drink it.

His eyebrows went up above the steel rims of his glasses reading the can, "Well, it seems appropriate, it says the champagne of beers."

We all clinked cans and I tasted cold beer and a job well done.

"We did it," Sanford said taking a seat in his stuffed leather chair. "You solved April Ward's murder and you didn't even kill anyone." He lifted his can and drank.

"Well," Billy said, "That one boy's in a coma."

"But he isn't dead." Alysa said. She turned to me, "Denny's in a coma from the beating you gave him."

The warmth I had been feeling was turning to fire in my belly. As part of my interrogation, the detectives made me look at pictures of Hitch and Lexi. Killed by police, their dead stares and pale grey skin was supposed to get me riled up. They had no idea how many times I had seen that stare and walked away. Lexi hadn't been the first girl I had held in my arms only to see her die and there was a chance she wouldn't be the last. I looked at Alysa, smiling and chatting with the group. She sipped her beer and ran her fingers through her blond hair.

Suddenly all the faces, pale, motionless, came rushing up at me. Not just the two Dead Ends and not just women I loved, but all of them. All the people I put in the ground by my hands came back. They weren't done, they had something to say, and their mouths hung open, breathless.

"Roger?" Alysa's fingertips touched my arm and it felt like needles in my skin.

I jerked, like waking from a bad dream, "Yeah. So…" They were all looking at me. "What?"

"You okay?" she said.

"Yeah, what were you saying about the rest of the gang?" I touched the back of my head, back to that scab once more.

A knock at the door got us all to spin around and the attention off me. Detective Camp stood dressed in her civilian clothes once again, a thin zip up hoodie and a pair of jeans.

"Am I interrupting?"

Everyone agreed she wasn't and invited her in. Sanford got up and got her a beer which to my surprise she accepted and drank.

She leaned against the marble counter saying, "This has been one hell of a week."

We all agreed once more and shared in a drink.

"I'm not sure you all have the details on the case. The department is keeping a tight lid on everything, and they should, we look like shit. I wanted to let you all know, Doctor Igo kept good notes. He wanted so bad to turn public opinion on the vigilante that he created a martyr, April Ward. Turns out she was a better investigative reporter than he ever was. She uncovered the vigilante, or vigilantes." She said, her head still but her eyes were on me.

Everyone played it cool except Alysa. She still didn't know how involved this office was in the murder of criminals all over the city these last few months. Her natural skills picked up in the shift in mood like a cold front rolling through. She looked around at each of us with concern but then seemed to let it go as Camp kept talking.

"April went to Igo with a victim that could ID Officer Florence and Waycross as the ones that attacked him. Igo decided to use the information to push his agenda against the police, but it quickly got out of control. He was no match for Waycross."

"Oh, you can come pick up your truck when you want."

I nodded. The Scout meant more to me now than before. It was a connection with April that in death I didn't have but now in life she would be there.

"What's Waycross saying?" I asked. The air sucked out. I was so far out of the loop; I couldn't see the edge anymore.

"Waycross committed suicide in his cell." Camp said. The others seemed to have already known this.

Revenge drove a big part of the vigilante. I used the natural fuel it provided to do a number of unspeakable things to very bad men. Now, I wouldn't get that revenge. April's killer wouldn't die at my hands, and I had to be alright with that.

"So, how'd the biker gang fit in?" Billy asked, finishing his beer and helping himself to another. He looked around to see who else needed one, but everyone was still drinking.

"It was some kinda social experiment Igo was already doing. It was a natural partnership, to combine forces with Waycross and Florence. They got on to Grimes and well that was a big mistake not even all of Igo's smarts could fix." Camp said.

We were all silently processing the final bit of news that brought the case to a close. Waycross and Igo were dead. Denny was in a comma and would go to prison if he ever woke up. Lexi and Hitch paid the ultimate price for wanting to be tough bikers. Wino seems to have escaped and I was alright with that for now.

I looked around the room, "You know," I said to the group, "in this office is everyone I know."

"Except Smitty." Billy said.

Smitty had been on my mind here and there. He usually popped up at some point with some news or just to shoot the shit. He even bailed me out when I was over my head. This past week had been a blur but thinking back beyond that and I couldn't place the last time I heard from him. Not even a phone call with the usual, *"How're you doing kid?"* Suddenly the crowded office felt a little empty without the old whitehaired mobster.

"You'd like Smitty," I said to Alysa who returned my smile. I looked over to Sanford. He was not smiling. He took off his glasses and pinched the bridge of his nose. He put his glasses back on and laid his long-fingered hands on the desk.

"Roger, somethings have come to my attention about Smitty."

We all knew Smitty was a crook. He had been part of the mob when it still had a hold on the jai alai and dog track. They left but he stayed and lived on his reputation as a mobster. He had always been there for me. My father was a sailor who I almost never saw, and my mom faded away into the sands of the Florida beaches before I graduated high school. Smitty, Billy and I formed our robber's trio and set about my education in being a criminal. He was part of my upbringing.

It had been easy for me to tell Billy I was quitting being a thief but telling Smitty kept me up for days. He took it well enough, considering he was out a major source of income. In fact, he took it too well.

Monique reached over the computer and picked up the file that had been open when I entered the office. I took it but didn't open it.

Sanford stood up from behind the large mahogany desk. With five sets of eyes on him, he said, "Roger, Smitty is going to need our help."

## To be Continued....

To find out what happens check out the next installment of *Grimes Redux* – Grimes is thrown back to his first case working for Willis Sanford. The prosecutions of the child traffickers have failed, now someone is murdering the top suspects. All fingers point to the Vigilante. Now Grimes is working along side the FBI to solve the case he created...
-HW